A Necromancer's Apprentice

BRIAN PHILLIPS

Copyright © 2018 Brian Phillips

All rights reserved.

ISBN:
ISBN-13: 978-0-9600703-1-2

DEDICATION

This book is dedicated to a long list of people who inspired me, supported me, and kept me company on this journey through life. Writing a book like this fulfills a dream that I have carried since my school days. When I was young, I loved stories. I loved books and games, and friends to share them with. These remain the among the highest joys in my life. So I dedicate this book to the whole gang. My weekly gaming group that has met in one form or another since 1984 remains the well that I draw inspiration from. My writing friend kept me motivated to finish this project. My children remind me why the imagination is vital to life. My wife Laurie makes it all worthwhile.

Thank You.
Brian Phillips.

AUTHOR'S NOTE

This is the first novel I have ever written. I have, however, been writing for years. I have published two magazine articles about role playing games. I wrote five academic conference papers, and wrote a 200 page dissertation for my doctorate. But this is the big one. Those other things were about real life (mostly), but this one is about dreams.

At its heart, A Necromancer's Apprentice is a story about becoming a grown up. It focuses on a journey, a journey most of us take whether or not we inhabit a fantasy world. It begins about the time we leave the safety of our home and quickly discover that we have no real idea what is going on around us. We assumed that we knew what to do when real life happened, but, then it actually happened. As we leave our comfortable roots, we encounter new things. Some of these things were taught to us, but perhaps we didn't truly grasp. Others emerge from nowhere. There is also a history to everything, and when we enter the world, we are engulfed in it whether we like it or not. In this story, as in life, a fledgling journeyer gains assistance in new friends they meet, and sometimes even from enemies. Life has an odd way of pulling some mismatched people together.

The story is also about me and the tales I am interested in. I love tales where the protagonist learns things and changes their plans. I love stories where forces from different sides take turns cooperating and betraying each other. I devour stories from the great authors that show a disconnected, chaotic world. You may see inspirations from Orson Scott Card, Alan Dean Foster, J. K. Rowling, C. J. Cherryh, George R. R. Martin, and most of all, Joe Abercrombie in this work. I like stories where things get complicated and plans go awry, when things don't exactly work out.

I hope you will enjoy my tale. If you get a chance, a review or an email would be appreciated! I've got a blog, http://whitehand.brianphillipswriter.com

Brian Phillips

A DIFFICULT JOURNEY

Miller climbed slowly up from the cold ground, his pants stained with the dark soil and grass where he'd knelt the past two hours.

A grave-marker stood before him, giving silent testimony to loss, grief, and missed opportunities. When she was alive, Miller had feared her. He had kept his distance, mistrusting her zealous nature, her aggressive strength, her warrior's soul.

Now, just two short years after her death, he was full of regrets. She had been right in the end, but she couldn't explain it. She couldn't, or wouldn't, subject herself to the judgment of others. He would love to go back and talk to her, to really get to know her, to show her what lay in his heart. But that was simply a daydream. She cared as much for his opinion as anyone else's, that being not at all, except Mistress Aileen's.

He stepped toward the stone. His hand, almost with a will of its own, reached out and caressed the damp gray rock. Only two words were carved into the stone. Two words to give witness to a heart that was once full of energy, full of fury, full of life.

MADAM K.

That simple name, shortened from the unpronounceable Klytaimnestra she'd been born to. It carried more weight with him than many others. It meant believing, really believing. It meant being ready to sacrifice self, family, or any other thing to accomplish a just cause. But right now, it meant sorrow. Sorrow on a damp, cool, fall day, with no other person present, nor welcome. He had come alone, and now he was here, he did not regret it. There was only one other person who could have ever shared this moment, and Faust had left this world to travel the Shadowlands beyond the final door long before she had. Other than Mistress Aileen, Miller was now the last of the fated group. The last who still traveled in the lands of the living, in any case.

Madam K had been amazing. She'd been a captain of the Eisenvard, a zealot, a true believer. She hadn't agreed with Aileen's decision to leave the temple; she didn't serve the White hand. She'd only followed Aileen into her secret war because of their close friendship. He remembered how she'd brandished that holy warrior strength. But she'd made the wrong alliance and it had cost her.

She and Mistress Aileen had been so close, until Aileen had killed her. Murdered her in a desolate snow-scape, hidden from all who cared. Aileen continued to say that it was for the best, and if she hadn't killed K, it would have gone much worse for her: K had made an enemy of the entire Order of the White Hand with her zealotry.

Miller didn't believe a word of it. Aileen didn't always report history as it was; sometimes she reported it as she wanted it to be. The truth was that Hermagon's cabal had been looking for a conflict with Easter's cabal. Aileen had made a sacrifice to head off their plans and support Easter. K didn't start the fight, but she did finish it by killing off a half-dozen of their apprentices which had put Aileen in a political fight between all the other

Masters, a political fight she would still probably lose. Someone had needed to take the blame, though, at the time; an ex-Eisenvard zealot was an easy person to sacrifice.

Aileen had truly joined the Order when she'd killed K. She'd made a decision that was irrevocable, and final. She'd put her own survival and political ambitions above the life of her ally and sometimes friend. It had happened to K without any notice.

It could happen to him just as easily.

He slowly released the stone, turning to take up his meager possessions. The saddlebag was newly made; its stitching rubbed roughly against his bare hand. His heavy carrying sack made the sound of a hundred mismatched things roughly awakened from their silence. Even his saddle, perched on the back of a riding mare, had the look of new craftsmanship.

Gear would fail, rope would break, and knives would go dull on these type of journeys. He expected two months of travel, was prepared for a year. Again, as he began fastening his saddlebag to the mare, he recited the list of things that would kill him, each one separated by a second of hesitation, and a vision of when his fate would occur.

"Could be burned alive. There's starvation, dehydration, falling from the horse, robbery. I could be poisoned, crushed by stones, or betrayed." And if he was lucky enough to finish his journey, and arrive intact, there was: "Master December."

He climbed into the saddle and grasped the reins, urging the brown mare forward. She began her trot, leaving the clearing and propelling Miller toward the town of Ingalls, or perhaps toward the Crooked Gate that guards the realms of the dead.

Miller's throat tightened, and his voice quavered a bit as he finished his litany of fears with the one doom that certainly awaited him in the end, the one he could never escape. He resisted saying her name for as long as he could. Fear, love, gratitude, and despair joined into his final syllables.

His hands trembled as he said, "Mistress Aileen."

He guided his mare toward his first stop, Clockshire, and passed quietly over the damp grass and onto a rutted two-track road. The road seemed to welcome his return. It stood open, broad, and in good repair. Massive trees stood at each side. The only sounds that came from the surrounding forest were soothing. They called to him to let down his guard just this once.

As always, Miller suspected that would be a bad idea. He liked being away from the camp, crammed alongside the other apprentices, connected to Mistress Aileen by just a few steps at all times. But being here, riding free in the wilderness, gave him comfort.

Miller always enjoyed the first weeks of a long journey. His nerves loosened a small measure every day he traveled farther away from this place. Adding distance between his fragile self and the duties of the Order always helped his mood—once one joined the Order of the White Hand, their demands were never far away.

It had sounded like a good idea once, joining the Order. He would apprentice to magicians who were masters at their art. He'd devote himself to serving the needs of the small people, healing the poor, and feeding the hungry. He'd travel the world and learn of new places and tongues. All of this came true, but so did the part they didn't tell him.

The Order of the White Hand was relentless in serving small people with small deeds, almost as if the apprentices very lives depended on it. Indeed, they did. It was one way to hold the madness at bay. Apprentices were taught to journey in the wilds, the towns, and the cities, bringing helping hands and small magics to soothe the hurts of the world. The Masters of the White Hand devoted their lives to healing the world itself. They removed spirit wounds from within the land and tried desperately to keep the foundations of the world from cracking and finally tearing itself apart.

But the cracks were where the horror lived. Monsters crawled within them. The cracks sometimes snapped open, releasing nightmares into the world where the small people lived, ignorant of their danger. The ability to travel into these cracks took a toll on a White Hand magician's mind, as well.

It did not take him long to discover what the bad part of the deal was: Masters of the White Hand went mad, one and all. The magical art they guarded so jealously allowed them to live for a hundred lifetimes, but each lifetime took a toll. They became less human. Miller had watched this happen to the Masters. He remembered watching as people he knew personally became more monstrous, their dark deeds piling atop each other, extracting a price from their soul. They were tainted by something and it terrified him. Masters were so accustomed to choosing between terrible options they stopped caring about the consequences of that choice.

Shortly after starting as an apprentice, he had lost interest in acquiring his own Master's ring. Small, good deeds kept the madness at bay, just a little bit, but not enough. Miller had been concentrating on just that for years now.

He knew about this madness first hand. His short time with Mistress Sword had taught him much of its cruelty, and hers. He still awoke hearing her laughter, sweating with fear, yet ashamed of it, yearning for her company for just one more night. Mistress Sword was a sadist, she was evil, and worse yet, she was chaotic and unpredictable. Miller had no idea how he'd ever been lucky enough to leave Mistress Sword's service and join Mistress Aileen's service. The politics of the Masters were mind-boggling. He suspected some deal-making within the two rival cabals had changed his service. He'd not been informed nor consulted until the decision had been made.

Now he journeyed from the temporary home he shared with Aileen and three other members of their cabal in the outer wilds, back toward the city of the goddess, Home's Hearth. Mistress Aileen had directed him back toward the great temple, commanding him to give aid to the sisters. Just three short years ago, they had allied to fight a new enemy invasion. Every few decades that unnamed enemy would come into their midst unseen, shattering the souls of victims and wearing their bodies like a skin. The White Hand had been fighting this enemy since they'd first met, three thousand years ago. They seem to have come from nowhere. They used no magic that was understood. The enemy didn't even have bodies; they merely stole the bodies of others. It was a difficult war, and the White Hand wasn't winning it. They could not find those enemies, or even name them, so the enemy was simply called "The Takers."

Miller had been lucky three years ago, during the last Taker incursion. He had found a way to identify those who were victimized and turned. Before he had discovered that insect spells could discover the infected, entire towns could be taken before anyone could act to stop them. The best defense now was to identify where the Takers were gaining a foothold, isolate that foothold, and then remove the infected.

Before his work, those infected would turn into mindless killers with no hint of their sickness beforehand.

The sisters had struggled to understand what had happened to the people. No one knew why the Takers had begun possessing common folk, nor how to defend against them. Neither did Miller. He'd just gotten lucky last time. He had made a chance discovery when working alongside other spell-crafters within the Temple. The Temple and the Order had had a tenuous alliance back then, brokered by then Sister Aileen. He had been tasked to remove a cockroach infestation and found that his spell also caused some of the Taken people to react. It was an accident, but a fortunate one; now he hoped to get lucky again.

No word of the Takers had reached him since they'd quelled the uprisings. He didn't know if any Takers remained. He believed they did; it just seemed logical.

Mistress Aileen hadn't dismissed the threat, either. Miller believed in her, and if she was worried, he was worried. So, he traveled to Home's Hearth.

DAYS OF TRAVEL

Three pleasant days of travel went by. Light rains decorated the sky as he moved through these familiar lands where he'd not trod for two years. He passed barns, open fields overflowing with grain, and creeks that irrigated fields and orchards.

He felt the call of the ring early in the evening, as the moon began to rise, painting the horizon in a welcoming orange. As an apprentice, he was linked to Mistress Aileen through this ring, so she could find him with only a moment's notice. Apprentices had large silver rings to show their attunement and cabal. Masters wore black rings of whatever shape and size they pleased.

The silver ring circled his right index finger. Its large outer surface reflected the dusk's light. The ring pulsed with a warning he had enchanted into its core. Aileen was preparing to contact him, to expose his inner hidden thoughts, and to speak directly to his awakened mind across the leagues. That contact scared the hell out of him. Mistress Aileen could reach out from across the miles and pluck his consciousness away, dropping it into a spirit medium. Such power terrified him. Someday, she might pluck out his spirit, and never return it.

Someday, she would go mad like all the rest.

The first time Mistress Aileen had used this method to speak with him, he'd been so surprised he'd fallen off his horse and limped for two days. The first thing he did after he could walk again was embed an alerting rune into the ring. Mistress Aileen had noticed it quickly and complimented him on his work. Now he received a few seconds' notice before she came to him, asking for his attention, instead of simply commanding it. It was safer that way.

He guided the mare to the side of the broken trail. Palm-sized rocks turned beneath the mare's hooves, threatening to spill both the he and the mare onto the ground. He dismounted carefully and tied the reins to a nearby oak tree. Then he moved into the meditation position, the one that Mistress Aileen had taught him many years ago, and waited. A few seconds later her voice came like a whisper from the corners of his mind.

It beckoned him, "Miller. Miller. Answer me, please, Miller, I have news. Please tell me if you are in need. Can you hear me?"

Miller relaxed. She wasn't just grabbing his consciousness. It wouldn't be a bad talk today.

He allowed his thoughts to mingle with the spell. It was like drinking warm syrup, then bathing in it as it poured down around his body. It covered all his senses, yet left him aware of his place in the world. He opened his awareness and saw Mistress Aileen. She came to him wearing the same black lacy dress, its conservative folds at odds with the custom needlework painstakingly sewn into its bodice. The dark colors of the dress offset her white skin and dark red lips. Miller was glad to see her well-rested. Her eyes danced with the smallest bite of impatience though.

He projected his magics outward, riding the flows of spirit.

"Mistress, I hear your call."

"Excellent!" Her welcoming smile broadened on her face. She used her fingers to brush aside shoulder-length blonde hair. "How is your progress toward Ingalls? Any problems?"

A twinge of worry appeared in Miller's confidence. She had told him that the road was clear before he left. Perhaps something had changed. "No, it's been peaceful, so far. I had expected to see some strangeness near the ruins when I went by, but it is still deserted."

"Did you go into Tweed's Castle?" Her eyes narrowed when she asked this simple question. After a moment of silence, she resumed. "No, of course not. Staying clear of the pit was wise."

The pit was where the final battle had been fought, pitching an army against an entire castle of infected, and beasts that Miller had never even read of. Madness, murder, and ground-burrowing things filled his memories and continued to give him nightmares to this day. He remembered close fighting beneath the ground. The ruling noble family had been corrupted by the Takers, and somehow managed to remain undetected for years. By the time the White Hand had found them, quite by accident, they had amassed a force of people infected with the Takers' will. Miller hadn't wanted anything to do with the place, so he just kept passing by.

Miller gave her a gentle smile. "I did talk to a few of the remaining locals. They tell me they have not seen any signs of Taker-infected, nor have they had any occult events. They stay clear, in any case. Patrols come by once or twice a month from the new lord just to check on things. So far, so good."

The remainder of the conversation passed quickly. He updated her on his progress, and she yet again praised his crafting skills. "This latest crafting, it will help a lot with the next wave of Takers. Phyllicitus will be very happy with you. It will help the next time they come from beyond."

Miller didn't respond, he merely bowed and accepted the acknowledgment. She had long since banned him from being humble to her. His enchanting and crafting skills were beyond most apprentices. He had a natural gift for it. Sadly, or not-so-sadly in the White Hand, that was insufficient for a Master's rank.

"They seem to be returning much more often than they did in the past."

Aileen paused to consider her response. There wasn't much to say. "Yes, they do."

She talked about Conclave politics, and Master December's impending trials. The Conclave was the great congress of all White Hand Masters. Many of the Masters showed up, representing their cabals or special projects. Miller tried his best to avoid being involved in cabal politics and avoided anything involving a Conclave.

Master December faced charges in this next one. He could be in deep trouble. His latest offense was murdering apprentices from rival cabals, and the other Masters were having none of it. There was open discussion of "banishment from this world" and Mistress Aileen seemed very nervous for him.

Miller didn't really care. They couldn't banish him far enough from Miller, that was certain. Master December was in his cabal. He knew him. He had never met a darker heart. The Order of the White Hand was filled with sick, twisted Masters. December was unique in his callousness, surpassing all others with complete disregard to life. It had been said that December enjoyed the company of the dead more than the living. Master December hated everyone, no matter what side of the Crooked Gate they were on.

Miller, and everyone who remembered the troubled times, had a healthy fear of the Takers. If they should return, it would sink the land into chaos. Takers infected people regardless of station, links to magic, lineage, or any other thing. The Takers swarmed into your blood, shattering your soul and taking control of your body.

Mistress Aileen ended the conversation after telling him to expect her next contact in ten days. She was eager to hear news from Clockshire. She seemed to love that place as it was never far from her thoughts, yet it had always brought her pain. Faust was buried there.

Miller arrived in Clockshire six days later. The previous sunny happy days had yielded to oppressive gray skies. Intermittent cold rain fell on him and his horse, coating his mood and gear with a dismal aspect. Tiring of the rain, he went directly to a warm place he remembered fondly, Durmitt's Inn.

The inn was a low building decorated with new additions added over the generations. It had a feeling of uncontrolled sprawl coupled with an innkeeper's declining family fortune. The remains of an old clock-tower jutted out from the left of the building, like a memory of much grander and happier days. Now it was covered in ivy and peeling white paint. The clock hands had stopped moving long ago.

He rode the mare up to the front of the inn where a boy stood waiting for customers. Miller had not seen this boy before. It had been two years since he'd last been here. He wondered where the old stable boy had gone. Hopefully, he had simply grown older and moved onto an apprenticeship. But bad things always happened, especially here, where the Taker-possessed were about the land.

"Oy!"

The boy turned and scrambled quickly to take the reins. His dirty trousers and horse-dung smell verified him as the boy that he wanted. "Feed her, water her, and clean her hooves. We leave after breakfast on the morrow."

"Aye!" He beamed up at Miller, peering through an unruly mop of dirty black hair. "She is a beauty she is. I'll take fine care of her."

He looked at his horse. It was a fine animal. Aileen had purchased it for him to speed him on his way. The horse had turned out to be a lucky break, indeed.

Miller reached into his first pouch, the one that typically got robbed, and retrieved a large copper coin. Then he reached back and fetched a second. "This coin is for your inn's fee, but this other coin is for you. I love this horse, so you have to tell me if anyone shows a fancy or interest in it. Understand? I want to know if anyone has plans for my beauty."

The boy smiled broadly. An extra copper just for him was a rarity. "Aye, sir! I'll check on her every hour, I will!" he declared as he slid one of the coins into a hidden pocket. The boy led the mare behind the inn to stable yard.

Mistress Aileen had gifted him the horse the day before he'd departed. He hadn't even named the mare yet. Miller had lost too many good horses to befriend them now. He had long ago resigned himself to the fact that these types of journeys tended to reduce horses' life-spans. Miller had begun sending them to pasture if they survived two trips. So far, he only had one horse in his pasture. He wanted another.

But someone needed to keep an eye on the horse, and especially on people who might be interested in it. Those people would be interested in him, as well. He needed as much of a head start as he could gather. If he ran, he intended to be out of harm's way before anyone could intervene.

Miller's thoughts dwelt on horses. He daydreamed of becoming a rancher in some deserted land, far away from White Hand politics and invading monsters that crept in from cracks within the world. Those thoughts were quickly interrupted as he entered the main room of Durmitt's Inn.

Six tables had pairs of farmers sitting at them, chatting about crops, weather, and the normal things that farmers discussed over a pint of mediocre ale. But the long, center table was full of trouble.

Four men sat there. The far half of the table was covered with gear. War gear, raiding gear, banditry gear, it all lay tumbled into a pile. There were things to help you kill people or to avoid being killed, and there was a lot of it. Two long swords lay atop a pile of boiled leather armor. Four long bows, along with their arrow quivers, leaned against the wall within easy reach of these dangerous men. A helmet sat on an empty chair. Miller spotted chain mail, a spiked war hammer, and three packs of camping gear. Clothing lay within piles of discarded bags filled with unknown goods.

The four men looked like they had been on the trail for a few weeks. Three had nascent beards. One had a gray-and-black beard that he might have been growing since his whiskers started to come in twenty years ago.

Miller paused in his steps. He knew of this kind of men. The roads used to be full of them. Then those in thrall to the Takers had ravaged the land, and yeomen and people of the countryside had taken to patrolling the roads, fighting possessed mobs, and keeping travelers safe. They were also the self-sworn enemies of the White Hand. Miller didn't know what they were doing here, but it probably wasn't a good thing for him to see them now. They should have disbanded long ago, when the Taker threat had passed.

He began a quiet turn to exit the room, hopefully to ride far away, when he was interrupted.

A loud cry leaped from behind the bar. "Miller! You're back!"

As he pivoted to see the caller, his gaze met the eyes of the long-bearded man. Those were cold eyes, hunter's eyes, killer's eyes. This man didn't care if he killed man or beast. He simply liked to kill.

A delighted young woman, dressed in her best tip-gathering ensemble: low-cut, green, and wenchery, rushed toward him. Her smile shined beneath long, raven-black hair. He was caught between visions of a beautiful, curvy, black-haired woman, and getting killed by the ruffians at the long table. Miller thought about running for the door, for the horse, for escape. But the die had already been cast.

Brita's embrace was as wild as her voice. She wrapped her

arms around his chest, and hugged him close, giggling with delight. Part of him was enthralled with the feel of her, the other part wanted to run from the room like a frightened rabbit.

"It's been years! Are you stopping by to see little Brita?" Her smiles and giggle filled the room, except the part with the armed men, of course.

Her long black hair swung wildly as she rushed forward. It had been two years since Miller had last seen her. He remembered a strong, athletic girl who liked to wrestle and tell dirty jokes with the boys. Now she had grown into womanhood. She was full of curves and loveliness. A tight corset gave customers a hint of what kind of beauty lay beneath those clothes. She looked like the dream of every boy who had ever crossed through puberty.

Miller stepped back, and only partially feigned a broad smile and his own mischievous grin. He did want to talk with her, but keeping his own skin intact seemed to be a higher priority right now.

A nervous pitch crept into his voice as he responded. "Brita! How you've grown! And you are so beautiful!" He pulled her into his arms while stepping toward the outer door. "Let's catch up out here."

Brita was not managed so easily. She squeaked in delight and spun to the room filled with customers. "Miller is a hero! So, keep away! While he is in town, he is all mine! He was at the temple when the trouble happened, you know. He was there when the evil came. In the fight to the last, he was! A hero, that's my Miller."

Miller was shocked. Brita had just given everything away, for no other reason than to brag to her fellow townsmen. But she had clearly not factored in the killers in the room. "Aw, hell."

STARTING OUT

The journey had started simply enough. Just a few weeks ago, life was functioning as normal. It consisted of waking up, doing chores, studying magics, and working enchantments. Life was as good as he could remember it. Mistress Aileen had even taken to giving him extra lessons just to pass the time during the heavy winter. Sadly, he had gotten skilled at the practice of meditation, mind-quieting, and other skills reserved for priests. He hadn't learned much of enchanting, nor of sending power through channels, of magic.

What did Master Easter always say? "You could take a priestess out of the temple, but you can't take the temple out of a priestess." The journey had started from a simple conversation.

A white ceramic pot sat cooling on the long oaken table. Chips of baked clay were missing from the old thing, with only the scraped ruin of what was once the image of a green fern decorating its face. Miller returned from the kitchen with three tall cups, each distressed in its own unique way. The green cup had a crack running down its length, but it still held liquid. The red cup featured small animal designs baked into its surface, yet the handle had broken off long before they had found it discarded in an old hovel near the wilderness. A sole metal cup stood alone it its cleanliness and polish. The only defect was the sharp dent in the side of the cup, as if it had been used to parry some sort of blade.

Aileen had put tremendous effort into acquiring the perfect long black dress that would accent her blonde hair and ebony ring, but she'd spent no effort making sure they had a proper functioning household; after all, this was only supposed to last a few months. They'd moved in two years ago. She never intended this place to be permanent.

Mistress Aileen, the newest Master in the Order of the White Hand, sat at the table. She was involved in an animated discussion with Master Easter, the leader of their little cabal, if they would ever admit to having one. It was confusing to him, and a little sad. The cabal had a half-dozen masters and none of them admitted to having a leader. The other cabals simply referred to them as "Easter's Cabal."

Miller approached the table, setting the cups down side-by-side. Aileen sounded weary of the conversation, yet the look on her face told Miller they were far from done.

Ignoring Miller, Aileen continued with her point. "It is convenient for them, slipping back home whenever they suffer a defeat. They can re-attack anytime they want, anywhere they want."

Master Easter spread his hands, accepting her point. "Thus, the need for us to keep watch. I'm telling you, the signs are there. We won the last battle. We didn't win the war."

"When is the last time we came close to winning the war? I really want to know. How long have we been fighting these . . . things?"

"We've never come close to winning the war. We win some battles. We lose some. So far we've won more than we've lost."

"Don't we ever attack? Isn't there something we could target?"

"Been looking for that for three thousand years. These enemies, they predate the Masters, the Order, all of it. I think the only thing older than our enemy are the First Gods themselves."

Aileen exhaled in frustration. "Then why don't the First Gods fight them? Why is it our jobs?"

Easter held up a cautious hand, urging her to control her words lest she bring some sort of doom on them. Master Easter wasn't the oldest of the Masters, but he was old enough to remember the days when the First Gods roamed the lands. He never spoke of them, nor allowed them to be disrespected in his presence. "The First Gods are animal spirits. They don't think the same way we do."

Aileen rolled her eyes, as if this was the thousandth time through this conversation. "I know. I've got it. The First Gods don't care about people. Their essence is the animal spirit, and the aspects those animals possess. Saving the world is our job."

Miller smiled as he poured the hot cider into the three cups. Winter had recently broken, but the night kept its chill. Soon the summer would be on them, and here in the north, near the border of Jarlsland, Ursland, and Cliffmark, the flowers would bloom, the wheat would grow, and the raiding season would begin.

Well, the raiding season would begin everywhere except here. The combination of White Hand Masters living in this village, and a recently returned goddess to Home's Hearth, a month's ride south, kept this part of Strathmoore peaceful and quiet.

Easter took the opportunity to sip on his newly poured cider, nodding appreciably back to Miller. When important decisions needed to be made, Easter would visit and offer her council. Yet, she rarely accepted his advice without a great deal of meditation and reflection. Something must have happened in the past, something that made her view every suggestion from Easter with suspicion.

Taking a step away from the table, Miller tried to retreat to the safety of the kitchen, far from important conversations that he didn't want any part of. He managed to achieve three steps toward that goal before Aileen called him back.

"You should stay. Believe me, you want to be part of this discussion."

Easter let loose a long breath. "Yes. She is right. You should be part of this one."

He froze in his tracks. Goosebumps traveled up his arms. He turned and walked back toward the table.

"Have a seat." Aileen motioned to an empty stool.

Spring was raiding season in the nearby lands. Here, it was traveling season, which closely lined up with getting-killed season. He sat in the chair, slowly, trying to get a feel for the mood in the room. "So, what are we planning?"

He used "we," even though Miller knew his voice wasn't going to be consulted. His job was to execute their plan, not to form it.

Easter jumped right to the point. "The Takers. We don't know where they went. It's been two years since we've had any report of their activities. Given the fact that the entire nation of Strathmoore was being attacked with possessions, murders, and chaos for at least three years that we know of, I'm thinking that we should get ahead of this problem. I'm confident we haven't seen the last of this."

Nodding slowly, he agreed.

Aileen reached out and covered his hand in hers. "Easter thinks we should send someone to help the priestesses. Your name came up. How would you feel about spending the summer in Home's Hearth?"

Home's Hearth was the city that Phyllicitus, Goddess of Love, called her own. The place was filled with happiness, cheer, and beauty. It had the most advanced school of magic outside of the Order, and even resources outside of the temple.

He hadn't been there in years, but still remembered it with pleasure. The food was excellent, even the wine was better than he could get within a week's travel of here. And better yet, there would be no White Hand Masters or their dark politics. It sounded lovely. So why was Mistress Aileen frowning?

"I'm not sure. Wouldn't you rather have me complete the enchantments we've been working on this winter?" He offered her a way out of Easter's plan, but she didn't take it.

"There is a down side to this journey. It will take you near Tweed's Castle."

"You don't expect me to go down there, do you?"

"No, nothing like that. We would like you to inspect whatever villages are left near there and look for evidence of possessions. That is all. I don't want you crawling around beneath the ruins of Tweed's Castle. Even if it is completely empty, cave-ins could trap you. Don't go down there alone, whatever you do.

"Here is the problem: I believe the Takers are regrouping, and have likely changed their tactics, and we don't know what the new attack will be, or when. We need a scout and offering you a few comfortable months in Home's Hearth in exchange for a day or two of work seemed like a good bargain."

"So, why just me?"

Miller waited for a dozen heartbeats before Aileen spoke up. "I don't want to go back there. It has been too long. If I go back, the goddess will try to keep me there."

"Seems like a soft and comfortable prison, doesn't it?" Easter commented.

"It's still a prison. I don't have time for the personality contests, the coddling, and the guilt. We've managed to stabilize the lands. Ursland is peaceful for the first time I can remember. Even Jarlsland has slowed down the raiding. If I go back there, I'll get sucked into her shadow. I might never return. Trust me, I know how she can be."

Master Easter added his opinion as well. "And we are seeing banditry again. Given the peacefulness of the rest of

Strathmoore, that seems like an indicator that something else is wrong, something we don't yet understand."

Miller remained skeptical. "Couldn't that be the remains of the Eisenvard? They have been turned out of the temple. How else would they make a living without some sort of war at hand?"

"Yes, Eisenvard could have gone rogue. But there are simply too many reports, from too many places. Most of the Eisenvard died in Jarlsland during their failed attempt to rebuild up there. There can't be more than a hundred of them left now. Not all of them would have turned bad. If the Eisenvard had anything, it was pride."

Again, Miller could not fault her logic.

"So, why am I going all the way to Home's Hearth? I could go to Tweed's Castle, scout the area, then return."

"Because I won't be here when you come back. I've got to go to a Conclave meeting. Master December is having some difficulties with the other cabals."

"It will take a few months to deal with this," Easter said, trying to help explain.

"Well, he did murder a half-dozen apprentices from other cabals. Maybe he deserves a little trouble over that." Miller stared at Aileen, silently accusing her of complicity.

Easter's sarcasm came out thick. "Sure. Let's all act like doing the right thing is more important than losing the most capable member in our cabal, and incidentally, the most feared by other cabals. I'm surprised at you, Miller. It's time to grow up and put away these childish fantasies. Our cabal survives because the other cabals are both terrified of Master December, and confident in my ability to be a reasonable negotiator. If December were to be exiled beyond the world's edge, life would get very difficult for us in a short time. I can't negotiate our way out of a conflict that we can't win."

"But why do we need to have conflict? Aren't we all in the same Order? Don't we have the same goals?"

Both Aileen and Easter laughed at that naive thought. Easter replied, after finishing his chuckle. "We are a guild of dark necromancers. None of us will let another tell them what to do. All of us have different plans, different goals, and unique agents. Oh, yes, sometimes we even cooperate while trying to slow the enemy-between-the-worlds. We have a Conclave that tries to police the worst abusers of our Order but has long turned into a weak political tool. Frankly, it's stunning the White Hand has survived so long. If it wasn't for the fact that Masters live for thousands of years, we would have disappeared long ago."

"So, what chance do we have, then?"

"None. Remember, the goal isn't to win, it is simply to survive as long as possible. It doesn't really matter what finishes us. It will be the Takers that can seep through the cracks between their world and ours. We could even fall to our own divisions."

Miller could only nod. He had suspected that for a long while. "I'll go. Home's Hearth doesn't sound so bad right now."

Aileen removed her hand. "I thought you would agree. Just be careful."

FLEEING FOR YOUR LIFE

Four chairs slid out from the long table as the men began fetching their bows and swords. Their leader, the older hunter, wasted no time. He simply vaulted over the table with one hand and used the other to stab at Miller with his eating knife.

Miller had already bolted to the door, avoiding the blade. He seized the door handle and pulled, but not quickly enough. The hunter grasped him by the shirt and threw him against the door frame.

Pain drove into his left shoulder blade where the oaken frame cut into his back. The knife flashed as it sped toward his throat. The hairy arm propelled it forward in a killing strike. Miller felt the blade cut quickly across his neck artery, sliding coldly away, lessened by the power of an enchantment, but the knife had given him a shallow wound. Miller had prepared for this journey as only an enchanter could. Small wards and protections decorated his bracelets and had just saved his life by slowing that dulled knife.

Three arcane words of channeling arose from Miller's throat. As he finished the words, he ducked his head away and closed his eyes. Even with his eyes closed, a fury of exploding light burned through. Screams of pain and confusion filled the inn. The light instantly blinded any who viewed it. Patrons were flung from their seats as the light burst into their midst. Miller ignored the spots swimming in front of him and sprinted out the door and ran forty feet to the back stables quicker than he would have thought he could.

The four men emerged from the inn door, staggering and shading their eyes as they recovered. Miller ran to his still-saddled mare and climbed on. The boy tending the horse gave Miller a surprised look at he pointed toward the panicked owner and his panicked horse.

"What are you doing? Hey! I was just getting ready to—"

The boy's words were lost as Miller dug his heels into the horse, and it leaped forward. Miller guided the horse away from the inn. He avoided the trail that passed in front of the inn and rode purposefully into the trees.

An arrow shot by him, so close he could see the fletching color: Black. Miller prayed to the First Gods, the New Gods, and any other supernatural force that might help him. He was terrified they could have mage-arrows, a bane to all spell-crafters. If struck by one, not only could it be deadly, but it would also rob him of his chief asset: Magical powers.

The horse galloped on, dodging trees and bushes alike. Yells filled the woods behind him as he urged the horse forward. Miller guided the horse on to a wide track. He knew if he didn't do something crafty soon, he would be caught and killed.

Miller used to like the brave yeomen who patrolled the roads. They tried to keep the roads clean of banditry when they were in the area, even when the nobles hid in their castles, shaking in fear. The people spoke highly of their kind deeds. If only they were not so dedicated to inserting an arrow into his brain right now, they could have gotten along quite well.

The horse took advantage of the open trail and began to gallop with new energy. Miller allowed the horse to pick its own route as he began the chants that would gather magical forces. His entire body jarred over and over again as the horse pounded down the trail. Magical words got mixed up with the smashing of his teeth and at least one tongue bite. Once through the spell, failure. Twice through the spell, failure.

He emerged from the forest at a mad gallop. He sped by a small chest-high gravestone, with moss growing on its top, and small violet flowers around its base. The horse was beginning to breathe hard when he looked at the reason for this deviation to Clockshire. Faust's grave stared back at him, reminding him of the consequences that distraction brought.

If anyone could understand such a brief meeting, it would have been Faust.

While Miller had intended to spend some time near his grave, he had not intended to join him beyond the Crooked Gate, at least not today. He urged the mare onward. The mare's breathing became heavy as she struggled up a bright green hill. Short grass and the remains of a shepherd's campfire told him what he would find on the other side of this hill. Nothing. A clear field for arrow fire. Death.

The arrows began falling again. The horse screamed as an arrow punctured his saddle bags. Miller judged that the point must have hit the poor animal. His spell craft had failed him when trying to ride a galloping horse. The enchantments were helping but they would not save him. He needed a new idea. He needed something fast.

There was one magic that he knew but it was dangerous. It could get out of control. He hated it. It terrified him. It killed and killed and killed, and it didn't care who or what stood in its way. He was far enough from the Inn, so the occupants weren't in danger. There was no shepherd to consume, nor a flock to be wasted. He could take a chance.

Miller pulled back on the reins, the mare reared. He turned

her back toward his pursuers, then raised his hand in the gesture of elemental linking and steeled his courage. In his magical consciousness, he connected the five points of elements and summoned. Miller spoke the word. The word he knew so well.

Fire erupted across the hill. Moments before the hill had stood green and full of life, now it was a blackening, burning chaos. Flames leaped upward, and smoke filled the air. Miller turned the mare and urged it to continue their retreat. The fire was frightening, but it would burn out quickly on this grassy hill. Incredibly brave foes could simply ride through it with minimal threat. It was large enough to be impressive, two hundred feet wide and twenty feet deep.

His pursuers didn't continue, though. They turned their horses and quickly rode back into the woods.

Miller shook his head at their stupidity. That was the wrong direction. Never run from fire into the woods. Other White Hand practitioners would not hesitate to remove an entire forest to end a few enemies, no matter what the cost to local residents.

But they would be safe enough from Miller. The grass would not hold the fire, and even if it did, it wasn't dry enough to spread. He hated using fire. He hated the damage it could do. He hated that it could get out of control. He hated the way the hill would blacken for most of a year. He hated the fact that when he finally passed through the Crooked Gate, it would most likely be fire that sent him there.

Fire was Mistress Sword's weapon, the core reason that Miller feared it, and he feared her more than he feared the flame. Mistress Sword despised him now, and she had a way of evening scores. That is why Miller knew the art of fire so well, even when he hated it. Fire was his doom. Fire was the first item in his doom-list. He needed to know it well.

But now he had another doom to worry about. He mentally added another to his ever-growing list.

Killed by an inopportune word, spoken by a girl who only wanted a kiss.

Miller smiled a bit as he trotted away. He thought of Brita's new womanly body, her long black hair, her face. If he was going to go through the Crooked Gate, then he could hardly come up with a better way. There had been days that he would embrace such an end. Today was not one of those days.

The fire would only delay the pursuers, not eliminate them. He rode on, paying attention to his mare's developing limp. Ingalls lay only a week away by road. This horse would need some help soon. His quicker pace would get him there in five days.

Three miles later, the trail passed in front of a farm. The yard had four chickens in it, a dog, and a woman busily washing the family's clothes in an overflowing tub. Her dark-brown hair was decorated with a few strings of gray. She sang as she washed. The symbol of the goddess Phyllicitus hung from her home. She was a true believer, then. Perhaps the gods were with him, or at least the goddess was.

An age-blackened barn stood fifty feet behind the house. Tall grass grew around it, masking old barrels and wagon wheels that had been long left to rot. It was a perfect opportunity. Miller quietly guided the horse around the edge of the farm, and then approached the barn from the back. A large door stood closed against the sunny day. He opened the doors and entered, tying the reins to a nearby post. Three other horses looked curiously at Miller and their new horse-visitor.

He dismounted and quietly began unbuckling the saddle and bags. He grabbed the arrow that still protruded from his bag, and gently moved it. The horse pulled its side away from him but did not scream or panic. The arrow had hit the mare, but the wound wasn't deep.

Miller pulled the knife from his side sheath quickly, while maintaining a hold on the arrow. A few cuts later and the arrow snapped, releasing the weight of his gear onto the floor. A small trickle of blood dripped from the puncture. This would not be critical if he could get at it quickly. He could help the horse and be on their way soon, if he could just keep his horse calm.

Miller began the channeling to calm her, sending her soothing flows of mana. His hands began to glow softly pink as the power flowed out of his own spirit. Spells of the mind did not come easy to him, but he concentrated, meditated, and continued his slow calming. The mare began to relax. He heard the mare's breath slow. The mare did not panic. Relief coursed through his nerves. As he gained some success with this mare, he widened the area of the spell. The other horses stopped fidgeting and began to appear sleepy. After ten minutes, all the animals in the barn were senseless and asleep.

Miller walked up to the mare, snatching a light wool coat that hung from a beam. Two quick cuts with the knife into the desensitized flank, and the arrowhead released its grip. He pulled it from the horse's flank and snapped the arrow in two. He allowed the feathered shaft to fall, then placed the arrowhead into his travel bag where it would be easier to carry. He'd show it to Aileen later.

Then he began the careful job of cleaning the horse's wound with water and that handy wool coat. It wasn't the best spellcrafting that Miller had ever done, but it was enough to make the horse ridable again.

Once his mind-channeling stopped, the horses began to awaken. He picked up the blanket, saddle, and bags, placing them gently on the mare's back. He dried the last bit of water left from the wash, then returned the stained wool coat to its peg. Then he slid the saddle onto the horse's back. Ten minutes later Miller was walking the horse to the door. He slid the door open and looked for any watchers. There were none, so he walked from the barn and returned to the trees.

As Miller walked past the corner of the barn he heard a painful cry. His gaze snapped to the house. The washer woman struggled with someone. Her dog bit into the assailant's arm, who flailed wildly in his attempt to remove the animal from his shoulder. The assailant lifted his other arm and plunged a long, broad-bladed knife down to the point where her throat met her shoulders. She slumped, grabbed her bleeding neck, and fell to the ground. He raised his arm with the dog attached to it, and quickly opened the dog's belly from beneath. Organs rained down from the poor loyal beast's chest and decorated the ground with guts. The attacker looked up from the dying dog, toward the barn, toward Miller.

He had taken too long. The men had found him. Miller pulled himself into the saddle and screamed at the horse to run

FLIGHT

Miller galloped away from the farm. The mare breathed hard as it sped faster and faster. Its hooves dug into the rich ground, flinging large clods of dirt in their wake. He urged the mare onward, slapping her uninjured flank. Branches sped by. Yells erupted behind him as he brought the horse to ever more perilous speeds.

The trail branched. Miller turned the speeding horse toward the wider, clearer trail. The way quickly became muddy. Boot prints and deep wheel tracks decorated the softening ground. Trees continued to speed by. Soon they began climbing along a gentle slope. When Miller reached the summit, he shot a panicked looked down. A long stretch of muddy trail led below to a small wooden bridge which spanned a violent river at the bottom of the hill. Rocks jutted out of the narrow waterway, cutting white breaks into the fast-moving river surface.

Miller saw a future where a broken horse and his maimed body slid to their doom, carried away by that river to be bashed against the rocky banks and drowned. He pulled back on the reins and the mare responded by slowing down. They were past the summit and onto the steep, downward slope. The mare slipped in the mud.

Miller grabbed the top of the saddle and pulled his leg back to extract it from beneath the falling horse just before it plowed into the slick mud.

The leg beneath the wounded flank buckled and went down. Miller and the horse began falling and sliding toward the narrow bridge.

The panicked screams of both horse and rider filled the air. Miller held on to the saddle with the tightest grip his fingers possessed. Pain shot through his hands as he and the horse began to rotate while sliding down the muddy slope. He clawed at the leather to stay near the horse. She kicked wildly, spraying mud in all directions, blinding him and bringing a stinging pain to his eyes.

As they approached the fast-flowing river, one of the horse's hooves connected with the remains of an old stump. The stump splintered, and a section of rotting tree came loose. But the kick had slowed the horse's movement. They came to a stop within an arm's reach of the river, just left of the narrow bridge that crossed it.

Both Miller and the mare lay exhausted, breathing hard, and trying to get their bearings. The horse scrambled up first, obviously disoriented by the tumultuous arrival. Miller crawled onto his hands and knees, then grabbed the mud-covered saddle, and stood up. He had no time to recover. The four riders had arrived at the top of the hill and were readying their bows. Miller pulled the horse forward across the bridge. He hoped they wouldn't shoot her. He was really starting to like her.

Arrows began to fall as they staggered across the bridge onto the opposite bank. Miller urged the mare to pick up speed, and she quickly moved forward a dozen paces before slowing into an exhausted walk again. Another volley of arrows fell around him, thudding into his warded cloak and breast guard. He felt the sting of the arrows striking his back, but its enchantment deflected their wide-barbed arrowheads from his skin.

The horse would not be any help. She could barely walk without a rider, never mind with one. He needed a few more moments to recover.

One of the men decided not to give them time. A younger one, with a newly grown beard and a threadbare gray cloak, handed his bow to a companion. He drew a short, wicked-looking sword from his side scabbard and began to carefully ride down the hill. Smiling, he drew nearer to Miller. The blade loomed large in Miller's vision. Two other raiders took inspiration from the bold one, and began a similar approach, leaving their bows behind as well.

Miller moved back from the bridge. There was an archer on the hill, but his immediate problem was the three men closing in on him, weapons in hand. They'd be in sword range within moments. An arrow struck the ground an arm's reach away; their bowman wasn't that good—he had a few seconds to do something.

He was tired, and had little spirit to devote to magics, but he had enough for this one effort. Miller calmed himself to enter the meditation space. He drew on the five points again, but instead of unleashing fire, he loosely tied the potentials of the bridge. A bridge was well suited to many things. Enchantments favored spells that tied to an item's potential. Miller quickly tied the bridge to a foreseeable potential, then began a quick retreat.

The first man sped up after he got past the muddy slope. Miller reached the mare and climbed into the saddle. He decided that owing a goddess another favor might not be the worst outcome for this day, and he began praying as he turned the horse away from the bridge.

Pain erupted from his shoulder. A long, black arrow had struck him, impaling him through his enchanted cloak. Burning pain quickly grew from the wound into his back and neck. Miller screamed in agony as he felt his spirit energy, the stuff of magic, drain away from his body.

A Mage Arrow. Where did they get Mage Arrows?

Miller disregarded caution. He seized the arrow shaft with his opposite hand, pushing fingers into the wound to find the arrowhead. He found the top of a narrow square. He struggled to grip it tightly. The blood made it slick, and difficult to hold.

The first man spurred his horse forward and reached the bridge. His cry of victory mixed with Miller's scream of pain as he pulled the long, sharp Mage Arrow from his shoulder. The mare saw the danger as well and began moving away from this new rider. The charging steed arrived at the bridge. Its iron-shod hooves pounded across until it reached the other side.

He saw the approaching danger through dizzy eyes and surging nausea—falling off the mare seemed like a good idea, but he kept his grip because there wasn't time to do anything else. He pulled the arrow from his shoulder, glancing at it before he tucked it away.

The charging raider came to the end of the bridge. A bridge has a clear function, and enchanters were excellent at manipulating the function of things. A bridge allows a person, a horse, or even a thing to transit from one location to another. This potential, one fate of many possibilities, was now fulfilled. Miller's quick enchantment triggered on this event and realized its own fulfillment. It ended the magic that constrained five connected elemental strands.

A tower of fire erupted from the bridge and drove upward, forming a swirling tornado of burning death, consuming wood and pitch within a few short seconds. The first rider was next to the base of this inferno. Flames surrounded him as he began flailing about, burning.

The mare gained speed as she realized how bad an idea standing next to this hell-storm was. Miller hung on to the saddle weakly, watching his attacker's horse collapse within the inferno. His heart filled with regret as he saw the man trying to crawl from the hell that he could never escape.

Mercy. Mercy is what the goddess would demand of him. He knew this even as he knew that Mistress Aileen would condemn him for it. His spirit had been drained, but there was no other path. He was on the way to Home's Hearth and the goddess might be there in person. He couldn't enter her temple with a fresh murder on his soul. He could only imagine how angry she would be.

He reached out toward the burning man. A few simple hand motions reduced the fire, giving the man enough time to crawl to safety, severely burned but still alive.

Miller had just started feeling good about showing mercy when blood began to drip from his nose. Spells demanded sacrifice. Normally, a caster sacrificed spirit, which could easily be regained. The Mage Arrow had stolen his spirit force. Miller had no spirit to give, so the magics demanded their price from his body. Just as Miller was rethinking the usefulness of mercy, the world spun, and he was unconscious.

The jostling of the horse brought him back to consciousness. The front of his clothing was covered in a chunky mix of drying blood and vomit. Vomit? When did I vomit? There was no river. The grassy river banks had been replaced by a forest. The mare strode upward, climbing a short hill. She seemed to be following some sort of game trail. The bright sun had begun casting long shadows throughout the forest as it prepared to set.

He didn't know how long he had been down. He just knew that he hurt all over. The only good news was that the mare was uninjured, and she seemed to have a plan. At least, she had a direction she wanted to walk.

Miller let the mare navigate for ten more minutes. He couldn't help but think the horse was doing a better job on this quest than he was.

They arrived at the top of the hill. The trees grew less dense here. Lights from a small village twinkled through the sparse wood in the far distance.

Pain lanced down his shoulder into his arm. Dismounting caused it to double in ferocity. He struggled with his saddle, released his bags, and removed them from the mare's back. Then he explored his injury. The arrow had sliced deep into his back muscles, puncturing the shoulder. He pulled off his shirt. Pain screamed. He used half the remaining water to clean the mare's wound, then the other half to clean his own. Then he removed the bit and bridle. Finally, Miller hobbled the mare for the night.

He grimaced, lowering himself to the floor of the barn. A wiser person would have left the hill and sought a good hiding place. Miller didn't do that. He was just too tired. The mare didn't look like she would make it far. He wasn't going to leave her, though, not after she had carried him to safety.

This horse was amazing. He had traveled with a Great Horse before. Mistress Aileen had gained one from the temple for a short time. When she lost it, she almost wept. These beasts, no, these horses, were highly intelligent, crafty, and normally very loyal. This was only the second Great Horse he had seen in his life. Of course, they looked the same as any other horse. But they weren't.

He wondered at his luck. This kind of horse was a treasure fit for any noble. He didn't know why Aileen had given her to him. He didn't fool himself, Aileen must have known. She didn't miss things like miraculous animals. She might have known how much he would need something like the mare. Sometimes Aileen could be too intelligent, too insightful. It was frightening. He had acquired the horse directly from a farmer. He guessed Aileen had set up that entire transaction. She might even be manipulating this entire journey from afar, just like a student of Easter's would. He shook his head. There were too many wheels-within-wheels to be believable.

He sat and thought about it. It seemed insane that Mistress Aileen would secretly arrange for a Great Horse to go on this journey with him. But Master Easter. That is exactly the kind of thing he would do. A Great Horse was a beast with some mysterious connection back to its Old God. The spirit of horses was strong in this mare. If she chose to help him, he had no choice to accept. He could hardly stop her anyway, even if he tried.

Mistress Aileen used to theorize that there was a family of horses still close to the First Gods. Such an idea seemed to make sense on the surface. Miller doubted that was the reason, though. The First Gods were animal spirits made flesh. Most had already left the world. The First Gods lived according to their nature. They tended to roam free in their own territories. He had never heard of one who'd share power with other animals, even of the same breed.

He unlaced the fastenings of a saddle bag and reached in. Bundles of dried straw came out as he searched for the prize. A small, black wooden box emerged from the straw. The straw was still dry. He was thankful that the goddess continued to be happy with him.

He unlocked the box with a hidden word and a sigh of relief. It opened, showing three silver vials, unbroken and beautiful. Each one was corked and sealed in beeswax. A skull head was embossed on each, causing Miller to pause. Mistress Aileen would have had to make some deals to acquire these vials, and deals with other Masters were expensive things. He hated to use them so early in the journey, but his wound would not be argued with. If it festered, Miller could die.

Stripping the beeswax off, Miller uncorked a vial. He drank the salty fluid and almost immediately felt the pain dissipate. A yawn erupted; he would be asleep soon. Two vials left, two drinks that could mend torn flesh. Two more chances to survive in the face of certain doom. He stretched out his arm, stretching the wounded shoulder and checking that the pain had fully stopped.

Standing up, he fetched one more of the vials. Then he picked up a shallow cooking pan and the canteen. His back had almost entirely stopped hurting by the time he arrived in front of the mare. Kneeling, he poured the water into the pan and then mixed in the healing elixir. He didn't know if the vial will do anything for a horse, but he thought she deserved the effort. He stroked her mane gently as she began drinking from the pan.

Darkness began to arrive as the horse finished her healing draft. The wound began closing on its own until only a small scar remained on its flank. Miller pulled his discarded cloak over his naked shoulders, and then curled up near the horse. He trusted that the raiders would be spending the night trying to save their burned companion.

A doubting voice bothered him, though. Sleeping in the barn could get him killed. He got up, walked around the barn and placed five charms on its outer walls. They would wake him if someone came close.

Those raiders had murdered an innocent farm woman. What kind of men were these? What had changed in the last three years that would drive them to do such a thing? These troubling thoughts did not stop Miller from finding sleep.

He awoke at dawn and gazed out an open window. The sky had begun to fill with low, gray clouds. He took some time to pack, and then hide the evidence of his camp. He wasn't entirely sure where he was. Tips of roofs emerged from the distance in the south, visible across the open fields. A village lay about an hour's ride to the south: gray smoke from early morning cooking fires decorated the sky above it. The forest opened below, and farms began to decorate the landscape. He would not be welcome dressed in a bloody cloak and coated in mud.

He would rather deal with suspicious farmers than murderous raiders, in any case.

Deciding he should at least arrive with all his clothes on, he reached into his bag and pulled out his special shirt meant to make him presentable to polite society. He looked down at his disheveled clothing. This was as polite as he was going to get. A few moments of cleaning and he looked like someone who'd previously done quite well, but now faced harder times.

The mare had no trouble navigating the sloping ground; it yielded under her hooves, showing dark, healthy soil farmers would adore. They passed through fields knee-high in wheat, even though summer had just begun.

The first farm he approached looked like it had been partially rebuilt after years of neglect. The last time Miller had traveled in these lands, the farms were barely surviving. Now they flourished. He looked across the yard and saw two dozen chickens, three goats, and a newly painted barn. Mistress Aileen had abandoned the goddess' vision. The goddess was a pacifist. Aileen believed in using martial strength for noble causes if she believed in anything. But here was some evidence that perhaps the goddess Phyllicitus had a better point.

An older, gray-haired farmer emerged from the barn. He walked up to Miller and smiled a gap-toothed grin.

"Welcome, Traveler," he said with a friendly note in his voice. "Welcome to Zeeter's farm. We've a well to drink from, and it tastes like mint and sunshine! Come fill your water jugs. I will share my water, and I will ask you to share news of the road."

Miller considered the old man. He simply asked for news from the road without weapon in hand, without fear. The farmer's greeting was a custom he had experienced many times farther north where Mistress Aileen had moved them. People had become a lot more trusting than they used to be.

"I'm grateful, sir. I much appreciate it," Miller returned, affecting his best peasant-farmer voice. "The road's been hard this last week, and your water is much welcomed."

The farmer paused in his welcome. His shrewd gaze rested squarely on Miller's face. "You look like you wrestled a bear."

Miller smiled back. "There's some that call it wrestling. I still think the bear should have kissed me first."

The old man laughed heartily until he ran out of breath. He walked up to a well and drew up a bucket, that he drank out of. The old man didn't even boil the water. Things really had improved.

Miller grasped onto the pause in conversation to change the subject away from his poor grooming, and apparent bear wounds. "Sure looks like the crops are coming up fast."

"Aye, we had a good season last year. This year might be even better. We might even get a second short season. Goddess be praised, it's been good since she returned to us, it has."

"I came through here two years ago. It weren't nearly so good. 'Twas war about, an' stories of creatures." He paused for dramatic effect. "An' sorcerers, too. Dark magic on the roads, there was."

The old man gazed at him, as if looking at another darker time. "Aye, things were hard back then. But the goddess, she fixed them. Sorcerers are gone, back to the cursed place they came from. The big storms have stopped coming. I haven't heard a true tale about the ground-beasts for months. I dare hope things are becoming normal, whatever that is."

He remembered beasts that could claw their way up from the ground. They would come in the darkness, rendering sleeping villages into just so much meat. Some called them ground-beasts, others called them Mole-Men. Miller thought the names were just stupid. Someone needed to come up with a decent name for those kind of things, as if the ordinary Takers weren't bad enough. The ground-beasts were twisted things. They may have been men once, but he doubted it. They looked more like cursed moles than any other life he had ever seen. He felt a slight quiver thinking about those strange monsters. Mistress Aileen didn't believe the army had eliminated them, and neither did he.

"How have the roads fared? I hear tell there are still patrols on the roads."

"Aye, but they've lost their cause." The old farmer shook his head sadly. "Those cursed sorcerers, the White Hand, they've been defeated by the local lords. So now I think they've lost their reason for being here and mayhap their way. Last year, a bunch of them went to Phyllicitus, and tried to enter her service. But you know the goddess. She would have none of it.

Made them promise to beat their swords into tools and take to the land. Now they might have three hundred men total, but they are loyal to their own way."

Miller thought that was odd, given he had recently finished running for his life in front of a group of raiders who were most probably leftovers from the days when roads were patrolled frequently, searching for signs of necromancy and possession. Good men go bad all the time. It wasn't surprising, especially if Takers had returned to the area.

"Any banditry?"

"Nah. You have been gone a while!" He smiled as he said it. "We haven't seen a bandit in these parts since last year. When the villagers finally caught them, it was clear they were a group of foreigners. The village fed them and sent them on to Home's Hearth, hoping the goddess could put them right."

"That is where I am bound. I'm off to the temple."

"Aye, a good time to do the pilgrimage."

"Pilgrimage?" Miller asked curiously. This old man was a fountain of recent knowledge.

"Last year, the entire town of Leeds-on-the-Drey packed up and walked to Home's Hearth. They were so eager to see the goddess they left their entire village unguarded. When they returned, none of their things had been stolen. The village is far from the well-traveled roads. The priestesses decided it was some sort of divine act, so now this year, there is supposed to be a larger pilgrimage from many towns. I'm not going, though. The goddess has better things to do than trade stories with the likes of me." He chuckled at the thought of talking directly to the goddess. Miller remembered how it felt to be standing in front of the goddess, only feet away. He had met her twice in the company of Aileen. It hadn't been funny at all.

The old man continued, describing the pilgrimage, and tales he had heard about it.

There would be crowds; there might be six or seven hundred more people than usual in town. He knew he'd better talk to Mistress Aileen. She might be able to set up some lodging. He chucked a little, thinking about how he was going to tell Aileen that the White Hand had been defeated by street patrols and city guards. She would probably need to make new career plans.

Miller chucked inside at the absurdity of it. The White Hand had been "defeated" at least three times in his life, but he hadn't seen any effect of it. The White Hand didn't take land, nor did they fight wars in the way that peasants or nobles understood. Their main battleground lay within the cracks of the world, whatever that was. He wondered if the Masters would inform him when he became eligible for his Master's ring. The masters certainly did babble on about it enough, he thought.

But he had already decided that he would probably not earn a Master's ring; the price was too high. It demanded a commitment that exceeded the normal "life-long" commitment of other guilds. In the White Hand, a life was an eternity, literally.

The apprentices were not given any details as to how to gain that rank, anyway. It remained a mystery until the day the other Masters began to refer to an apprentice as "Master." There was no ceremony. When the apprentice received his or her Master's ring, then they were a Master. He had no idea how that happened. The masters simply repeated, "We will know when you are ready, and so will you." Other guilds had exams. Miller had even heard of magical houses where master level was awarded based on the ability to enchant magical items, a skill he was sufficiently advanced with.

It seemed that the White Hand had no rituals, processes, or deeds that made one a master. It might be simple seniority. But how does seniority work in an Order where the masters live forever? Why don't they simply tell us? Why don't they let us leave the Order? Apprentices can't even get kicked out. The Masters would prefer to simply kill the failures and move on.

But the Order of the White Hand offered one thing that no other magical guild ever would: The secret of unending life. When he was young, Miller had considered that the ultimate prize. Now, after seeing small hints of the darker parts of the world, he wasn't so sure.

The truth was that most apprentices would leave given the chance. The White Hand was a frightening group. It was a guild of dark sorcerers, steeped in mystery and not afraid to shed a lot of blood for their abstract, hidden plans. Most of their "eternal life" seemed to involve resurrecting zombies and terrifying the common folk. The Masters were the most terrifying of all. There weren't many stories of Masters finding their mates and creating families. He couldn't think of a single one.

A FRIENDLY MEAL

Miller talked with the old farmer for another hour, offering up news from the northern fringes of the kingdom. The Jarl to the north had been silent lately. The yearly raids had not yet occurred. A new iron mine had opened, but its trade remained small, and weapon smiths were building farm tools. It was a time of peace.

When old man Zeeter offered Miller a meal, he couldn't refuse. The family didn't seem to mind his freshly scarred face and hands. The children asked questions continuously of the now-mythical bear attack. Miller invented tales about bears in the north near the borders of Jarlsland and told real tales about how the northern lands kept to the Old Bear God, while continuing to honor Phyllicitus when her priestesses came.

The company made him happy, and Miller was delighted by the fresh leafy greens, rich tomatoes, and sweet cheese that decorated his plate. The family consisted of three sons grown into adulthood, two young wives, and five grandchildren. They sat happily around a long rectangular country table excitedly discussing the new music that would appear this year at the LaDeeDah, the finest song-hall in Ingalls, and probably the entire land.

Sadly, the great bards would arrive at Ingalls the same week as the pilgrimage of the priestesses. Leave it to the priestesses to spoil a good time. Perhaps he could discuss this inconvenience when he arrived in Home's Hearth, if any priestess of rank would hear him out. Most of them were pretty understanding. But if Phyllicitus heard that the pilgrimage interfered with a good party, she would probably just cancel the pilgrimage and attend the party. She liked a good time.

"What's that ring for?" one of the children asked and Miller was stopped in his mental tracks. Miller felt his gut dropping out of his chest. Oh, no. Please, no.

Apprentice rings were wide silver bands with a thumb-tip-sized cameo, set on a thick band. The cameo showed a human skull. The ring identified him as a member of the White Hand. Rings were enchanted, only people who could gather and focus spirit could notice them. A normal person's mind could be trained to notice and remember them, but it would take a few weeks of dedicated effort. A natural sorcerer would take note of them immediately—and the ring in turn helped identify those who could become apprentices.

This child was eight years old. He was a small boy with golden hair, thick arms, and a wide, cocky grin who had just unwittingly volunteered to enter the Order of the White Hand whether he wanted to or not.

Experienced sorcerers knew not to interfere with the White Hand, including their apprentices. "Thank you for the dinner, but sadly, I must go." Sad was the word of the day.

"But what about the ring? Tell me the story!" the boy insisted.

Miller gently smiled at the little fellow. He didn't want to ask his name. Names were funny things to White Hand Masters. The less he had of them, the better. "I can't share the story today. I will promise that next time I come this way, if we should meet again, I will tell you a tale full of surprises and marvels. And yes, about my Mistress's ring."

Miller rose from the table, thanked the family again, and left. He lifted his loaded saddle, along with his bags, onto the mare, fastened them tight, and quickly trotted away from the lovely farmstead. After he rode a half mile away, Miller turned the horse to point back at the farm. He sat there for several minutes committing the farm to memory. Then he bent down to the mare, and said, "If I ever stumble on this place again, remind me to leave immediately."

The horse flicked her ears as if she understood. She just might understand, at that.

Miller swore an oath to Phyllicitus that he would never reveal this child to the Masters, and then he prayed that he could keep it.

They traveled into the evening, avoiding the other nearby farms. A road crossed their trail, and Miller turned onto it, toward Ingalls. They made camp near the side of the road, just within a thick grouping of trees. He cleaned his traveling clothes the best he could, then repacked them. He didn't want to ruin his formal wear.

As he traveled the road he remembered more and more of it. The next morning, they left just after dawn arrived. He had eaten the last of his cheese, and now would subsist on dried hardbread and a few donated tomatoes until they got to Ingalls.

After two hours of riding passed, he noticed the tell-tale signs of his mistress reaching out to him. She didn't seem panicked, but she normally kept to a rigid schedule. If she was contacting him early, something must be happening. Miller pulled the mare onto the side of the trail and tied it to a nearby tree, giving her access to some ample grasses. At least the mare could relax a little.

Miller had barely entered his mental preparation state when Mistress Aileen was there in his consciousness. She was far away, but in his mind, she stood next to him. She didn't seem panicked, but she seemed very edgy, like she was walking on a very thin rope over a very deep chasm.

"Miller, where are you?"

"About three days from Ingalls, Mistress."

"That's too far. You should be there by now."

He bowed deeply and respectfully, preparing for the next wave of rebuke. He knew it was going to be a one-sided conversation; there would be no use fighting against it. He had become skilled at recognizing these situations.

"Mistress, you have my apologies. I became distracted when I nearly got murdered. I will try harder next time."

Aileen immediately halted her diatribe. She stopped and inspected Miller. She saw his blood-soaked clothing, and his dirty skin.

"Are you injured?"

She was hard to deal with, but she cared, at least she seemed to. He thought for a second that Aileen might be the only one of the masters who could feel good emotions. It was probably because she had just recently attained her ring. Maybe it was because her earlier life was in service to the goddess before Easter converted her to the White Hand. Either way, Miller knew he was lucky to have her as his Mistress. His first service had been to Mistress Sword, and he never wanted to go back to her service again.

"I am fine now. But I had to use two of your potions."

Her eyes went wide. The previous calm dissipated to be replaced by a greater storm. "Two? How did you survive long enough to drink two?"

"My horse needed one, too."

It was too much for her. Her hand came up and slapped her forehead as the pitch of her voice rose. "We've talked about this. I can get you another horse. Don't die, Miller. You aren't a Master yet; you don't get to come back all by yourself. Don't make me look for your decomposing body. I swear I will pickle you for a month before I bring you back."

It wasn't a pleasant vision, but better than some alternatives.

Miller didn't especially want to come back if he passed through the Crooked Gate. He had seen what had happened to Faust and didn't want to share that fate. No, he had long since decided that when he passed, he would simply lie down and rot away like anyone respectable would do. Besides, she couldn't get another horse like this one. Miller wasn't going to let her know that.

"Thank you for your concern for my safety. I am recovered now. I will be in Ingalls in three days. I had an encounter with four raiders who decided to start a second career as highwaymen. One of them had a Mage Arrow."

"Did they hit you?"

"Yes, but I got it out in time."

The color slowly returned to Aileen's face. Her blonde hair looked unkempt, as if she had been up all night. But she was very afraid for Miller. For just one moment, he could see it.

He attempted to change the subject. "You had news, Mistress?"

"Yes," she responded thankfully to Miller. He had steered the conversation back to where she wanted it. "Word arrived this morning that the next Conclave will consider the matter of Master December."

Miller didn't care about Master December, other than to stay as far away from that murderer as he could. That maniac had managed to kill off at least a dozen apprentices, only one of them being December's own apprentice. The White Hand gave a large degree of freedom to their Masters, but apparently killing the apprentices of other Masters was now frowned on, at least if done in volume. Master December was one of the strongest Masters in the White Hand, and the other cabals respected him. Miller would be more than happy if the White Hand decided that it was time to do something final to Master December. He was a sadist, and the worst sort of necromancer—the kind that enjoyed his work.

Miller smiled on the inside yet kept his face and voice neutral. "Oh?"

"Oh? And perhaps my apprentice is not aware that we are nearly in direct conflict with Master Hermagon's cabal? Perhaps it has escaped your notice that our leader, Master Easter, has been devoting his every considerable skill to stop this trial? What reality have you been living in?"

"My apologies, Mistress. The affairs of the Masters are beyond my comprehension. I understand that you have an alliance with Master December. Of course I am your apprentice. I will support your every requirement. What do you need of me?"

Mistress Aileen clearly understood the message. He didn't care what happened to December, as long as it was bad.

"Ah, I see clearly now." she replied slowly.

Miller would never win a duel of wits with Mistress Aileen. He didn't attempt the folly. He merely bowed low, accepting her lowering opinion with grace.

She abruptly changed the conversation. A slight smirk appeared on her face. "I just so happen to have something for you to do, Miller."

Miller didn't like the sound of this tilt in the conversation. "Yes, Mistress?"

"Master Easter would like Master December to be somewhere out of sight and out of mind until the Conclave meets. He does like to cause trouble. Master Easter would like to minimize such troubles over the next few months. So, I need to find something for him to do." She paused, gesturing at his clothes and appearance. "By the disarray of your dress, it appears to me that you are having a hard time of it on the road."

Miller began to dread her next words. He saw what was coming. There was no way out.

"I think I will ask Master December to accompany you on your journey to Home's Hearth. I think he would be competent if a conflict presented itself."

Miller scrambled, searching all his mental trickery for some tactic to avoid traveling with the lunatic. He had to play long odds. "Mistress, there is no need. I will be in Ingalls within three days. There I will meet with Drane and the Free Mages. I hope to gain their support on my journey. I suspect his presence would not be welcome there."

"Drane of the bloody fingers? He would travel with you? Have you somehow become popular?"

"We once got along famously," Miller announced, stretching the truth enough to be useful yet still believable. "I think he'd be interested in a quick trip to Home's Hearth, if for no other reason than a change of atmosphere."

Aileen was right, it would be difficult. Drane would need to be pried out of that town; he loved it there.

"Really? I thought he liked it in Ingalls."

"He does, he just likes to go out and, well, you know, collect new songs." The lie was sounding weaker and weaker as he uttered it.

Mistress Aileen paused, and then began to play with her shoulder-length blond hair. She smiled at him, as if the cat had just caught a mouse. "Very well, go ahead and reach out to Drane. I will also talk to Master December. You might need some help and I would like someone nearby. And, Miller, you did test them, didn't you?"

"Test them, Mistress?"

"The raiders, for blood parasites. The ones you've been devoting your every waking moment to find a way to fight for the past two years. You did check the crazy murderers for them, didn't you?"

"I thought they were finally gone." He was surprised. He hadn't even thought of it. Had he grown complacent?

Aileen looked at him coldly. "A funny thing about bad events that simply go away: they tend to come back all by themselves.

Stay alert, get to Home's Hearth. I will contact you after I get Master December's first report."

PREPARATION

The discussions had gone as Easter had predicted. Miller took the bait. The promise of a few months in Home's Hearth had proved to be too much for him to resist. Aileen didn't feel good about it, though. It seemed too manipulative, too sneaky. It had the marks of something Easter would do.

It was something Easter would do. It had been his idea, after all.

Aileen turned to the necromancer who had once been her own White Hand Master. He had always been more of a mentor, almost a friend. She wondered how much of their relationship had been an act, how much continued to be an act.

One of the most difficult things to learn about Master Easter was that you never knew you were doomed until it was too late. She had allowed Easter to get his hooks into Miller. There was no use trying to avoid it. If she had protested, Easter would manufacture some other pressing need and put her in an even more defenseless position. At least now she could claim to be part of his plans, even a willing participant.

"What do you think his odds are of making it to Home's Hearth?"

"Making it? Pretty high, actually. Getting possessed by Takers before he arrives? That's what you're worried about. I'm confident in the young man. I'd say he has two chances in three to arrive in Home's Hearth intact."

Aileen's voice turned to ice. "That much? Seems a little aggressive."

"Oh, no. I'm more than confident in his abilities. Plus, he has a natural sense of when he's in danger. He knows when to run away. That could get him through this entire ordeal by itself." Easter smiled his thin, spiteful smile. "Why? Do you want to make a wager?"

Aileen didn't want to let Easter see her fear. She was terrified that Miller would be infected and turned by the Takers. If he was killed and left at the side of the road, she could find him and perhaps revive him, even pull him back through the Crooked Gate, if need be. There was no remedy for being taken, possessed, turned by the enemy-between-the-worlds. Miller would just cease to be. Even his spirit would fray into corruption. But she couldn't let Easter see her fear. He would use it, capitalize on it for his own goals. She had to keep it hidden.

"Don't even think about it. The last thing I need to worry about is you cheating on a bet."

Easter shrugged, raising his hands in mock surrender. "Cheat? Me? When have I ever cheated you?"

She tossed his comment off with a laugh. "It just hasn't been my time yet. I'm sure it will come." She smiled to soften her rebuke.

She remembered very well some of his cheats. She remembered dealing with bandits, tracking them down across frozen tundra. They had stolen artifacts left from ages ago, maybe from the old priests of the Stag God. Easter had sent her to make a deal with the thieves, accompanied by only four people. When she found them, it hadn't gone as they'd expected it would—they'd expected to negotiate a price with a priestess of Phyllicitus, Goddess of Love.

Instead, they'd come up against a White Hand Master waiting for them on the trail, with a pack of huge dogs. Master Easter had guided them. The dogs were taller than waist-high, and hungry. Two dozen men were ripped to shreds that day by a pack of dogs guided by a Master who never walked within a mile of them. When she found the scene, the terror of the ripped-up bodies haunted her for months afterward. Easter never gave his enemies a chance. He used agents to do his bidding, either his dogs, or his cabal members. He cheated his enemies out of any chance of defeating him, as he never fought directly.

Back then, she was dedicated to Phyllicitus' cause. She'd found the bodies of those men scattered in a field near the trail. They lay atop a foot of red- and brown-stained snow. She brought the bodies together, crying the entire time, performing last rights for these unlucky men, which was when she'd noticed that not all the body parts were present. Someone had collected and kept souvenirs, pieces and parts of murdered men, for their own dark purposes. She never found out what Easter did with those parts. She'd never dared ask. She didn't see him for a year after he recovered the artifacts. She didn't mention them again, either.

Her attention returned to the room. She sat at a dark, round table, covered with a half-dozen cups. The remains of a pitcher stood dirty in their midst. Miller had been gone three days. He should be approaching Clockshire any day now. For a moment, and not for the first time, she wished she'd gone with him. Easter was staring into her eyes, trying to read her. He was good at that kind of thing. "I should have gone with him."

"We've been over that. If you went along, the Takers wouldn't try anything. We wouldn't find them and the entire reason for the trip would be lost."

"I'm not worried about the Takers." That was a lie. She was fearful about the Takers. "I'm worried about Phyllicitus. It is conceivable that Miller will arrive in Home's Hearth, and Phyllicitus won't even receive him. What happens then? She can be petty. She is more than capable of holding a grudge against me, then taking it out on Miller."

"No. She's the Goddess of Love. That doesn't sound like her."

Easter was smirking again. It drove her mad at times. He never seemed to speak plain truth.

"Oh, yes, it's definitely like her. I lived in the temple, remember? She is the Goddess of Love, as in everyone loves her. Sure, she is full of love and soft emotions for everyone around her. Don't forget, it's mostly about her, though."

"What? Have you truly abandoned your goddess now?"

"I think you saw to that a long time ago. Like it or not, I'm in the fight now." She held up her hand, showing the narrow Master's Ring encircling her finger. She could feel power channel through it, potentials, collections of raw fate.

"It never was about the power with you. That's why I liked you. You understood what was at stake, and why we had to fight. The whole necromancy thing was just another annoyance to you. I've thought that way for centuries."

That was a strange admission. Aileen was intrigued. Lifting the old pitcher, she looked in, searching for some remains. It had long since dried away. She decided to investigate a little more. She set the pitcher down and moved into the kitchen to find a new bottle of cider, wine, or anything else that wouldn't make her sick for a week.

Innocently, she carried on the conversation. "So, what brought the great Easter around to my way of thinking?"

"Great?" He was always sensitive about that title, one he had so far avoided.

"Yes, but not Great Master. At least, you aren't one yet. We both know the Conclave would give you that title if you'd simply ask. But get back to my question: Tell me about the change in philosophy. I'm interested."

"I was a pretty normal Master in the earlier years. I was new to my powers, and arrogant. I got involved with some dangerous magics kept hidden in a desert city. It didn't go well. I also found out what it was to be in love, and rejected, in the same month. It was a growing experience. What I discovered was that if I didn't have a chance to solve something without magics, then I probably didn't have a chance with them, either. Magic just gave me more force to apply. If the problem couldn't be solved by force, then my magic didn't help much."

She picked up a bottle of wine and returned to the room. Waving her dark Master's ring over the bottle, she watched as magical forces gently pulled the seal from atop its neck, freeing the dark liquid within. Easter shook his head side-to-side, unhappy with her petty display of magic.

"You shouldn't waste it on such trivialities."

"What better to waste it on? Reviving the dead, perhaps? No. I'll stick with my perfectly reasonable needs. Thank you."

She poured the wine into the cleanest cup. Easter walked forward, presenting his own.

"So, I told you my little story. I'll have one in return."

Her heart started beating faster. Easter wanted something from her.

He continued, acting like everything was normal. "What made you leave the temple?"

She had always assumed that he knew. His powers of reading minds were famous. "That's an odd question. I thought you knew."

"Humor me. Believe it or not, I don't dance through life reading everyone's thoughts. It would take a lot of effort. Plus, it shows a real lack of trust, don't you think?"

"Oh yes, lack of trust. We can't have that in a perfectly respectable necromancer guild, can we?"

He smiled back at her sarcasm. At least it was her happy sarcasm. Her angry sarcasm was harder to smile at. She decided to take his bait. After all, if he wanted that information, he could get it whether or not she decided to cooperate.

"I loved the goddess. I loved being with her. I loved her cause and her vision. But when I went north into Jarlsland, it changed me. I had seen too much. Takers were more real than I had ever imagined. The Stag God! I saw it with my own eyes! An Old God! And it still had followers! I saw horrors that love could never conquer. I saw terrors unimaginable to the people in peaceful Strathmoore."

Easter kept his silence, urging her to continue with a nod.

"On one trip out to the ruins we found something bad. It was a machine. It fed on souls to do its magic." Her voice began to tremble and grow louder. "Can you imagine a machine made of huge hooks? Impale a young child on each hook. Use magic to keep the child alive forever, then collect its pain to power the machine. Then tie a demon to the machine, pulling rage from it, and growing in power for a hundred years. Years later, long after Phyllicitus had returned, I talked to her about it. I asked her to raise the Eisenvard and go north into Jarlsland, to free the people of those horrors. Do you know what she said?"

Easter shook his head. He did not know.

"She said that the people in Jarlsland needed to solve that problem. They let the Takers in, they had to push them out. She tried to sound strong, but I saw through her game. She was afraid. She was unwilling to risk the perfection of Strathmoore to help those in faraway lands. At that point, I knew she was hollow. She was about love all right, but just the love she could see and feel. None of the fear, terror, or despair of those far away changed her."

Easter shook his head. "I doubt that. Maybe she knew that by going in there, she would start a generation-long war?"

Aileen didn't let herself get drawn into a debate. "Then you came into my life. You showed me how small Home's Hearth and Strathmoore really are. Then you showed me how to make a difference and fight the fight that actually matters. Let's face it, not many fights in the world do. But the enemy-between-the-worlds, the Takers, they matter."

"Do you know when I was meeting with you long ago, when you were still a priestess, December advised me to recruit you?"

"December?" Her voice was full of surprise.

"Yes. He believed that if we didn't recruit you, you would join the Eisenvard, or some other equally crazy crusade, in a vain effort to die in the most glorious battle possible."

Maybe December had been right. He was insane, but he might have been right. Back then, she wanted to fight so badly, to do the right thing. She just didn't know what the right thing was. Now she had a Master's ring, and her friend was going in harm's way. She still didn't know what it was. She only knew she had to keep fighting.

TAKING BRITA

Brita polished the table. The wood had begun to shine. She hummed to herself. It had been an exciting day. She spent time dreaming about Miller, and what kind of man he had become. He was tall, and she found his brown hair lovely. He had muscular arms, accustomed to hard, yet intimately detailed work. He reminded her of a goldsmith, yet she had no idea what his craft was. She hoped he'd stay near town as she wanted to see more of him.

She giggled at her wicked thoughts.

Brita pondered whether Miller would make a fine husband, and decided that he would. She liked the idea of a man who was well-traveled, and who knew people from all parts of Strathmoore, and even other lands. Miller had the potential to be an influential man when he grew into his craft, whatever that was.

She knew he was apprenticed to a woman named Aileen, and that she was once a servant in the temple. Aileen had actually met the goddess! Face-to-face! The thought exited her.

She spent a few minutes dreaming about a small wedding near the goddess' shrine. There would be flowers, and children! She smiled as she finished setting the table. She spent a few seconds imagining new and exotic names for the children. She didn't have them, yet, but it was best to be prepared. After all, she didn't want to leave that kind of thing to last-minute decisions.

Her original names sounded much better than the new ones though, so she kept them. He had done this same imaginary journey many times. Laurent, Becka, Valence, Dena, two boys and two girls. She smiled to herself then moved to the next table, continuing her cleaning.

Brita began imagining different ways she might capture her apprentice's attention. She knew she was beautiful. She had had four proposals this year so far. Sadly, none of her potential grooms could hold a candle to Miller. They were a collection of farmers, ranch hands, and craft-less boys with minimal prospects. None of them were like Miller.

It was no secret that Brita had dreams of exotic princes from far-off lands. Even her mother scolded her from time to time about her imagination and standards that could not be met. There were plenty of perfectly respectable men in the villages, and no need to tear off across the world looking for what might not even be there. Brita had found Miller, though, so that made her mother wrong.

She had thought about the young man many times since he had lived among them just a few years ago. She liked that he was a hard worker, and he was a gentle soul. He traveled with people who were important. His teacher was respected throughout the countryside. That counted for a lot. And, oh yes, she liked his strong arms, broad shoulders, and beautiful smile.

She heard the inn door open. It should have been locked.

"We're closed. . . ." Her words died in her mouth when she saw who had entered. Three men walked in. She recognized them as the woodsmen who'd chased Miller away.

The older one, the one with the beard, held a long hunting knife in one hand. The door had been unlocked, its crossbar defeated by that long knife. The man had forced his way in. Sliding its blade between the door and the frame, he pulled the crossbar upward so silently that Brita had never heard a squeak.

She panicked, then sprinted toward the kitchen, screaming a warning to the other patrons. "Help! Bandits!"

She only made it five strides before she was tackled. Her body hit the floor, forcing the breath from her lungs for just a moment. The younger man with a scarred face climbed onto her back, straddling her, pinning her to the unyielding wooden floor. He grabbed her by her long black hair and pulled her head up. She cried out as her neck was forced up.

"Gentle now, no need to get so excited. We just need a little help from you, then we'll be on our way." His words tried to be comforting, like he was calming an animal. The knife in his fist spoke differently.

"Please, don't hurt me." Her voice shook with fear.

She stared at the knife, and at the three men. Two held her down as the bearded man looked on. Terrible images came into her mind. She knew what happened to women who were alone. She knew what men like these might do.

She began to sob. Her future, her life, her dreams, and her future children, were all about to be taken from her. She felt her heart break from despair.

The bearded man knelt next to her head. He looked down at her, meeting her tearful eyes with his empty gaze. "You know that lad, don't you? The one we were chasing."

There was no use denying it. She had already spoken the truth in front of these men. All she could do now was hope these men had no interest in ruining her. She knew what could happen to her if they did.

"Yes. We all know him. He was here when the troubles were

about." She tried to say more, but her sobs had transformed into panic. Her guts felt like they had turned to lead. The scarred man's weight on her was making it hard to breathe.

The man reached under her, grasping at her arm that was beneath her. She screamed when the scarred man touched her. His hand had slid across her breast. She kept screaming as loud as she could.

Footsteps pounded across the floor upstairs. The innkeeper emerged from the stairwell. He held a thick club menacingly in his hand. Two men followed him down the stairs.

"What are you doing?"

More sounds emerged from upstairs. The inn had awoken to Brita's screams.

The leader nodded once, and a raider lunged forward with a long knife and stabbed it into the innkeeper, who tried to scream, but only a soft bubbling gurgle came out. A thin jet of blood sprayed out, springling red across the wooden floor. The other two men who so recently thought to help the innkeeper backed up the stairs, yelling for help all the while.

The young raider shut the door, then wedged it closed with his knife, jamming the metal blade between door and frame.

"You better hurry up, not much time."

"Aye, I'll make it quick," the long-bearded one said as he walked toward Brita, knife in hand.

Then the knife arrived in front of her face. She stopped screaming and tried to cower, turning her face into the floor. All she could do was whisper. "Please, no. Please, no."

"No need for hysterics. Be calm. All this will soon pass."

His voice was calm, reassuring. She had heard similar tones before, when ranchers butchered their sheep.

The innkeeper had gone still. Blood continued to form a puddle around him.

She felt the scarred man pull her blouse down, exposing her neck and most of her bosom. She didn't feel brave. She wanted to fight, but just couldn't. Terror had her in its grip. She began shaking.

The bearded man patted her now naked shoulder. "That isn't the way. In just a moment, it will all be a lot easier. Don't you worry."

Brita felt the sting as the knife sliced across her shoulder. It made a slice half the length of her ring finger. It was a shallow cut, with only the smallest droplets of blood arising from it.

The bearded man pulled the knife away from her face and held it point up. He took his other hand and grabbed the blade. After a few moments, he released it, opening his hand to show a larger and slightly deeper cut. Blood covered his palm and ran down his life line toward his wrist.

She was confused. She didn't understand what he was doing. It felt wrong. For a fleeting instant, she started to fear sorcery. She screamed in terror, calling to the goddess.

Visions of arcane rituals invaded her imagination. The troubled times were full of such tales. But these things had never happened here in the village. They were always far away.

The man's bloody hand pressed against the wound in her shoulder. She squirmed and struggled, but the man held her tight. She felt herself growing warm, and her shoulder had begun to tingle.

Brita had heard the tales, but until a few violent minutes ago, hadn't believed them. She remembered when the Knights of the Eisenvard had come to warn their village two years ago. Threats like this seemed too remote, too far away, too unworldly. Now the threats had come for her. She remembered the tales of dark wizards hidden in their underground lairs. She remembered their name finally, although it was too late. She prayed again, begging for mercy, and for protection against the dark sorcerers of legend, the White Hand.

THE TAKEN

But the White Hand had not come for her. The Taken had.
Her shoulder felt warm, then it began to burn. It wasn't a burning sensation like she had a flame by her skin, more like a rash, like a swarm of insects were crawling beneath her skin.
She began to reach for her shoulder, to push against the weight of this man atop her. Her hand stopped moving before it was half-way to her shoulder. Her vision blurred.
"What?"
She didn't get the rest of the though out. A deluge of ideas and thoughts sprang into her mind. She knew the man atop her. His name was Gardin. She knew he was the leader because the friends told her it was so. She had never heard a voice inside her own mind that belonged to someone else before. Now there was a new thing with in her. It didn't use words, but it let her know that the voice was her friend, and everything would be

fine.

Visions continued to batter at her. She felt Gardin's weight ease from her. He stood and stepped aside, allowing her room to rise. Somehow she knew the others now. Ebber and Terp rode with Gardin, and had for months. Terp had joined their family this year, but Ebber had been one of the family for the longest time.

None of her thoughts made sense, yet she delighted as they poured into her. It was as if whatever gave her this knowledge also gave her pleasure in receiving it. The forth man of their number, named Ignus, licked his lips while he stared at her. He seemed fascinated by her. She knew that something was changing inside of her, and Ignus wanted to witness it firsthand. Somehow she knew what Ignus was feeling. That surprised Brita for a moment, then the surprise vanished as if someone had wiped it away with a cleaning cloth. She began to take joy in the other four. She reveled in their presence, and in the fact that she felt completely free. Nothing would be denied to her, nothing.

Gardin held out his clean hand. She took it without hesitation. He pulled her from the floor and she took her feet with no difficulty.

Shouts of alarm continued from up the stairs. Gardin offered her a broad smile. His brown teeth hadn't been clean in years. Somehow she could feel his emotions, his satisfaction, his goals. "Welcome to the fold." Gardin said as he offered the knife to her handle first.

She smiled back. Joy, almost rapture, coursed through her body as she touched its handle. After a moment's hesitation, she wrapped her hand around it's sticky blood-splattered handle.

She pulled the knife into her hand, settling it there for the long night's work ahead. The voice in her head sung out. Brita knew what she needed to do.

Brita gazed around her. Almost a dozen bodies lay scattered across the floor. She remembered it all yet could not believe it. The men, the raiders, had gone upstairs. They'd killed those two brave men who'd tried to help the innkeeper. Then they'd forced the rest of the patrons downstairs.

Then she had the knife. The long, wonderful knife. She remembered Gardin handing it to her. She knew what to do. There was no hesitation, only joy as she stabbed and stabbed and stabbed. Gardin, Terp, and Ebber kept the people imprisoned in the room as she murdered them. Ingus ran about outside, hunting down any who had fled.

Spending a moment with a calm head, she wondered how she knew the names of these men. She didn't remember talking to them, or making introductions, but she knew them, all of them. Somehow the world had turned strange.

She looked down at the still bodies of her neighbors and friends. She had no feelings as she stared into their terror-struck faces. She knew them all. There was Alycin, her brother's sweetheart. Mook the cook lay sprawled across a table; his face had been cut open like a fillet. Brita felt nothing as she looked at the bodies. There was no remorse, no sadness.

She didn't feel right. She expected to feel something, some emotion, some remorse, some sadness. There was nothing. She knew she should feel something, but she didn't. It wasn't as if she couldn't think. She simply could not care. It felt wrong, but there you have it.

And then tears began streaming down her face. She had killed her friends, her neighbors, dead. They lay scattered across the bloody floor, silently accusing her of treachery.

The shaking began with a small intake of breath. It rapidly became worse as she fell onto the floor and began sobbing. Her heart felt like it was going to erupt from her chest.

Then she began screaming. Her body locked into a knot while the screams continued to sound. Her life was over, just as surely as the rest of the people who now lay on the floor with her. She would never have a husband, children, grandchildren. She was a murderess and she didn't even know why. She began to wail as her tears pooled onto the floor.

Then she was abruptly calm. Brita opened her eyes and looked at a pair of boots. Terp stood in front of her.

"I know this is hard. We've all been there. I hate to say it, but it gets easier."

She was completely calm. She could not understand how this happened. Looking at the smeared blood on the floor, she could not even understand why she wasn't still in hysterics. Staring up into his eyes, she could only ask, "How did you do that?"

"The calming? That wasn't me. That was the Friends. We all have them, now you do, too. Sometimes they encourage us to do things for them, and other times they help us out. I think you just got helped."

She calmly stood, looking up at Terp's face. A chill went through her back. She remembered the troubled times. She remembered the Taken. He stood a head taller than her. "I don't think I want their help."

"None of us did. But they are with us now. We can either get along with the Friends, or like others who came before, we can simply die. I know that it is tempting to give into despair. But believe me, a whole new chapter of your life just opened. You have been given a gift. My advice is to embrace it."

She replied in a near whisper. "But why me? Why did you do this to me?"

"Don't get the wrong idea. It isn't you, it's the apprentice. You know him. Perhaps he likes you? Maybe you can discover a few things for us. Maybe the Friends think you'll have an easier time getting close to him. Truthfully, there are a thousand reasons, none of which make much sense to people like us. Just accept reality. You're one of us. The Friends have chosen you. That's all you need know."

A SMALL REPREIVE

Gardin emerged from behind a villager's hut. She knew him, even knew his name, but she had never met him in her life.

He strode up to Brita, towering over her sitting form. His beard was unkempt, decorated with gray and a collection of woodland debris. An outdoorsman. A hunter.

Brita looked up and met his eyes. They were cold, uncaring. She felt like she should be afraid, yet she wasn't. Strange.

"Did Terp explain what happened to you?"

Gardin's voice was hard. It was composed of sharp syllables that struck like an ax against a soft tree.

Brita started to respond, but Terp interrupted. "Nah, she's just at the first part. You know, welcome to the family and all that. Thought she might need a moment to, adjust, you know."

She could feel Terp's urgency. He needed to do something, and fast. She could sense his impatience, but he had given no verbal cue to his impatience. She shook her head in confused wonder.

"We don't all have that luxury." Gardin gestured toward the trail leaving town. "The young White Hand is out there, riding farther away as we speak. It's time to get in the saddle and ride."

Brita caught her breath as Terp stood. He started walking toward the horses.

"But what is going on?"

Gardin's answer was direct. "We are going to find your friend, then bring him into the fold. It's that easy."

It felt right to her. She thought about Miller, and how little she knew him. Her inner voice spoke, telling her how this fantasy had always been doomed. She had only known him for a few months. There was no reason to grieve.

Her chest began to spasm. She sank to her knees. Her gut burned and she bent down, trying to quench the pain, pressing her face against the earth. She gasped for air. Miller, she thought, he was the one. He could have been a husband, a father. Now all her dreams were gone. Her children, gone. Her home, gone. Her life, gone.

Brita's wail of sadness filled the air. She screamed as she realized what these Friends were. They were the Takers from the old, troubled times. They had her in their grasp. She wrapped her arms around herself and tried to vomit. It hurt deep in her chest. She tried to scream out and plead to the goddess, but only wails of pain emerged.

Then the pain was gone. It left faster than it arrived. She looked up at Gardin from the ground. She thought again about her family that had only lived in her dreams, her plans for life, and the people she loved. She felt nothing. She tried to recite the names of her children, but they would not come to mind.

Gardin looked down at her with an impatient stare. "The Friends will keep you calm. It's just another thing they do. You are not fit to ride yet, so you can stay here with Ebber. Catch up with us when you get a better handle on your emotions."

She didn't understand how these Friends could control her

emotions. They were inside her, though, that was obvious. She didn't know how or why. But she knew what the Friends were. They were Takers. They controlled her emotions somehow. She had to ask. "I thought the Takers turned people, us, into mindless slaves."

"You think too much. First, we call them Friends. Second, the Friends came to help us. And third, well, the whole taking-over thing didn't work so well, did it?"

"Why do we call them Friends? They don't seem friendly. Curse it, I even call them Friends, and I don't know why."

"Because they want you to call them that. This is just a hint of what the future holds for you. Get used to it."

Gardin turned and walked briskly away, leaving her sprawled on the ground.

"But I have questions!"

"Ebber will fill you in. I have sorcerers to hunt."

11

STRANGE ALLIES

Ebber danced into view. His gaze swung in a wide arc, meeting everything and everyone about him with a maddened smile. He laughed out loud while he executed a skilled pirouette. Three, long-dried bloodstains decorated his oversized shirt, marking the remains of an unlucky owner.

His voice leaped out, loudly, as if from ambush. "Well, how are we today?"

Brita could only stare back. Another person she knew, but had never met.

"How is it? Friends talking to you in your sleep yet?" His eyes seemed to laugh at her, mirthful, maybe insane.

"Er, no." She backed away from this short-haired maniac. He was tall, and his figure was narrow and full of wiry muscle. A bent earring dangled from his right lobe.

"Don't worry, it won't be long now. But you've joined with

the new ones? Lucky you."

Brita had to wonder. Does he know something? Can he share? Is he even right in the head? Forcing herself to relax, she began to question him.

"New ones?"

"Sure, you remember the troubles? Come on, you aren't that young. Back a few years ago, the Friends, well, they weren't very friendly. At least their brethren weren't, so the voices in my head tell me." A quick chortle emerged as he thought of some oddly amusing secret thought. "Now we have the new Friends! You should be excited! They can be so helpful!"

"What are they helping me with? Why are they helping me? Where did they come from?"

Ebber gazed calmly back and shifted to stare into her eyes. As she met his gaze, she could feel an odd sense of communion, as if he were trying to share a thought, but it was obscured in a cloud of noise. Then he sat on the ground. Brita stared down at him. She knew him, but she didn't. Something about him was broken, she could see that.

"They are going to tell you soon enough. The new Friends want to be your allies in this war. You didn't know you'd been at war, did you? Most of us don't."

"I remember the tales. They were, um, I don't know, what was I saying?" She tried to say "Takers," but it would not pass her lips. "They possessed people and turned them against their families, their neighbors. It was, um, uh, the words are fighting me." She struggled with the words, she couldn't find them. She could not say them. It was so horrific she couldn't speak the words.

Ebber's eyes lit up with delight. "Oh, there they are! You found them! You just got helped by your Friends!"

Her next words were clear. "I don't understand. What are you trying to tell me?"

"Tell you?"

Ebber stood. Now he towered over her. She remembered how strong he was. She remembered when he held Janie down against the floor of the inn. She remembered driving a knife into Janie's chest. She remembered Ebber holding Janie down while she cut her up. He'd whispered something into Janie's ear the entire time.

Her sobs began again. Ebber offered a theatrical bow and walked away, uncaring, or perhaps respectful of her grief. She couldn't tell the difference with him.

The grief retreated a few seconds later. Her emotions calmed, but it left her thinking. She wondered if the Takers, Ebber called them Friends, would rule her feelings? Would she go mad, like Ebber?

Terp returned. He spoke with Ebber in quiet tones. Finally, he placed a hand on Ebber's shoulder and guided him back where the horses were being readied.

A few moments later her emotions were under control. She felt no sadness, no anger, nothing. She knew what happened. She remembered most of it. She wondered why she couldn't feel anything. It wasn't as if the sadness had softened, then left by small steps in the night; sadness normally left that way. This was like throwing a bucket of water on the campfire. The sadness had been banished in an instant. It wasn't just her sadness, it was her heart. She had lived her entire life listening to her heart. Her kindness and love had always guided her way. Now that voice was silent.

She let her gaze wander. The others were preparing horses. Gardin hurriedly filled arrow quivers with steel-tipped shafts. His face was completely calm and impassive as he prepared to launch death in the near future. Ebber tightened his saddle as Terp paused in his task and turned to her.

"Are you fit to ride? It might be rough terrain and fast movements."

Oddly, she understood her non-readiness completely. She had never ridden a fast horse. She remembered ponies, mules, and carts. "I don't think so. I might need a little time. How can I explain this? I know I need a few more days before I am, well, skilled. But I don't know why." She could not explain how she knew, but she did.

Terp nodded as if he'd expected that answer. "All right. We need to move fast. I need to catch up with Gardin. I will leave Ebber with you. You might need some guidance as you grow into this. It will be good to have someone around who can give you council."

"But, Ebber? I'm not sure."

"Yes, he's a little bit mad. But his madness can sometimes yield wisdom. He was first taken by the old Friends; somehow he managed to befriend the new ones. Pay attention to what he says, not what he means, and you'll be fine."

"But, well. He is a murderer." She tried to wring her hands and show her fear. Men always came to her rescue when she played at being in distress.

Terp only smirked back. "Did you forget? So are you."

LOST

"I'll get the horses." Ebber walked to the barn and brought out the two mounts. Ebber's was a shaggy-maned brute of a horse he had named Haircut. Haircut had black fur, with long spiked tufts of hair springing out in random patches. The horse had been burned in the past. Burned badly. How was it even ridable?

She walked up to the beast, gently stroking it where its mane survived. She whispered a child's song to it, trying to befriend it. She didn't know why she thought of the song, but her heart had inspired her. It was speaking again, and she didn't want to silence it.

After a few moments brushing the animal and speaking to it calmly, Ebber went deeper into the barn, beyond a tall pile of hay, and retrieved two saddles. He dropped one of the saddles on the ground, and then slung the other on Haircut's back.

Haircut jerked with surprise but Ebber stood by and calmed him down. Finally, he attached the saddle to its straps and tightened them down.

Brita looked on helplessly. She had never saddled a riding horse alone. Ebber made no move to help her, and she knew that she must. She could feel the need to move faster, to ride toward the farm, wherever that was.

"Are you going to saddle your horse? Or do you have a more pressing engagement elsewhere, M'lady?" His last words were filled with scorn. She noted that Ebber didn't like people who couldn't ride well. That would be good to remember. He must not have been a noble, before the Takers.

The other option was that he simply didn't like her. Brita had a moment of fear, then relaxed. Whether or not Ebber liked her didn't matter very much in this new place. The Takers, in their heads called Friends, would make sure they were nice to each other, wouldn't they?

She paused a moment and looked at the saddle. Then she glanced at her lovely brown horse. Diamond was its name. She had a white spot in the shape of a diamond on her forehead. She was easy to ride. She didn't bite, and she didn't run off. Brita couldn't imagine a more perfect horse. But now she had to saddle her.

Ebber walked up next to her. Haircut followed a few feet behind, at the end of a long tether. "You are thinking too hard. Just let the Friends tell you how to do it. It will take a moment to get used to, but they do know how to saddle a horse." Suddenly Ebber began laughing hysterically. "They must have gone to horse school!" His peals of laughter filled the area. "I'm betting they can't get out of Friend apprenticeship until they pass horsemanship lessons!" He continued laughing as he pulled himself up into the saddle. "I wonder if they know how to ride sidesaddle, too?"

She could feel herself react to his glibness, angry with him for belittling her. His laugher was annoying her. She wished she could push him away. Her thoughts came to an abrupt stop.

Then there was nothing. No anger, no rage, no plans of petty revenge. She was calm, reasonable, and terrified of how quickly her emotions had been controlled. *They control what I see. They control what I feel. Do they control what I think, too? No, if they did, I couldn't think these thoughts, could I?*

Ebber continued on with his maddening laughter. She wondered how he did it. Wondered why the Friends didn't calm him down; something was very broken inside of him.

She wanted to get a hint where his insanity came from. Hoping for a small clue from the Friends, she gazed deeply into his eyes. She tried to reach out to him, to reach out through the Friends and connect. It felt like a swarm of bees were flying around her head, each one droning a different pitch while traveling its own chaotic path. The Friends couldn't help her see inside him.

It should have worked. She didn't know why, but it should have worked. She should have been able to see his emotions, but she either couldn't, or his emotions were all helter-skelter. If that were the case, how could Ebber have any sanity at all?

Then he paused. A huge grin spread across his face as he gazed back at her. Their eyes met, and Brita felt . . . something. It seemed like he was trying to tell her something and protect it at the same time.

"What?"

"Shhh. None of that. Those flowers have yet to bloom. Best to grow your own."

He is mad. Stark raving mad. Why do the Friends keep him around? Was he that useful? Why not leave him behind? What was motivating the Friends?

Panic began to spread through her body. Her hands began to quiver with fear. She tried to talk to him, but no words emerged. She could feel the Friends exerting their power over her.

Brita grabbed her head and screamed, "NO!"

Ebber just smiled back at her. He bent down to pick a small yellow flower, more of a weed than anything else, and handed it to her.

She didn't want the flower. She didn't take it from him. She wanted to keep her thoughts, not be confused by the Friends and their workings. She desperately wanted to safeguard her memories.

But Ebber had found a way to keep his thoughts. The Friends didn't control everything! She saw him and knew there must be a way!

She tried to commit that to memory. She kept whispering "Ebber has a way" to herself. As she continued her self-made memory charm, Ebber moved forward and placed the flower into one of her button hooks.

"A pretty girl should always have a flower."

Then the calm descended on Brita. She was motionless for a few beats of her heart. Then she looked down at the strange flower that Ebber had attached to her button loop.

She was momentarily confused. But then she understood completely. "Thank you for the flower. It is very lovely."

She reached down to stroke the soft yellow petals. She was very calm. She'd just been given a flower. It made her very happy.

"Brita, keep that flower for a few days, all right? I want to show you a trick."

She smiled up at Ebber. He was so rugged, so handsome. Why was she just noticing this now? The flower, perhaps?

Returning to the horses, Ebber continued to prepare for their journey. He packed both saddles with provisions and camping supplies. He tied a tent to the side of his saddle, and a short spear covered with a leather sheath on the side of hers.

She stood there in amazement. The horses were so interesting. The supplies were so interesting. Why had I never noticed this before? Everything fascinated her.

He returned and took her by the arm. He pulled her gently toward the waiting horse. She had ridden mules and donkeys, but never a full horse. She didn't think, she didn't fear. She simply walked up to the light-brown horse and grabbed the saddle, laying it on Diamond's back and quickly fastening buckles until it was firm. She placed her foot in the stirrup, then confidently pulled herself up. A moment later she reached out to take the reins and directed the horse out of village, toward that mysterious farm.

Ebber mounted his horse as well, then caught up with her. He fell in behind and let her lead the way. It was only mildly surprising that she had the skill to ride this horse. But things were different now, and surprises never seemed to end.

MORE THAN WORDS

They passed a few miles with no deep conversation, only Ebber's tuneless humming and mad comments to mark the time.

"So, what happened? Why are you so different?"

Brita had been with Ebber the entire day. He had transitioned into and out of three different forms of insanity within that short period. Sometimes he was the showman, announcing his petty observations to the world. Other times he was the dark watcher, brooding with troubled thoughts and staring at her with uncaring eyes. He mixed in the third personality in small portions. This third Ebber presented some form of all-seeing oracle that never got the visions right.

But it was more than words. She could feel him. He was trying to be sincere, but Brita couldn't figure out how to say the things he wanted to hear. When she tried, the words got all jumbled.

The Friends always helped with the communication problems, but they didn't do a good job trying to piece together Ebber's words, gestures, attitudes, and volatile moods.

Ebber continued. "Not different, unique. What is more different than being different, you understand?"

"Sort of. The Friends give me the feeling that you are trying to tell me something important. But they don't know what it is, either."

"Yeah, no, neither, both. The Friends, well, they want to be Friends, right? But hey, not my fault. "

Great, back into moodiness. She needed to pull him out of this. "Terp says you need to show me some skills, or something." Her words sounded strange to her own ears. Somehow they would make sense to Ebber though, she hoped.

"Exactly! Now you're cooking!" He smiled excitedly, like she had had some sort of breakthrough. "It's all about your mind. Not your eyes, not the voices, not the water. Definitely not about the water."

He's starting to drift again. She needed to keep him lucid. "Come on Ebber, tell me more. Tell me about the water."

"No!" He motioned with his arm, imitating cleaning and scrubbing. "Never take the road, always take the forest trail."

"I have no idea what you're talking about. I need to understand what's going on."

"If you want to understand, you need to stop listening. Open your eyes and see what is around you for once in your cursed life."

She almost spoke harshly to him. But then she felt it. She believed that he wanted to help. But why couldn't he? He was frustrated, yet impervious to doubt. It was like he was sure in his way, and in his approach, and he was just waiting for her to figure it all out.

Thoughts began to roam in her head. Questions were spawned that couldn't be answered. Why did Ebber have to act like this?

She kept thinking about him as they rode past a wall of green. The thick bushes formed a barrier between those few on the trail and the rest of the world. A village lay sprawled ahead. They rode into it.

She decided to simply take his advice at face value. She turned from Ebber, ignoring the uncomfortable silence that had set in. She began taking inventory of everything about her. There were nine villagers. Two of them had Friends within them. There were three draft horses, eight huts, a wooded craft hall, and a large open forge area with a rickety wooden roof over it. The village was surrounded by two sets of fences, and between them at least two dozen sheep grazed.

"I don't see anything unusual."

"Really, what do you call unusual nowadays?"

"Can I get a straight answer out of you?"

"When you see what you are looking at, I'll give you a crooked one."

Her anger spiked, but it dissipated two seconds later. The Friends were helping her again. Helping her not to punch him. They were oddly considerate for Takers who possess people, she thought. Then remembered the inn, and how she had murdered her friends.

She continued gazing at the same things, looking for a clue. People, animals, homes, sheep. What is unusual? What is different?

These Friends hadn't given her magical vision. She could only see what she could see. How can she see more?

She started working through the list again. Sheep? Are they different? Fences? No. People?

The truth struck like a hammer. Two of these people had been taken by the Friends, yet she didn't even remark on them. They seemed completely normal. These Friends were controlling what she perceived. Even if she saw whatever Ebber was referring to, the Friends could change how she understood them. Her eyes might spot an oddity, but she might never notice it in her mind.

She opened her mouth to announce this fact, to tell Ebber she understood. Her mouth would not form the words. Pausing, she tried to recover and get her head straight. Her imagination kept intruding. An inner voice argued with her about issues gone long ago.

The pain caught her by surprise. Ebber was standing above her with an open palm. He slapped her again. "Wake up! Don't drink the water! Pay attention!"

She scrambled away from him, leaping up onto her feet and pulling a knife from her belt. She felt the Friends telling her she was safe, and Ebber just scowled angrily at her.

"I think our lesson is over. It's a good thing. We are being summoned, in any case."

"What in the name of—?" Then the words were gone. What was she going to say? The goddess? "Why did you slap me?" she yelled at him.

"I told you not to drink the water."

"There is no cursed water! Can't you see that?"

"So, there is one more thing you can't see."

She turned from him angrily. "You are barking mad. I can't believe they left me with you. You need a keeper! No, an asylum!"

His next words were calm and full of malice. "And you need to listen to the Friends when they summon you. Servants who don't listen aren't in high demand, if you understand."

She stopped in her tracks. Was that a threat? A warning? A plea? What was Ebber feeling? Could she sense him through the Friends? But was what she sensed true, or merely what the Friends wanted her to perceive as truth?

It took a full minute to calm herself. Finally, she could sense feelings. She wanted to travel. She wanted to ride. It was the Friends, they were calling. She could see her goal in her mind's-eye. She was looking for a barn but didn't see one in front of her.

She guessed this was what Ebber was trying to explain. How does one even attempt to put this into words?

"There was a farm? There is a farm? I'm not sure."

"Close. There is a farm about a day up the road. Something is happening there. We should go check. Maybe Gardin and Terp need help."

"Maybe they found Miller?"

She dismissed it from her mind as soon as she said it. Thinking Miller's name brought back hope, joy, summer love. She would not let these evil things take that from her. Not her love. It was all she had left.

14

INGALLS

Hooves splashed through the puddles and dark mud coated Miller's legs and boots. Low clouds, filled with rain, had begun obscuring the setting sun. Miller rode the mare down the high road of Ingalls, passing empty market stalls, darkened craftsman shops, and bakeries where only the hardest working families continued into the night. Townsfolk kept their fires hot to guard against the cold night. Miller agreed. It was always a good habit to guard against darkness. Strange things live there.

Torches held back the night in a few places along the street. The watchmen had done a good job ensuring they were burning tonight, even with the earlier rain. The streets were quiet nearby but he could hear the sounds of music and revelry in the distance. A section at the far end of the street was bright with a much greater number of torches. This part of Ingalls refused to let the dark of night interrupt their revelries.

A small crowd of twelve people had gathered outside the building. Its three stories stood surrounded by a gallery wide enough to drive a cart down. Doors decorated the upper landing, allowing easy access. The roof jutted up another twenty feet with four steep angles and three chimneys. It was painted with illustrations. Figures, animals, and musical instruments stood boldly against the building wall. There were other taverns in Ingalls, some cheaper, some more refined. But this six-gabled three-story gaudy inn dominated the end of the main street. This was the LaDeeDah.

What's that? It wasn't here last time. There was something new in the middle of the street. Miller squinted at the figure as they approached. It looked to be almost twice the size of a man. It had claws, huge malformed arms, and a head that looked like an old stone. The statue stood in the center of the town circle. Newly constructed buildings surrounded it.

Ingalls had been settled before the New Gods walked on Strathmoore's green soil. Miller looked down the main street and saw building after building laid out. Each of them had new construction. Some were completely rebuilt from the ground up. Miller remembered when older, grander mansions, crafter halls, and bell towers stood in their place.

The Stag God really did a job here.

Miller stopped the mare to look around. He was surrounded by dozens of buildings that had been completely reconstructed. Their new features stood in contrast with the older dwellings that surrounded them only a few blocks away. This destruction took place before Mistress Aileen had taken him in; a part of her past she didn't share easily.

He approached the statue. It was built within the boundaries of a shallow stone pool, empty except for the illustrations of children on its wall. Mistress Aileen had earned her valiant reputation when she'd defended this city from the northern winter demons and she had also gained Master Easter's attention.

He wondered if she would rather have lost the town,

immediately rebuking himself. What am I thinking? She is an excellent Master. She is everything a Master should be. I am none of it.

Here was a memorial of the last battle between the First Gods and the new. The tales survived and were still sung in this town. A fledgling priestess had held off a rampaging Old God and its shamanic followers. It sounded like a fantasy, a tale for children made for the theater.

Miller gazed at the statue creature. Even as a work of art, it was terrifying. It stood more than twice his height. One of its arms was thicker than his leg. Fangs stood out from the mouth, curving upward almost to its eyes. The statue carried a club as tall as his horse. He imagined dozens of these ice giants running about this town, smashing buildings, smashing people. Aileen was a powerful Master now, but back then, she was just an initiate of Phyllicitus with a half-dozen retainers.

But how did these giants come here? And why? How did she defeat them and drive these winter demons from Ingalls? He continued to stare at the statue.

Aileen had power, the power to heal, the power to know secrets. She wasn't a fighter, though, at least not enough to defeat giant demons. He couldn't imagine how she could have defeated monstrosities that large, and that strong. He doubted she'd killed the demons back then. She probably couldn't defeat such a thing now. He'd thought he knew the history; pretty obvious he didn't. Did she really kill such a thing? The thought filled him with fear. He felt close to Aileen but sometimes a darker power would come on her. He couldn't predict when, or what would happen when it did.

Miller made a mental promise to never believe what bards say. This tale was built on lies and tears, just like everything else the White Hand touched.

He urged the mare to continue on, toward the bright lights at the end of the street. Once he spotted the stable boy he made his way toward him. The boy came to him and after a few coppers were exchanged, the boy took the mare away for a special feeding and a night's stay.

Then he turned toward the LaDeeDah. It had been repainted sometime in the past two years, and all evidence of the fire damage removed. Its roof now sprouted wooden statues of bards and musicians plying their craft. He walked toward the front doors, allowing the happy tunes from within to improve his mood.

The doors had been upgraded as well. These two thick oak doors could be used to guard a small Keep. Newly carved decorations stood out from the surface of the stout door. The carvings showed patrons dancing and drinking. The LaDeeDah had learned some lessons from the past. Apparently, investing in solid doors was one of them.

The door swung open easily enough as he pushed into the building. It was only half full this night, which could have easily been two hundred people given the immense size of the place. A trio of musicians occupied the grand stage. In other towns, they would have been regarded as one of the great musical troops. Here, they were merely average.

The smell of the savory food being prepared combined with superb music to awaken old memories of days gone by. He approached one of the least populated tables with a small trio of craftsmen relaxing after a long day's labor. He pulled out one of the four empty chairs, giving the occupants a slight bow. Their conversation broke as he sat.

"Welcome, stranger!" a craftsman with a belly the size of a beer-barrel announced.

Miller smiled back. If his craftsmanship was as huge as his belly, he must be talented, indeed.

"Forgive my intrusion. You have the most open seats."

"It's because my friend here," the fat man said, gesturing at his neighbor, "chases all the visitors away!"

The laughs flowed from the craftsmen. Soon the conversation was back. Discussions ranged from who had the best chance at courting the local beauty, to the best pegs to connect different types of wood. Miller began to relax, shed his wariness, and after a few shared glasses of wine, he had genuinely begun to let the more terrifying parts of the journey slip away from his immediate thoughts. Sometimes it was good just to be safe, and to feel safe.

"Excuse me."

The voice came from behind Miller. He snapped his head around, searching for the next danger. A short young man stood there. His clean embroidered tunic and servant's cloth proclaimed him to be an apprentice cook. Miller loosened his grip on his knife.

"Please excuse me for startling you." The young man took a step back. Concern mixed with fear showed through his eyes. "The masters of the LaDeeDah have asked me to offer you our house table. It is, shall we say, an honor."

The craftsmen at the table began looking at him with a different kind of respect. Their plump leader was executing some kind of calculus within his mind as he looked at Miller, a person obviously too young and too poor to demand such place.

"There must be some mistake. I'm just a traveling apprentice. I'm no one important."

The servant bowed, keeping his eyes firmly toward the floor. "The proprietors say that they owe some sort of debt to your mistress and wish to repay a small portion of it by hosting you."

He had been recognized. The two owners of the LaDeeDah knew Mistress Aileen from years ago. How in the world did they recognize him? He had met the two owners twice in his life, and it had been two years ago. Either their memories were longer and sharper than usual, or he had been marked long ago.

Miller regretfully pushed his chair back and stood. After bowing and exchanging farewells with his table mates, he allowed himself to be led to the house table with its twelve empty seats. Outlines of animals decorated its surface. He was surprised to see images of the First Gods. It made sense, considering the age of the inn. The goddess had plenty of followers, even as far out as Ingalls. Why hadn't they been removed? This inn had seen a lot of years go by, there must be a reason.

Human gods came and went over the centuries. The First Gods were permanent. The First Gods were forces of nature. He didn't know if they were imbued with aspects of animals, or if animals had somehow inherited something of the gods. Aileen believed in them and treated them with respect. Master Easter even more so.

He remembered sitting at this table years ago. At the time, he had not noticed that it was a place of some honor. He had thought it was simply an expensive table with a good view. It was the same table, but he could see so much more now. Well, there was nothing for it; he might as well play all the cards in his deck.

A small clay jug of wine arrived within minutes. Miller sampled it and enjoyed its peppery flavor. It was delicious. Soon after, a half rack of lamb arrived, along with a freshly baked loaf of bread. A bowl of herb-decorated carrots made its way to his table soon thereafter. The servants would simply deliver, bow, and mumble something like "With compliments," or "For your enjoyment." Hopefully, the owners were kind enough to offer this as a free meal, otherwise he would be going hungry. He didn't have enough silver to afford the next inn.

But Mistress Aileen had always advised him to accept generosity when offered and assume it would never come again. Miller began to take small tastes of the meal laid about the table, surrounding him with its aroma and flavors. The tasting quickly transformed into a full-on assault as he devoured its contents.

An older man approached the table as he finished his meal. His rich clothing testified to his social status, and his apron to his station. An open bottle of wine occupied both of his hands. The LaDeeDah was owned by a partnership between two men. This was one of them. After a moment, Miller remembered his name, Quint.

"Might I?" Quint asked. His gentle voice was calming, while its deep tones commanded attention.

"Innkeeper Quint, you are always welcome. Please."

Quint pulled a chair out and sat down. He smiled as he presented the bottle of wine. "Apprentice Miller, isn't it?" Quint motioned to one of the servants, who approached with a pair of silver-gilt goblets. Quint carefully poured the wine into these goblets before continuing. "I haven't seen you here in a few years. How have you fared?"

Miller began feeling oddly cautious. Since when does an apprentice stand out in this place? Perhaps there was more to this. He took one of the goblets from Quint, smiled, sipped the wine slowly, enjoying this excellent blend. This was not the blend one normally served apprentices. Quint remembered who his masters were.

"I have been hard at work these past few years. When I passed by Ingalls, I simply had to stop by and enjoy your hospitality. It is beyond perfect, as I remember." He offered a reassuring smile.

"And how fares your mistress?"

"She fares well. Her duties keep her busy most days now, but I saw her a few weeks ago. She was in good health and humor." As much as ever, anyway.

Quint smiled again, indicating some level of genuine relief. He turned toward the main stage of the inn. Scores of audience members listened happily to the jaunty tunes coming from the ensemble. "This town still remembers the service your Mistress Aileen gave. Many continue to remain silent, but we all know it. She saved this town. When the northern ice gods came, she was one of the few who pushed them back. I won't ever forget it."

Ice gods was it now? When did they get the promotion? "Ah, the Stag. I wasn't in her service when she did that. I heard it was a horror." Miller was in service to another mistress then, but even then, he'd heard the tales. Aileen had faced down an Old God. In one battle she had saved the town and sealed her fate as a target of the White Hand. Now Easter owned her, and she owned him. How was that even possible?

"Yes, it was. This town has a deep appreciation for her. We

remember well." He paused for almost a minute. The musicians finished their quick tune and began a slower one. Violin music filled the space as Quint continued. "We remember the Order here. I wanted you to know that, by and large, most people don't care for it."

Miller pushed his chair back, quickly scanning about him, alert for danger.

"No, no, no, you are not in any danger. I just wanted to make sure you were aware that the town isn't a safe haven to your kind. Mistress Aileen will always be welcome here, but the others less so. I thought it would be good if you knew what you were getting into, while you are visiting." Quint gestured at the open wine bottle.

Miller took the hint and poured a deep portion into his own glass, and then into Quint's. "Er, thanks, for not, well, killing me."

Quint raised his glass in a mock toast. "You are in no danger in this house. There are those out there who still follow that old way, to cut out wizards from the world. The days of the Eisenvard have passed, though. You won't find the town crawling with knights seeking to burn you at the stake. But again, that doesn't mean the other Masters would find us easy prey. There are a few of your Order we remember very well. If they step foot here, well . . . let's say we have improved our city guard."

He wondered what they were planning. Miller knew exactly who Quint was talking about. Were they insane?

LA DEE DAH

Miller considered breaking off this conversation and simply leaving town right then. It was not safe to be here with this going on.

He chose a different path. First, he finished the goblet of fine wine. Then he poured himself another cup, drinking it as fast as he could. He refilled Quint's glass when he began staring at him, trying to read him like a card player. He felt his hands grow clammy, and a bead of sweat spring from his forehead.

"I assume you are talking about Master December?" Miller spoke in a calm voice, while his insides threatened to dump its contents onto the table.

"Indeed. It would be best if this Master December did not visit Ingalls again. He is an evil wretch, a necromancer who summons the dead. He uses dark magics to capture the minds of good, free people. He is no better than the Takers. We won't have his kind here."

Miller took a moment to sip some more of this excellent wine. He was starting to feel the warmth in his belly, calming it down. Perhaps a little liquid courage would be a good thing tonight. "What will you do if he simply decides not to take your advice? Perhaps he will be drawn here by some errand? What then? Do you think he will listen to your requests?"

"No. We have already tried him. Judgment has been rendered. We have witnesses to his dark magics. If he comes here, we will take him."

"That's where you're wrong." Miller looked deeply into Quint's eyes. He wanted Quint to take him seriously, and hopefully guide the town of Ingalls away from such a foolish plan. "Do you know why he is named December?" he asked, dropping his voice low to avoid any eavesdroppers.

"What? Why do I care?"

"You care because he is a Master of the White Hand. Every Master eventually takes a name that means something about them. He isn't a new Master, so he is powerful. I mean, really powerful. This town can't face him and hope to win."

"We are not seeking this Master December out. But we will defend our town. That is a hard-learned lesson."

"Then you have learned nothing. Master December took his name based on the month he killed his own home town. His town was much like this one. It was a thriving community full of hard-working farmers, townsmen, and crafters. When he finished his apprenticeship and became a Master, he celebrated the event by slaying every inhabitant there. Not a man, woman, or child survived. Each citizen became his servant in death, and the slaughter continued until there was no one left to kill or eat. To hear the story, the feast took days."

Quint looked stunned.

"But Aileen"—Miller reached out and held his arm in a comforting grip—"Aileen is now Mistress Shield, at least until she finds a new name. All White Hand Masters take new names. She is no different in this way. She still has great love for Ingalls and would be saddened by its destruction. But you must understand, her days of being a priestess are over. She has converted to the White Hand in all ways."

He paused for effect.

And now for the bad news. "She has made alliances within the Order to preserve her status and advance her cause. I say this to you now so that you can avoid a fight that you won't win. Her chief ally is now Master December. She does not support his heavy-handed ways, but she does value his alliance. She would be sore put to come to your aid if this town insisted on confronting him. Think about it. An entire town devoured by their own walking dead. Home's Hearth is too far away. Your priests can't help you. The goddess can't help you. Take my advice and let me help you. Let December alone. Let him pass by you like a cold wind."

Miller remembered the LaDeeDah from years ago. He counted its music among his favorite memories. Now he was making more memories, just not good ones.

Quint nodded, finally realizing how dangerous the situation would be. Ingalls would have no help from Aileen, and they would be at the mercy of a madman. He rose from his seat, picking up the nearly empty bottle of wine before turning.

"Before you go," Miller inserted, "could you tell me if Drane is still in town?"

"Aye. He's here. Good luck getting a favor from him, though. His opinion of Mistress Aileen has never been as high as mine. Now I see why."

Miller exhaled in resignation. The thoughts of the Masters were beyond him. He couldn't criticize townsfolk for not understanding them either. The Masters played a long game where their goals were shrouded in secrecy. Even Mistress Aileen had started to become silent about many things. Anything that could frighten her into silence scared the wits out of Miller.

More people began to flow into the LaDeeDah. Miller didn't particularly feel like giving up his excellent table until he was asked to, so he unpacked his journal, ink, and quill from his travel bag. He began jotting down short thoughts about the events that had occurred on the journey so far. The raiders bothered him specifically, so he spent time pondering what might have happened in the Order to convert them to banditry.

Miller stopped after scribbling a random thought. "How did they get Mage Arrows?"

He guessed that some of those arrows could have been given to them by the Eisenvard, but they'd left the lands years ago. Each of those arrowheads could be sold for more silver than a raider would likely see over their entire lifetime. But they keep them handy to shoot into a random apprentice? The more he thought about it, the less sense it made. There was no chance that any random robbery victim would have enough treasure to warrant using one of those arrowheads, yet they used it on the first apprentice to walk by?

Or was he the first? Were they waiting, looking for casters to slay? Did they have other Mage Arrows? Given that only the Free Mages traveled about these lands now, and they were almost respected locals, could those mage arrows have come from Free Mages?

The White Hand traveled through as needed, silently, without attracting notice. Why were those men there and why were they being so aggressive?

Those raiders were in that town for a reason. They were armed with a Mage Arrows for a reason. The only thing that Miller could envision was they were there hunting Mistress Aileen and the others within her cabal. The others, like him.

But where did they get the Mage Arrows? Those had been crafted by an artificer who knew his constructions, as well as his wizardry. These weren't charms he could buy from the local hedge witch.

He blew on his notes, trying to quicken the drying process. After a few moments, he turned the page of his journal and began to draw. He had only glimpsed the arrowhead for a moment after he pulled it out of his shoulder; he could hardly pull it out here, in front of everyone. He needed a clearer memory, so he reached for a skill that Mistress Aileen had insisted he learn. He calmed his mind, removing errant thoughts from his awareness until only the image of the arrowhead remained in it. Miller began drawing. The shape of the arrowhead formed quickly on the page, it's jagged edges standing out, differentiating it from other arrows that he had seen before.

It wasn't a narrow war arrow. It wasn't a wide hunting arrow. The arrowhead had been two fingers wide, and just longer than his index fingers. A tiny edge was smooth and sharp along the front side, and the middle was filled with some sort of design.

Miller tried to concentrate on the design. It was made of protruding metal lines that danced within interconnected triangles. It was hard to tell where the design started and ended. He tried to copy how it fit on the arrowhead, how it started near the point, and how it tapered near the shaft. Each time he concentrated, the image changed. It would not remain fixed in his mind's eye.

He tried to remember the pattern and failed. It was frustrating. He wrote that thought within the journal, drawing a light line between those words and the unfinished sketch of the arrowhead. After a half hour without a useful drawing, he changed tactics. Instead of trying to remember the pattern, he decided to try to notice what was missing.

Miller knew how to construct a Mage Arrow. It required a water sink, a flexible mind channel, at least four essence accumulation runes, and some Mage Stone of three different types. These kind of enchantments normally required specialty diamond-crafting tools. He should see scoring from the Hard Smith but none was visible. His vision of the arrowhead remained obscured, but he knew what was missing, just not what was there.

A shiver went up his spine as he scribbled down more notes, joining them to the sketch with more arcing lines. Is this enchanted to prevent remembering? Why? Is this a new enchantment technique? Who else has done work like this?

Miller stretched with fatigue, rubbing his palms against his curly brown hair. He looked up from his work, noticing that the inn had accumulated another three score customers. It was getting busy. He had been drawing almost an hour without noticing how the crowd had grown, and how the musicians had changed at least once.

Quint had left the table to him. The place of honor was his, by conquest.

He spent some time drying the ink that decorated the page. It didn't help much, but he'd have something to show Mistress Aileen when she called on him again. Perhaps she knew what this strange enchantment was. Perhaps it was a secret only a Master would know.

After Miller had dried the ink and bound the journal within its leather case, he returned his belongings to the travel bag. He looked into his disappointedly empty wine goblet, then across the main area within the inn. There were several people here who had some level of wealth, and at least three knights. But Miller had remained at the high table, uninterrupted. *My, how Mistress Aileen's influence has grown.* She would be delighted to hear that. She did love it when people thought well of her.

Not all of her priestess training had vanished yet. That was a good thing. How long would she follow it, though?

Miller found the person he had come here to talk to, and hopefully enlist. "Bloody Fingers" Drane arrived at the head of a long entourage of what he called "companions." A dozen of the most beautiful women this part of the country could produce followed him in, attentive to his every motion, ready to offer smiles, laughs, or flirtations as the situation allowed. A few the musician's companions followed the parade into the LaDeeDah as well, hoping that this would be one of the rare nights that Drane would sing.

Miller breathed out slowly, gathering his thoughts, hoping he could convince Drane to accompany him. The alternative travel companion, Master December, didn't appeal to him.

IN SEARCH OF ALLIES

Miller approached a twelve-person table below, close to the stage. It was overflowing with beautiful women, newly opened bottles of wine, and laughter. His dark-brown woolen cloak and travel clothing contrasted with the lively colors and soft silks that inhabited this new kingdom. Miller walked around the edge of the crowd as it made a point of ignoring him. He forced a smile to appear on his face as he nodded as he went around. None of the people recognized him but their revelry made them welcoming. After a few minutes of being ignored, jostled, or invited to join in some sort of mysterious "after party," he saw Drane sitting at a table like the bard kings of legend.

Drane sipped wine with a smile as two lovely women laughed and continued their wildly humorous stories about some noble woman that Miller couldn't care less about. Drane was a handsome man, perhaps beautiful. He was tall and broad-shouldered, with a narrow waist. He managed to maintain a good balance of muscles and grace even when feasting and drinking almost every night. His long black hair grew straight down his back, ending just before his belt. His smile was genuine and contagious. It put people in a friendly mood and urged all his neighbors to open up to him. Miller hated this about Drane, yet still loved him. Everyone loved him. Everyone wanted to be him. Miller could not stifle his jealousy.

His apprenticeship training proved too strong to allow a direct approach. Instead, he stood dutifully to the side, awaiting Drane's attention. The other people in the crowd noticed his odd stare first, and then called out to him.

"Aye, lad! What's yer business?"

The table crowd grew quiet with concern, all eyes on Miller.

Drane turned to look in the speaker's direction, then at Miller. At first, he stared in confusion, then recognition. His smile was replaced with a scowl for just moment, followed by resignation. He recovered quickly, standing up to reach out his hand. Miller stepped forward to offer his own but was surprised when Drane stepped closer and grasped his shoulder to pull him forward.

The crowd seemed to regard this as some sort of good thing. Conversations resurfaced only to be overcome by the musicians on stage. Drane shouted to him in an effort to speak, giving in to the music and noise.

"By the five channels! Miller! Where's everyone else?"

"It's just me. I'm running an errand for, well, you know. Can we talk somewhere less, er, loud?"

The look on his face told it all. Miller had just confirmed Drane's worst fears. Drane did not look eager to be part of any more Aileen-drama, and definitely any part of the White Hand. He gave Miller a broad, open and mischievous smile. He leaned over the table to begin unclasping his lute case, instead. The table crowd began cheering with excitement as he opened the case to reveal fur lining and the most beautiful lute Miller had ever seen. Its polished wood reflected the candlelight as he drew it out. Even Miller became excited just thinking about the songs that Drane could conjure from the magnificent instrument.

Drane walked up to the stage. The musicians began to falter as the best known, and perhaps best loved, living artist the LaDeeDah had ever hosted motioned a silent question. Can I join you?

The band broke out in smiles as they made room for one more. Drane walked to the stage, handed the lute to an audience member, and then climbed up onto its dark wooden surface. He retrieved his instrument and walked into the musicians' midst, lazily attaching the long red strap to the lute and joining the harmony as he did so.

The crowd broke out in a vast cheer.

The skill level of the band seemed to rise as their new member joined in, bringing a new vitality, new confidence, and a new art to their music. The song did not end. It transitioned into a new melody. Drane launched into a high-speed duet with a second lute player. Notes flew from the lutes. Drane's fingers rippled across the strings, evoking complex tunes that sped the heart. The other lutist struggled to keep up, then retreated into melodious chords, instead. The vocals were beautiful, transforming the small stage into an epic story about a lost love and a hopeless battle. The music went on and on. Drane contributed, helping the entire ensemble to a new level of artistry.

People began arriving from the streets. The inn soon filled past capacity. Locals were coming in to hear this new show, and to be part of what would surely be the next story born at the LaDeeDah. Workers in sawdust-coated jackets just in from shutting down the mill mixed with well-to-do ladies in their festive dresses and jewelry. Every face lit up in cheer and delight as Drane stepped to the front.

He strummed a few chords to begin the next piece, a song celebrating some of the loves and deeds found in the books of Phyllicitus. Someone had transformed it into a song both bawdy and touching.

Then Drane began to play in earnest. His fingers began at the slow pace of the tale and leapt into a tune faster than Miller had ever heard.

Bloody Fingers. He'd got that name by playing so fast his fingers sometimes started to bleed.

Dancing erupted in the audience. It was wild, unkempt, simply amazing. The energy of joy washed over Miller, drowning him in its intensity. Before long, he was dancing with a lovely older woman, whose graying hair had been let down as she whipped it about.

The hours continued to pass within the blur of revelry. Drink flowed, his feet ached, but Miller was unwilling to stop his dancing. It was near midnight when Drane brought the show to a close. The exhausted and sweating musicians bowed to applause.

Miller stood there for some time, wondering if Drane had just successfully avoided his conversation. Drane eventually emerged from the crowd and walked up to him, bending to speak in his ear.

"Walk with me."

With those three simple words, Drane continued on, passing by smiling well-wishers and dreamy-eyed young ladies alike. For some reason, the crowd did not form around Drane as he walked out of the LaDeeDah with Miller briskly in tow.

He had the crowd trained. There wasn't a follower in sight.

Miller caught up with him as he entered the darker streets. They were leaving the main part of the town and entering the living areas. Miller knew where he was bound. Drane lived at the Free House, a refuge and home for the local Free Mages. Drane's ability as a bard and entertainer were renown, but his reputation as a knowledgeable magician less so. It had suffered because of his fame as a musician, and perhaps his laziness. Drane was a competent practitioner in those areas where he cared to excel, but he didn't have the discipline needed to become a true master of the magical art.

At least that's what Mistress Aileen had told him once.

"Why the huge show?" Miller gasped as he came next to Drane.

Drane smiled down at Miller. Miller stood almost six feet tall and Drane towered over him, conquering Miller's height by more than a hand span. "That wasn't huge. If you want to see huge, then come on the LaDeeDah birthday celebration. That's huge."

Miller smirked at his attempt to minimize his latest "small" affair. "You didn't have to do that."

"Are you serious? I can't hide anything in that place. And if you can't hide something, well, you just create something else to talk about. You know how people like to talk."

Smart; he hadn't thought of that. "What now? Do we wake up the entire house to have our talk?"

"I thought we should spend some time drinking a glass or two of wine and catching up before Aileen shows up."

Miller shook his head slowly. "I'm afraid I'm all there is tonight. Mistress Aileen is busy doing errands for Easter. Don't look for her on this trip."

They walked for two more blocks. Drane slowed his walk and tilted his head, turning Miller into the object of his complete attention. "Well, well, look who got promoted! You're a journeyman now, eh?"

"We don't have journeymen. I'm an apprentice."

"Miller, my friend, when are you going to learn? These titles that surround us," he said, waving his open hand in a half circle, "they are as meaningless as yesterday's fire. You are journeying. You are on a task for your master. It doesn't matter what other people call you. Right here, right now, you are a journeyman."

Miller hated it when he started making sense. Mostly because he usually agreed with Drane.

"You need to live for right now, my friend, and live for what you see. Isn't there someone else you'd rather be with? Some other thing you'd rather be doing?"

Miller took a few steps as visions of Brita came to mind. He barely knew her, but she had been haunting his dreams of late.

Of course, the absolute worst thing he could do would be to pay attention to her. Mistress Aileen made it clear that a girl like Brita could pay a heavy price for any attention he offered.

"Still thinking about Sister Joy, eh? Don't worry, the sting will go away."

He remembered Sister Joy, the young accolade of Phyllicitus. He remembered meeting her at the temple in Home's Hearth, introduced by Mistress Aileen. Miller remembered losing his heart to Sister Joy the instant he met her. That wasn't the best idea ever, but he wouldn't trade it. The last he'd heard of Joy, she was traveling the lands, tending to the sick. He felt like an idiot for letting that relationship go, but what chance did they ever have? The story of his life.

He had half hoped, and half feared he'd find her on this trip. In truth, Miller didn't have any idea what he would say, even if they did reunite. He couldn't do much besides show her how much of a buffoon he was.

"No, another girl I met in the country. She caught my eye, but I don't really know her."

A safe subject, Brita.

A house appeared as they turned a tree-decorated corner. Its steep roof dwarfed other houses in this wealthy part of town. The house served as a base, a shelter, and a meeting place for any Free Mage who needed it. It had been built in a time where there were many more Free Mages than there were today. A dozen windows stood dark in the night, with light emanating from only four. Its three dark stories towered over the road. During the night, the surrounding iron gates and stone pillars, decorated with magical protections, were cold and slightly frightening. They walked through the gate, heading toward the thick, grand door.

Drane attempted to keep the conversation going. "That's great! Good on you. We'll save your soul yet. What is your mistress doing? Is she still cuddling up with K?"

Miller simply replied with the truth. "No."

FREE MAGES

Drane approached the door and opened it. He used no key and uttered no mystical phrase. The house simply knew who it should or should not admit. Miller had always been impressed with the enchantment. The skills needed to build such things had left the Free Mages long ago. He was glad to see some splinters of greatness survived.

The house was an excellent piece of enchantment. It consisted of spell-layer after spell-layer, each cast by different people, with different skill levels, at different times. Yet the house stood a cohesive whole, its architecture and spell-crafting well-anchored in the world. He would like to meet whoever crafted this house. There were generations of artificers who added their touches here and there. But those days were gone, and that mage had long since turned to bones and dust. If he ever practiced the art of speaking with the dead, this was going to be the first spirit he'd hunt for. Normally, the thought of speaking with spirits who'd passed through the Crooked Gate terrified him, but the idea that he could have a long conversation with such an artisan, and perhaps learn new techniques, was enthralling.

"So where is K now? She was very intense, if I remember correctly. That separation could not have gone well. Eisenvard training, and all."

"No separation. K passed through the Crooked Gate."

A few seconds passed in silence.

"By the goddess's teeth, I bet that didn't go over well with Aileen," Drane said as he walked into the front room.

A cluttered mess greeted them. Furniture built in various styles over the past two hundred years was spread about the floor. The haphazard organization of the room looked more like a child's tantrum than any planned design. Old papers, tapestries, and even an old plate of cold pheasant lay in odd places across the grand sofa, the game table, and the triplet of chairs. One of the chairs, or at least the oddly shaped pile of blankets, moved as he entered.

"Aileen was the one who sent her there. There was some issue between them, and it went bad." Miller paused, feeling the sorrow of K's loss. "It shouldn't have gone that way, but it did."

"You really need to get out of there."

"I know."

The blankets decided to erupt at that moment, stopping the rest of Miller's statement and uncovering a short woman in a night shift with light blonde hair that hung disheveled just below her shoulder. Her eyes gazed out sleepily as she sat up, looking at the two arrivals. Her shoulder-length hair remained mostly straight as it struggled to keep its posture.

"You two could try being quieter," she scolded.

Drane playfully returned her banter in his sexy voice, "Were you waiting up for us? You shouldn't have."

"Pig." She saw Miller at his side and leaned back into the chair. "Miller? You've grown a few inches. Welcome back." Her smile was broad, hinting at mischief.

"Yeah, it's been a few years. How have you been, Chamise?"

His guard senses came up. If she was anything like she was three years ago, he didn't doubt that Chamise would try to have him in bed. Then on to the part she really cared about, spilling secrets. Two weeks after that, every Free Mage in Ingalls would probably be dead. The White Hand liked to protect its secrets.

"Drane and I need to talk business. Can we have the room?"

"Not going to happen, cult-boy," she responded with a shake of her head.

Drane joined with her, shaking his head in support.

"Sorry, Miller, your business is house business. That's just the way it is. Everyone should be up to hear what you have to say. We don't deal with your issues alone anymore. Last time we almost lost the entire town."

He didn't know when these became his issues, instead of White Hand issues. It wasn't worth arguing now. They probably didn't know there was a difference between the two. Or they didn't care.

"What? Mistress Aileen didn't . . ."

Chamise immediately cut him off. "Not Aileen. The other one."

"Ah," was all Miller could say before he closed his mouth and began rearranging clutter to find a place to sit. He discovered a rich red sofa beneath a pile of unraveled scrolls. He moved the scroll parchment onto a small table and sat. It would be best not to bring up Master December in this crowd.

Footsteps emerged from the next room. Hartgen Brute and a Free Mage Miller didn't know entered the room. Hartgen had heavily muscled arms covered with bear claw tattoos. When he was younger, he thought those tattoos were to make him look intimidating. Now he knew better. Those were the marks of the Bear God. They gave testimony to Hartgen's faith, and his family history. After living closer to Jarlsland for two years, he knew them well.

Miller held his right hand up in the sign of the Bear God

used by the people in the north country.

Hartgen met Miller's eyes and returned the salute. Dark ink stains in the form of a bear claw decorated his forearm. "Miller, you've been learning things on your journeys?" he asked in his deep voice. His throat was covered in the designs of bear teeth, tied together with ceremonial knots. It showed that his family might have been close to the Bear God back when it walked in the world. Those designs were a high honor.

Drane smiled. "That's what I told him. See if you can get him to listen."

The unknown mage produced a crystal decanter of brandy and set it on a table. He had a short beard, and well-honed mannerisms. The man bowed slightly and introduced himself. "Piers Fronge, at your service."

Chamise interrupted. "Don't promise him any services until you hear what he needs. Then don't promise anything, in any case."

Piers could only stare back, eyebrow raised.

"I mean it. Nothing," Chamise continued sharply when Piers tried to interject. "Just be quiet and learn something. It might save your life."

Drane broke the silence by handing out a set of short clay mugs. He then took up the decanter and poured each of them a strong dose of brandy. He raised his cup. "To unforeseen guests."

"You know we love you," Chamise added coyly.

Miller was sure she'd give him the chance to find out.

Drane raised his glass and the rest followed his example. Miller took a sip of the powerful brandy. It burned as it met his lips but left a pleasant pear-flavored aftertaste. He'd normally refuse any drink gifted to him by another spell-user. All kinds of bad things could happen with free drinks, another skill the Order had drilled into him: How not to be poisoned. He'd learned that skill the hard way.

"To business, young Miller!" Drane urged. The others took their seats, moving various knickknacks out of their way to form an entirely new obstacle course. They sat and gave Miller their attention.

"Well, I'm in a hard spot. I have business in Home's Hearth. I've been doing some research and have some new information about the Takers, and how they tie into the strange weather events and the like. Mistress Aileen thinks the priestesses should have this information, so she sent me to teach them what I know. I ran into trouble on the road, though. I almost got killed by some raiders. I was hoping I could convince Drane to be my escort to Home's Hearth."

None of the Free Mage's appeared confused. They'd all been paying attention to what was happening over the years: People had become infected, taken, and had begun turning against their neighbors and families.

"Well, that's an easy one," Drane replied quickly. "No. Thanks for stopping by, though."

Miller had to make the pot sweeter.

"Drane, you know I can make this a rewarding trip. Perhaps a small permanent enchantment? A ring? A waterproof lute case?"

"I know better than to make deals like that. What aren't you telling us?"

Miller hung his head. "They had a Mage Arrow."

A low whistle came from Piers. "Dear me, you weren't joking when you said to avoid entanglements with him."

"You know I wouldn't bring this to you unless it was important. I can save lives if I get this information to the priestesses. You know I can."

Drane was not going to accept this mission. It was clear. There would be no Mage Arrows sprouting from his back.

A full minute passed in silence as they stared at their brandy or finished it.

Chamise finally broke the silence. "I'll go." Everyone in the room spoke up to disagree. Finally, she raised her voice. "Look, you remember what happened before. How many people died? At least fifty were from this town. And I'm not going for free. I need something from you, Miller. This house demands a price."

The other Free Mages began listening again. Miller felt like he was suddenly out of his depth.

"You are the finest enchanter this house has seen in a generation. You arrive as our guest and leave in friendship. Occasionally, we help each other. I need, no, we need the same thing the temple does. We need a little bit of your mind. I need to improve my craft and I need to grow my enchanting. And the house needs me to bring that skill home and pass that knowledge along. I will accompany you if you teach me your craft when we reach Home's Hearth. I will require at least a month of your time and you must train me in your enchanting practices. I already have some skill, so you wouldn't be starting from the absolute beginning."

A month would extend his stay there for an entire season. Miller nodded gravely. An entire season in Home's Hearth would not be a bad thing. Plus, he could talk to Mistress Aileen and get permission to teach her some small things. With permission, there wouldn't be any retribution, hopefully. Miller raised his gaze toward Drane.

Drane spoke. "I am not going. I have already learned my lesson. I'll stay here where it's safe. And Chamise, I predict you won't be happy with this bargain. If you're going on the trip, bring something sharp and pointy."

There were no other volunteers. There were no uncomfortable offers to stay the night, either. Miller finished his brandy and stood. "Meet me for breakfast at the LaDeeDah. We can leave after we eat."

Miller let himself out, walking through the deep night back to the inn. He stopped to whisper another prayer to the goddess. He had help, but he would need to guard Chamise as much as she needed to guard him.

18

THE FARM

The farm was quiet. Light winds moved the tops of wheat stalks. A house that grew a marriage and a family lay quiet just beyond. A woman's blood-covered body lay discarded in the yard.

A dog lay unmoving beside his owner. A trail of blood testified to the animal's bravery. The dog had used his last breath to defend her and died at her side.

Brita looked down from her saddle. She felt disgust, and a slight bit of heartache.

"Knife to the throat." Ebber supplied the obvious explanation. "At least it didn't take too long, for her, anyway." He shook his head when he saw the blood covered dog.

She dismounted and walked closer to the bodies. "That is one way of looking at it. Another way might be, well . . . is there another way? It still looks bad."

Her focus had gradually returned during her two-day journey. She remembered it all. She could think clearly, distracted by nothing, guided by a sense of purpose. Somehow, she had known the way, even though she hadn't been given any directions, or even an end goal. She had just known. They'd made a cold camp the first night, not even bothering to set up the tent. Instead, they simply curled up within its canvas. They didn't bother keeping watch or patrolling for strangers. After all, the Friends would warn them if someone approached.

Now she stared down at the woman. She was mature, but not elderly. She looked like someone who had lived a good and full life. Someone had put a lot of work into this place. And a lot of love.

She looked up at the house. Three sleeping rooms would take up most of the main floor, with a cellar below and bare wooden beams above. It had a barn beyond it, then another field of wheat beyond that. Small patches of vegetables decorated the grounds nearer the house.

She was sad. "I think this was a widow. The wheat fields look like they are only tended once in a while. The vegetable gardens show some attention, though."

She looked at the house. A perfect house for a small family. A dream. Her dream.

Ebber dismounted, then took both horses to the house, tying them to a hitching post near the door.

He seemed to sense her sadness. "Best not to put yourself in their place. This could have been us. But still, it wasn't."

She didn't reply. She walked up the painted wooden stairs toward the entryway. The door stood slightly ajar, showing a well-kept house within. The goddess' symbol was mounted on the door.

"This woman, she was a believer."

"Fat lot of good it did her." He moved past her to push the door fully open. The house looked like it had been looted, but gently. A chest of drawers lay open, with clothing and dishes removed, but organized in some semblance of order on the floor. The dining table had been moved, and all the candles from the candleholders were missing. Plates and silver stood on a side cupboard, stacked and neat.

"It's Gardin. He always likes to use supplies left behind. He really hates waste."

She could feel the truth in his words. The Friends were confirming Ebber's guesses. Gardin had claimed items he would need on the trail, yet left things he would not. He did not destroy them, he had left them so the next group of travelers, or family members, could find use in them.

She continued to look through the house, going room to room, searching for some reason why this woman had been killed. She arrived at a smaller room with a rough, unskilled painting hanging on the wall. It showed a small boy about ten years old, holding what could be a pole or spear in his hands. The head was un-proportional to the body, and a dozen other details testified to the inexperience of the artist. It must have been difficult for a country family to afford such colored paints. This was a painting done with love.

It was such a treasure. She could feel the love of a mother to her son. She felt her heart beginning to break. "Gardin, eh? Why do you think he killed that woman?"

"I'm not sure it was him; it might have been another of us. It was definitely one of us, though. Not sure why. It's all about the war, right?"

"The war? Really?"

"That's what the Friends tell me, anyway. And I can hear them better than most. Don't forget, I've had a lot of practice."

She turned from the painting and walked from the room "All right, I guess I should ask. What is this war anyway? And who are we at war with?"

"Oh, that is the question, isn't it?" He sounded delighted to talk about this. "We are at war with death itself, of course!"

She stopped and turned toward him. "What?" How can you be at war with death itself?" Somehow, she felt the truth of it, or at least the truth that the Friends wanted her to feel.

"Well, the agents of death, anyway. You do remember the necromancers called The White Hand? Those are the enemy, and we are the foot soldiers in a long war against them."

"Necromancers? How are we supposed to fight necromancers?"

"I think there's more to it than fighting. I've been in the family for at least a decade, maybe more. I've picked up on a lot of things, but most of it doesn't really agree with each other."

"I still don't understand. Can you explain so a pretty peasant girl like me can understand?"

"Well, you are pretty, that's for sure. But your peasant girl days are behind you now." He winked at her.

She suspected he was flirting. That was the last thing she needed, this maniac flirting with her. But how can he flirt? The Friends? They weren't exactly the romantic types.

For a moment, she imagined Ebber trying to woo her, and it made her laugh. Ebber joined her a moment later, and they laughed until the oddity of it passed.

"Come on, let's check the barn. Keep talking about these White Hands. I remember when the Eisenvard sent messages across the lands back in the troubled times. They were serious about rooting them out of the countryside. Whatever happened with that?"

"The Eisenvard lost."

"Lost? How can they lose? They had a thousand men under arms. They had knights, and castles, and everything else. How do they lose?"

"Well, right now, all the Eisenvard are dead. There are no survivors we know of. Yet the White Hand survives. I would call that a loss on Eisenvard's part."

She had to stop and think about the enormity of it. "How does a group of necromancers kill off an entire army? It makes no sense."

"You're thinking about this wrong. We aren't fighting a group of maddened hedge adepts. We're fighting a group of evil wizards, each being up to a thousand years old, each being immortal, and dedicated to dominating all magic, and all life. You don't see them because they don't want to be seen. They touch your life every day and you don't even know it."

"I think I would notice a grubby necromancer digging up graveyards, thank you."

"Really? And did you notice any grave dirt on that young Miller lad? You seemed to like him a good bit. Is it the smell of fresh corpses what lights you up?"

Brita could only scowl, then the Friends took the sting away. She forced the scowl to stay on her face. Small victories counted, too.

She approached the barn with doors left open. There was enough room to stable a half-dozen horses but was empty now. Gardin had collected the horses, and just about every other piece of gear he could grab.

She thought about Miller. She thought about the deserted house, the farm, and the names of children she would never mother. She still wanted all of that, but the Friends told her the truth of it. Miller was connected with them somehow.

Ebber scoffed, as if he could read her thoughts. Maybe he could.

"Miller serves Aileen. She is one of the worst of them. She was in the service of the goddess. The White Hand convinced her to betray all that was holy and good. Can you imagine what that would take? To move loyalty from a goddess to a group of necromancers? Especially these necromancers? Don't fool yourself, there are dark forces moving against us. The Friends can smell them; they hate these dark wizards."

"But how can we fight them? If they are so powerful, how can we make any difference?"

"It isn't about directly fighting them. We need to keep them in check; I get that sense. But the real fights are happening somewhere else, somewhere people like you and I can't see."

They spent another half hour exploring the barn, then she decided to walk around the perimeter of the farm. She wanted to get away from Ebber and spend time with her own thoughts.

She didn't know what this war was about. She could not conceive of how such a war could be fought, let alone won. How were the Friends involved? Were they inventing this truth just to enlist their cooperation? She spent time thinking, then broke that time up with frivolous behavior, trying to confuse the Friends. She would stop and dance, or simply lie on her back. Any time she felt distressed, or angry, or worried, she would distract herself.

Hopefully, she could distract the Friends, as well. It seemed to work for Ebber; maybe it would work for her.

She continued through the wheat fields, lost in thought. She was surprised when a boy stood up a few paces in front of her. He appeared to be ten years old. He favored his mother's looks. His hair was light brown, and it had collected various sticks, leaves, and other detritus while the boy had lain in the fields. He must have been here for hours. Did he even know about his mother?

"Uh, hullo."

His country accent was thick, but she knew it well enough. She smiled back at the boy, hoping to calm him.

"Hullo, little boy. Why are you hiding in the fields? Did you get planted here?"

Brita frowned as she tried to understand the boy through his thick country accent, "No. Me mother, she sent me out. I think bandits came. I heard some yelling." He looked down at his feet. "I don't reason you look like a bandit."

The poor boy, he had no idea. His mother lay dead on the ground not fifteen minutes' walk away, and he'd been out here all day.

Her heart went out to him. It would be a terrible blow. She didn't know what to do about his mother, but she could give some small bit of comfort. She opened her arms to embrace him. "Come here, good heart. I've got terrible news you aren't going to want to hear."

The boy looked into her eyes. *He does know, or at least suspects.* But where would he go now? He really needed some help. She stepped up to him and embraced him, holding him tight against her. What could she do with this child? How would she take care of him? Should she send him away? To where?

But she already knew the answer. The boy had seen her. He had probably seen Gavin and Terp when they came through. He might've even seen Miller. She knew what to do. The Friends had told her.

Embracing the boy tighter with her left hand, she slowly dipped her right hand toward her belt to find the hilt of a short dirk she kept with her for cooking. She knew what to do. She knew how to make this painless and quick. She could see it in her mind, one quick cut on the boy's throat would solve both of their problems.

She could see his confused look in her imagination. She could see the blood covering her bosom.

"Not going to happen!"

Brita's scream startled the boy. He stepped back from her as she began to dance. She danced with all of the fear and passion she could muster. The Friends called her to finish the child, to end the dilemma. She danced harder. She danced to drown them out.

"Are you well?"

The boy's confused look was priceless. She must look like a complete madwoman, dancing about the wheat field while his mother's body lay cold just fifteen minutes away.

"I've got a gift for you, so keep it close! Ask no questions, just take it and use it wisely!"

She spun and bowed before him, depositing her dirk at his feet. "Take it and be off with you. Trust me, the bandits haven't been good to your mum. You don't want to go there. Go find your friends, but don't come back here. The bandits will get you!" she screamed at him, unleashing a maddening roar of anger and fear.

He ran. He had left the dirk behind and sped away through the wheat.

She watched him run, becoming happier every step the boy

took. She didn't want to know where he went. She didn't want to end up chasing him, stabbing him. She decided to just keep dancing.

She danced. She danced every childhood dance she'd ever learned. When she ran out of dances, she improvised and created new maddeningly awful dances just for this moment, just for her.

Soon she saw Ebber walking through the wheat field. He was moving fast, but not at a panicked pace. He looked amused. Was he feeling smug? She thought so. She tried thinking about the Friends that connected her to Ebber. She wanted to know how he was feeling.

And the Friends answered her. Ebber was feeling satisfied, and oddly aroused. She guessed he liked her dancing. She giggled a little, wondering how the Friends were dealing with romantic feelings. She knew that the Friends were actually Takers, and she was in their power. At this moment, she reveled in the experience, in the feeling of belonging to something larger than herself.

Ebber continued until he was in front of her. She stopped dancing as he held out his hand. She placed her sweaty palm in his and began to giggle. He understood. He was quite insane, but he understood..

DANCING IN THE DARK

Morning arrived with a bright sky filled with birds. Miller spent a quarter hour with his mare, tending to her needs, brushing her mane and cleaning her hooves. He shared an apple treat with her. Then he stood for a half hour gazing up at the birds, looking for signs of ravens. Ravens could be harbingers of the Raven God, and that would be a poor omen for his day. He saw no flock of ravens. What were they called, an Unkindness of Ravens? Rather fitting.

When he finally arrived back in the main hall of the LaDeeDah, Chamise was there waiting on him. His brief experience with being a high-status guest had apparently ended. When he asked for a table, the servant merely shrugged and motioned toward the crowd of low-sitting tables, half of them covered with the remains of previous meals. Chamise waved to him from one of the least crowded tables far to the side.

Miller had managed to clean his traveling clothes last night before falling into a deep sleep, and had even had time for a shave this morning. He could get a lot more done waking up two hours before dawn, though. He would pay for that efficiency later. The night had not left him untroubled.

"Good morning, sunshine." Chamise looked ready to travel. Her sleep shift had been replaced with a padded undercoat, its pale-yellow cloth highlighted by black stitching. A pile of traveling gear lay sprawled on the floor next to her. A hardened breastplate of boiled leather, a short, narrow sword, a leather satchel, and a wicked-looking crossbow stood ready within an arm's reach. She was taking this seriously. Good.

Miller sat down at the table and pulled over a long wooden bowl half full of eggs. It had been carved into the shape of a northern long ship. Surprisingly, it even had the Stag God's head on its bow. He didn't think he would ever see that again around here. He fetched one of the eggs and began peeling the shell off until he had nothing but its firm inner treasure in hand.

Silence stretched for five uncomfortable minutes until Chamise broke it. "Things seem odd between us. Talk to me. I am going on this trip with you, after all."

"Sorry." Miller began after he finished his first bite. "Last time we were together, in private, things got, well, a little intense."

He remembered clearly her naked form, curled up in his bed. Mistress Aileen had been out that night on Order business, and Chamise had decided that Miller would be a good companion.

"Yes, I remember."

Miller paused a few seconds before continuing, "You caught me a bit, well, flat-footed."

"I know that I came on strong. I'm sorry for surprising you. But didn't you see anything you liked?" she asked with a mischievous grin.

Was there going to be three weeks of flirtation on this trip? He suspected they'd get killed if they didn't keep their heads thinking straight—at any rate, that's what Mistress Aileen would say. Miller remembered that night clearly and regretted every instant of it since.

Chamise began laughing at his confused look. "You really don't get out much, do you?"

"No, not really."

She sighed in surrender. "Well, let's agree not to make this trip a party, and just get you to Home's Hearth. All right?"

Miller nodded his head, the red blush slowly retreating from across his face. "Eat up, it's going to be three weeks in the saddle. The waypoint inns don't appear until the second week."

They dedicated themselves to their breakfast. Eggs, bacon, ham, sausage, biscuits, fruit, and every other morsel not currently claimed met its fate as either stomach contents, or hidden treats to be unwrapped later. The journey should offer enough forage, but they could not count on it.

They had consumed their meal within a half hour. Miller went to the innkeeper and paid his remaining tally. He also purchased two bottles of wine just in case the weather caused them delay. There might be food on the way, but there definitely would not be any good wine.

Miller went to the stables and retrieved his mare. After checking her hooves and teeth for problems yet again, he paid the stable boy a copper bonus, along with the inn's fee. He placed the brown saddle on the mare's back, and then reached under to tighten it. The boy attempted to help with the rest of the gear, but Miller waved him away. Ten minutes later, Miller had prepared the mare for travel. They walked from the paddock, the mare following meekly behind him.

Chamise stood in the middle of the street, tapping her foot impatiently. She had changed into her boiled leathers. Her blade hung menacingly on her hip. The crossbow had been attached to her saddle by a strap. Her horse, a black stallion, appeared ready to fight as it stared at Miller. If someone were going to attack them on this trip, the horse might just scare them off.

She was impressive in her warrior attire. Her lithe body moved like it was made for the saddle. She was strong and graceful, demonstrating it by setting her foot into the stirrup and vaulting into the saddle. Her shoulder-length light-blonde hair reflected sunshine as it contrasted with her dark brown leathers. Chamise was at her best when she was in action, moving. She was like a cat, no, a lioness.

Miller simply turned to his horse and climbed up onto the saddle. It wasn't graceful, but it didn't result in any new embarrassments. He turned to Chamise. "Ready?"

"Born that way. Let's go see your temple friends."

They left Ingalls. The sky continued to be sunny, open, and full of birds. Small clouds could be seen far to the north, decorating where the lands of the Jarl lay. They trotted on a well-traveled road heading east, away from Ingalls. Small wooden signs marked their way. This was the fastest way, but probably the most likely to find trouble. Miller took the lead, allowing his mare to set the pace. They soon entered a trot that seemed to last hours.

"Miller! Slow down!"

Chamise had come up beside him. Her horse was breathing hard; its mouth had begun to gather foam.

"Oh, sorry, I didn't notice." Miller guided the mare to a slower pace.

"What kind of horse do you have there? She is barely sweating."

"She's just a loan horse Mistress Aileen gave me. I like her a lot. I hope I can keep her," Miller replied as he patted her back.

"What's her name?"

"She doesn't have one."

"What? Everything has a name. You didn't name your horse?"

Names were a funny thing to the White Hand. Yes, everything did have a name, but that name could have a power over what it named. It was best to be careful giving things spoken names, lest you accidentally find its true one. The mare had not yet shown her true name. Plus, the mare might not survive the journey anyway.

"I'll get to it. Don't worry."

They continued their journey at the slower pace. Each hour they would stop to rest, changing who took the lead position. Each rest found Chamise speaking her mantras, trying to recover whatever spirit energy she had tapped so far. Miller had no need of such techniques. His White Hand training had given him the ability to restore fatigue and spirit merely by sitting quietly for a few minutes. Chamise tried hard, but her magical learning as a Free Mage was inferior in almost every way. It was no wonder she wanted training.

Free Mages are an odd collection of people, Miller reflected. They could access spirit powers, but they didn't understand those powers. Their deep learning had been hoarded and protected over the years as a set of steps, or recipes. This approach was like owning a small farm; as much work, but it created smaller harvests.

The White Hand treated the spirit powers like a river, where all powers contribute to the overall magical forces in play. The White Hand talked about magic as flows or streams. The Free Mages talked about it as a set of steps. The Order had large collections of magical tomes. Their Masters wrote their own books and conducted their own research. The Free Mages had a few impressive magics left from years gone by, their learning was meager compared to White Hand apprentices'. They also didn't share, even with each other.

The White Hand possessed not only magical books, but the wizards who had written them. Some of those books were hundreds of years old. Some of the writers were, too. Free Mage secrets gave some advantage to individuals, but the entire group suffered for it. The White Hand had secrets, but much different ones.

The sun had begun to set as they rode into a small clearing. The center was occupied by an old abandoned fire pit that had been used thoroughly over the years. The surrounding grass was long enough to feed the horses. A thin stream passed along the edge of the campsite, providing refreshment to the weary riders.

"It isn't going to get much better than this," Chamise stated simply as she scouted the edges of the clearing.

Miller took her lead and dismounted. He removed the saddle and gear before pitching his small tent. He took five silver chains from his bag and hung them at five surrounding locations, seeking the places of best resonance. Chamise rode over to stare intently at his creations. Each one supported a silver bell smaller than a thumb. Small intricate runes decorated the outside of each.

She peered at the closest charm, staring but not touching. "Amazing! What are those? I've never seen these before."

"Yes, probably not. I made them last month."

She had no reply. Instead, she squinted in the fading light, trying to capture every detail from the bell. "Is it some kind of alarm?" She looked even closer. "Where is the power core?"

"Yes and no. Yes, they will ring when strangers approach. I didn't use a core, though."

The thought stopped her questions. "No core. Well, I definitely want to talk about that during our lessons."

"I gave you my word. You will have whatever lessons you ask for, if I have the knowledge." She wouldn't know how to ask for the really dangerous arts in any case. Best not to resist her learning this trick. It was simple, much like using small windmills to capture the power of the wind. The theory, though, that would not be a good thing to share.

Free Mages didn't care for theory, anyway. They were very interested in application. That was another of their many weaknesses. Theory mattered, even when it was wrong, it mattered. Without it, there could be no first principles. And discovering the first principles of magic was central to understanding and using magic itself.

The night's rest was uneventful. Stars shone throughout the sky, lighting the trees and fields with a soft, dim illumination. No other travelers came that night. They had intended to share watch duties, but morning found Miller waking up next to Chamise. She lay at his back, her arm draped over him. While he didn't like waking up to such surprises, he could not pull away from her warm embrace. Soon enough the sun began to shine into the tent, waking them both to their morning's business.

After a quick breakfast of their smuggled leftovers and fried ham, they mounted their horses and resumed the journey. Low clouds had begun to gather on the east. Great, rain. Just what they needed.

Rain clouds continued to gather but did not release their sodden cargo on them. The next evening passed in silence, the small fire heating their meal. Miller stood watch until sleep began to claim him. His thoughts would not leave the strange arrow, though. He thought about the interlocking pattern that decorated it, and the lack of magical links that could power it. The item was unique. He had never seen anything constructed in that manner. First principles analysis would have at least given a hint of its capabilities. But he couldn't understand it.

He stared at the tent. Its small frame stood illuminated by the firelight. Chamise lay within that tent. She had begun haunting his thoughts, too. It wasn't like with Brita. Thoughts of Brita were filled with passion, but not much else. Chamise was different. She was more . . . complex. Out here in the camp, he had nothing. In there, would he have something? Someone?

Eventually, he had to admit that he was becoming groggy and losing the ability to keep a useful watch. He stood and called out to Chamise. A few seconds later she crawled out of the tent, pulling her assortment of armor, weapons, and gear with her. She began donning it while she asked questions about the night's activities.

He kept the conversation going while gazing at her near-naked form. She slid bits of leather armor on and buckled them together. She kept talking while dressing with no thought to Miller's presence.

When she finally stood ready to take the night's watch, he entered the tent and lay down on the thick wool horse-blanket, then pulled a thin blanket over himself. He thought about Chamise, then Brita, and then every other woman he had been fond of in his life. As long as he was in the White Hand, he would never truly have someone. Even as a Master, he would simply outlive those he loved. He would be alone, forever.

ORIGINS

The campfire was down to its last embers. Brita watched the dying flames trying to consume the last of the wood. The group was beginning to gather. It had grown by many newcomers over each of the past few days, passing sunset sprouting new branches of men and women, all taken. Brita had lost count of the horses and men a few days ago. There wasn't any real reason to keep track of it all. She had merely been curious. At what point did they transition from a group of raiders into an army?

The camp had begun to quiet down as its occupants took their places by the fires and in their sleeping blankets. She could feel a soft call to sleep, to rest, to pass the remainder of the night. By now, she had become accustomed to how her Friends controlled her by offering suggestions and wants as if they came from her own heart. Instead of fighting some sort of meaningless resistance, she merely began unrolling her blankets, preparing for a quiet sleep that arrived every night, without fail.

Ebber stared at her across the fire. She felt his emotions as much as saw them on his face. Brita knew she was beautiful. She'd been aware since childhood of men's stares and lusts. Ebber didn't look at her like that. He looked at her with sadness.

"What's wrong?" she asked, a hint of annoyance in her voice.

"I'm just thinking of the old days, before all this. Back when I was mostly normal and round."

"Round?" Here he goes again, talking without talking, never giving a clear answer. She had learned to follow his circuitous patterns, though. She wondered what shapes had to do with this

"Yeah, round." He continued on with his shape analogy. "You know, something with all the edges and sharp points filed off. That's how I am now. I've been changed into something that I wasn't supposed to be."

She rolled over to stare at him, resting her head on her arm. "This is starting to sound like a pretty normal conversation even though it's complete nonsense. We don't normally have those. I think your way of thinking has started to effect me."

Brita tried not to think about it. Her normal life wasn't far behind her, but it seemed to be receding more every day. Why was this any different?

She continued with her thought, as if uninterrupted. "I've spent a little time staring up at the stars and talking with my Friends about how we were meant for some special fate. It never came true. If I ever had a fate, it wasn't a good one."

Ebber keyed in on what she said. "Not sure what normal is anymore. I'm not even sure what voices are mine, or if I even have one." He tapped his head, indicating that same inward conversation she had been struggling with since she had been taken. The fire crackled, sending smoke lofting into the air toward the stars winking down on them. "In the past, in the stories I tell myself, I had some dreams. In some of these dreams I became a woodcarver, in others, a brewer. When I was younger, before life changed, I had it all planned out. None of it worked out, though."

Brita thought for a moment about the children who lived in her dreams. Sadness descended on her for a moment as she thought about all the joy that would never come to pass. "I understand what you are saying. I used to have dreams, too. Of a family that will never be. It rips at my heart. I still want it, so badly. But things are different now."

"Yes, they are."

The fire continued to crackle, dying off as the night sky grew darker. Dusk had retreated, allowing the night to take up residence in the sky. Stars in the east had begun to fade. Brita could see a line of low clouds obscuring their light.

Her inner voices were kind to her tonight, allowing her to drink in the sadness of her lost dreams. Even if they were sad, they were her lost dreams, not anyone else's.

Ebber spoke again. "It isn't as bad is it could be."

Was he trying to cheer her up?

"What do you mean? I've got these . . . Friends, now." She tapped her own head, willing him to understand without trying to spell it out in words. He knew perfectly well what she was saying.

"No, it was worse before."

An icy chill spread across her back. Ebber had never talked about "before" with her. "You've been at this a while, haven't you?"

"A while. I'm not sure how long. The early days are a blur. Thankfully, the memories didn't stick. I remember walking around a lot, essentially shambling from target to target. I ate a lot of strange things. I remember eating roots, dirt, and people." His eyes gazed into hers, desperate that she not turn away.

She knew he wasn't lying. It was obviously bothering him right now. "I'm not surprised. I heard the tales a few years ago. It was pretty horrible until the goddess came back." Her curiosity began to gnaw on her. She wouldn't have many opportunities to get real information from Ebber. He was in a talkative, somewhat sensible mood right now. It was time to ask the hard questions.

"So, you were there, at the end, three years ago. What did the goddess do to stop it? How did she stop the hordes? The Taken had grown in size. They were marauding everywhere in Strathmore, then, like magic, they weren't. What happened?"

"Nothing that Phyllicitus did, that's for sure. There was a battle at this place called Tweed's Castle. I don't know how the King of Strathmoore found it, but he did. He sent a few barons, along with some northerners from Jarlsland, to sack the Keep. When they came, they found all the secrets we'd hidden, and we were disrupted."

"Were you there?"

"No. I was out doing my normal thing, shambling from one vague place to another, wreaking havoc on the locals. You know, monster things. I was a monster back then. I guess I still am."

She didn't know what to say. No use allowing him to drift off into self-pity. "You are less of a monster today than you were back then, if you ask me." She offered a generous smile, and he returned a small one. "So, what happened? Why did it all stop?"

"I don't have the full story. I think someone figured out how to detect people who were taken, and how to protect people from being taken. The temple had something to do with it, but there was more to it. We were fighting someone lurking in the shadows. I never learned who our true enemy was."

Brita stopped, cold still. She lay still, staring at Ebber across the fire, thinking of her young beloved, Miller. He and his mistress, Aileen, had been involved with the temple back then. Could they have something to do with this invisible enemy?

She felt her emotions calm. She wanted to talk about Miller and Aileen, and what they were doing when she met them. Recognizing the feeling for what it was, manipulation, she decided to keep asking her own questions.

"Let me get this straight: One day you were shambling about, eating grass and such, and then what? You just got better?"

He nodded. "I remember waking up one morning, wondering how I had gotten in the middle of the woods. I was lost. I found others around me. Some were sleeping on the ground like I was. Others weren't."

She didn't want to ask what the others were doing. But she blurted it out before she could stop herself. "Weren't?"

"Yes. When I woke up, I was surrounded by seventy-three dead bodies, and eighteen live people. I counted them all. The strangest thing was that I couldn't remember ever walking into the woods. I didn't know any of the people, either, living or dead. I didn't know what to do. After a bit, I started having a nagging feeling that I should be moving south. I talked to a few of the others, and we agreed to team up and try it. They'd been thinking the same thing I was. I thought I was lucky at the time. Now I know it wasn't luck."

"You survived and went south. Then what?"

"Then I started figuring out the new rules. Before, there was no choice. I was driven by feelings; controlled by them. Somehow the Takers moved my arms and legs without me. I didn't have to think; I just did things. I couldn't think, not because I didn't want, because it was impossible. Can you imagine having no thoughts at all? I could only do as my emotions told me. After waking up in the forest, the feelings were a softer thing. The things inside me had transformed into the Friends. They didn't control my every move anymore, they asked me nicely. It didn't take long to figure out that not listening was a mistake. We lost six more people before we came to Cliffmark."

"Cliffmark? That's a long way from here."

"Yes, but for some reason, I knew that I had to get far away from the temple. By then, Phyllicitus had returned. I was worried about getting hunted down by Eisenvard, but it turned out I didn't need to; the Eisenvard got killed off by the same enemy the Takers were afraid of, the necromancers."

"They got wiped out in Jarlsland. The jarl himself invited the

Eisenvard to take up residence in one of his old fortresses. I heard he killed them when they arrived. Are you telling me that the Takers were afraid of the jarl in the north?"

A laugh escaped Ebber's lips. "No, oh no. The jarl might have supplied the men and steel, but necromancers put him up to betraying the Eisenvard. Removing the Eisenvard turned out to be a decisive blow for the necromancers. After that, they could travel unmolested through the lands. It wasn't too smart, though. Soon enough, the Takers will come again. Now there will be no Eisenvard Knights to slow things down."

It was a frightening thought, even if she was one of the Eisenvard's targets. There would be no defenses this time. The temple would fall quickly against a massed horde of Taken. The only one in these lands who might stop it was the goddess, and she had no idea how. "What happens now?"

"Now? We mass, we prepare, and we wait to see what the necromancers have in store for us. After we spot them, we move. If we find the enemy first, we will take them. If they find us, well . . . ." Ebber paused to be dramatic. "This will all go off the trail, and it will be pure chaos." Ebber began laughing, holding himself in crossed arms as he giggled away.

REPORTING IN

"Then I arrived in Ingalls."

Miller finished updating Aileen on his progress. His body sat on the cold ground under the stars, in front of a dying campfire. His spirit, his awareness was in the company of Mistress Aileen, far away yet nowhere, propelled there by her magics and will.

Aileen had constructed a phantasm in her mind, an illusion, of a place that she was intimately familiar with, the Closure. It was a special place in her memories, harkening back to days when she spent quiet contemplation of the goddess. The white stone walls of the Closure stood decorated with scenes of piety and worship. She used as a place of refuge, even if it was just a phantasm. She had acquired her Master's ring three years ago. It was not far enough in the past for her to give up all her previous identity. The vestiges of her temple lore surrounded him. She kept it close in her heart yet had never shared a single story of those days with Miller.

He was in the Order of the White Hand, as well. It wouldn't be wise to share her heart unwisely, if ever. This room was a private place for her. Its dark, ornate wooden door held carvings that told a story from her life, if he could ever learn to decipher them. Although the temple of Phyllicitus was a welcoming place, this alternative in Aileen's mind was a place of peace, contemplation, and loneliness, unsullied by visitors. The fact that that she let him see it at all was a sign of trust.

But after Madam K, it surprised him to ever come here, especially within her own mind. Aileen had been turning more and more into a White Hand Master ever since she'd killed K. Her priesthood days were fading away. Seeing this place made Miller happy for a moment, imagining that there might be a way for her to come back, somehow. If there was a way for Aileen to turn back, then perhaps there would be one for himself.

The Closure was a way-room that joined three others. In the real world, it connected the entrance to the studies house with the room of contemplation, and the bakery. The odor of fresh bread seemed to linger here. It held five luxurious red chairs that surrounded a short table. Dark wood with intricate carvings contrasted with the red fabric and white walls to create a scene of peaceful elegance. Aileen reclined on one of the chairs, her ebony dress contrasting with the room in a painfully obvious way. She held a teacup in her hand, white with gold scrollwork. The teacup contrasted with the small band of black that encircled her delicate finger.

"Ingalls. I love that place. Is the LaDeeDah doing well?"

Miller smiled back. It was going to be a good talk, the kind that he always looked forward to. When Aileen smiled, somehow it lit up his heart. She could make him feel safe, and beloved when the mood was on her.

"Like always. It wasn't as busy as I remember it being a few years ago. Quint made me feel welcome, even though he seemed a little worried about my arrival. I think we left some bad memories behind from a few years ago."

Aileen nodded. "Unavoidable."

He decided to skip the details of his discussions with Quint, and instead, went right for the meat of the conversation.

"I found Drane there."

"That's good news. Did he agree to go with you on your little journey?" She was smirking while she said it, as if she had already known what Drane would say no long before Miller asked.

"Sadly, no. Yet again, you were right."

"They call us Masters for a reason, you know?"

He smiled back, taking the traditional bait. "I thought you preferred Mistress for your title."

She giggled a little bit, as if he had made a new joke instead of continuing one three years in the running. "I'm just standing up for women necromancers. There aren't a lot of us. We've got to stick together."

Miller's face soured. "I've only met one other. That didn't work out well for me."

Aileen didn't want to talk about Mistress Sword. Instead, she changed the subject "You left Ingalls all alone?" Visions of possessed mobs plagued her imagination. She thought about Miller and wondered how he was faring.

"No. I stopped by the Free Mage house and did a little recruiting. I managed to get Chamise to volunteer in exchange for a promise for some enchanting lessons. Do you remember her?"

Aileen's brows pushed together. The lighting in the room dimmed, reflecting the mood of its owner. "Chamise? The Eisenvard exile?"

"Well, she was the only volunteer I could convince. None of the others wanted to come along. I'm glad to have her. She seems pretty competent, even if her spell-castings are a little primitive."

"The Eisenvard exile?" she repeated. Aileen's voice rose an octave with panic and concern. "She is an Eisenvard! An Eisenvard witch! I can't imagine anything more dangerous to have near you. You need to send her back."

He shook his head. He was fully aware of the risks that came with her and was also freshly aware of the dangers they faced. He needed the help. Mage arrows didn't favor the unready. "The war is long over; she's just a Free Mage now, trying to make a name for herself. What's the harm? She doesn't have an army of knights at her back."

Aileen didn't respond. She stared at Miller with a gaze that could bore through armor. The lighting in the room dimmed until it bordered on deep night. Aileen's black dress wrapped her body in darkness, leaving only her paleness of her face unconcealed.

"It didn't take you long to forget, did it?" She spit out her response, letting the hate ooze on to every word.

Miller was stunned. He'd never seen her so upset, and he had seen her in full rage. This was a cold fury.

"It seems that I need to update my apprentice with a few history lessons. Do you agree?"

He didn't know what to say. It wasn't really a question, though, he knew that. "History? All right, I guess so." It was going to go bad. Whenever she asked him if he agreed to something, it was dangerous in some way.

Aileen grinned a mocking and bitter smile back at him. Just as he nodded back, a pounding sound erupted from behind him. He turned his head, glancing backward and taking in the room behind. The wooden entrance door stood there, its surface covered with carvings. Masterful images of northern warriors from Jarlsland, snow-covered castles, and caves whose entrances were decorated with icicles stood out from the door's surface as it jumped against its frame. Something was out there, pounding hard to get in.

"What is happening?" His voice cracked with a hint of nervous panic.

"A history lesson."

The door burst in. Shards of wood sprayed across the room. One struck his face, slicing into his cheek and drawing blood.

Miller leaped from the chair, turning to give the door his full attention. Just as he swung around, an armored man rushed into the room, reached out, and grabbed him by his head.

Miller reacted on instinct—he opened his channels of heart and rage, pushing the man away with pure magical force, but the man continued into the room faster than Miller could react to. Miller could feel the forces he had conjured simply wash over the intruder with no effect. Somehow the man could deflect spell-craftings.

Miller tried to turn away, but the man shoved his head forward, then down. Miller screamed as his face was pushed down toward the floor. He lost his balance. Reaching out, he tried to steady himself by grabbing a table. Miller felt the kick on his feet as he tumbled to the floor. A steel-clad boot kicked into his face.

The man, no, the knight, laughed at him. Miller tried to scramble up from the floor, but he was moving too slowly. Blood dripped from his mouth where it had hit the floor. He could feel a gap in his gum line. Three of his teeth were gone. His teeth were broken open. He could feel sharp points near his gums where the teeth were just moments ago. Sharp pain filled his jaw, then his entire head. He couldn't craft any spells.

Aileen sat in her chair, aware of what was happening, but not reacting.

Miller was stunned. He just had to last long enough for Aileen to react. There must be a way to escape. But if he couldn't cast any magic. Could Aileen?

The man grabbed at his ankle. Miller felt himself being pulled across the floor, then flung out the remains of the entrance door. He skidded to a landing in a muddy street. Struggled against the nausea and slippery mud. Tried to stand. Tried to free himself, to help Aileen. He'd never had a chance.

"What?" He was confused. A moment ago, he'd been in Aileen's personal Closure. Now he was in Home's Hearth. He saw the buildings and he recognized the shops in the Crafter's Quarter, one of his favorite parts of that city. But this Crafter's

Quarter was different. It was engulfed in fire.

Flames shot up from the windows of shops. Signs, displays, and wares burned along with the buildings. The heat poured out into the street along with dark, choking smoke and flaming cinders.

Miller tried to get up again and felt the hand return to grab his head. It pulled his head up from the muddy road, then violently thrust it back down, thrusting his wounded face into the mud puddles and hard stone beneath. He could hear screams from horses, livestock, and people trying to flee for their lives. He saw armed men everywhere he looked. He saw long swords, chain mail, and Eisensvard coats of arms.

There might be one way to escape. He pulled magic into his body, moving channels to encase himself in a protective cocoon of force. It wouldn't do much against a sword, but it would protect him against fire. He could flee into the burning buildings that surrounded him, their smoke and flame belching out a horror onto the streets.

A scream cut through the scene of horror. Miller glanced up before marshalling his strength. He had to run away right now. The spell completed, and a cool feeling descending on his skin. Whatever shielded the Eisensvard from his spell attacks did not stop him from casting enchantments on himself.

Then he saw a little girl, maybe eight years old. She wore a thick wool dress died blue, the kind of favorite dress any commoner girl might wear for market day. The girl stood crying, holding her older sister's hand. An Eisenvard knight looked down at them. Blood dripped from the long sword he held upright in his hand.

"These two?" the knight demanded.

The man next to him, dressed in a common brown travel coat, responded with a choked voice. "Just the little one." He grasped a long staff close to his body, as if gripping it for some form of salvation.

The sword-wielding knight snarled down at the pair of girls. "By the code, I declare you witch! As such, you must die!"

Miller's eyes grew wide as he recognized the voice, the tall stature, and the long, thick mane of black hair. Drane, the Free Mage, stood there, gripping the staff tightly. Tears streamed down his face as the Eisensvard knight brought his sword down on the child. She screamed as the blade cut into her shoulder, exiting her body at mid-lung. The girl's older sister screamed in horror. She stopped when the Eisensvard thrust his sword into her body as well.

Drane screamed out. "Why? She wasn't a caster! Why did you kill both of them?"

The knight laughed. "Because of the code. They were both doomed as soon as they left their mother's womb. The little one was a witch. The older one loved her even so. The code is clear."

"Drane? Drane? What is happening?" Miller tried to speak, but he was overcome with grief.

Something grabbed him by the back of the shirt collar and pulled back, back, back away from the slaughter, the fire, the hate. He saw the carved wooden door slam shut in front of him, thankfully hiding the burning town. It didn't hurt as he slid across the cold floor, and he could no longer feel the mud that had been caked onto his hands and chest.

The pain in his face subsided, then vanished. He used his tongue to search for his missing teeth. The teeth were unbroken. It had all been a phantasm, a working of Aileen's mind in her private place, her place of power.

As this was her place of power, then he knew whose fault that scene was. He struggled to stand, but his limbs shook in fear, anger, rage. Yes, he had agreed to a history lesson. That was hardly a history lesson. It was more an assault.

"What was that about?" he managed to sputter out between deep breaths.

"That was the history lesson. Yes, you were with us during those hard times when the Eisenvard rebelled, but you never truly got to see them in action. You saw the evidence and heard the stories, but you never experienced their burning directly.

Even Mistress Sword, as poorly as you got along, managed to protect you from the worst of it. Never forget what men who believe in a cause will do. Never forget that you are not a Master yet. If they seize you, you would die uselessly and in pain. Your magical defenses will not be as useful as you assume. The Eisensvard train daily to fight people like us, like you. Truthfully, even the Masters tread carefully when the Eisensvard are around. Our best defense is the ability to return from the dead. And let me tell you, getting killed hurts a lot, and the Eisensvard are good at killing."

"But the Eisensvard are long gone!"

"You poor boy. You think it was the men and their armor and their sharp pointy swords that brought their death? It wasn't. It was their ideas that made them dangerous. Those ideas still live in this world. So you had better be careful with your little Eisensvard companion. As much as she might deny it, she was born, raised, and bathed in those ideas since birth. Remember what I showed you here when you deal with her. Don't trust her to be anything other than what she is."

Miller couldn't respond. He stood up, swayed for a moment, and began shambling back toward the carved door. He wanted to leave this place and return to the trail. Just as he opened it, he heard Aileen call to him.

"For what it's worth, I'm sorry I was so rough. I just, well, I just don't want to lose you, not like that."

For a moment, he felt a twinge of hope. He nodded, then opened the door. The burning town was gone. In its place stood a lonely road, a campfire, and Miller's peaceful body resting against a tree. Without looking back, he walked through the door and back to his own body.

ABOUT MAGIC

The sun began to wane. Its tired red glow fell behind the tall pines. Miller's rear end was sore from all the riding. He was simply ready to be done for the night. Chamise didn't look like she was ready to stop any time soon.

"Don't you get tired?"

"Sure. I just don't let you see it."

"Well, I'm tired."

She let out a laugh. "That's because you're weak."

He grimaced and kept riding. Sadly, it would soon be too dark to ride. Finally, it was his mare that made the decision to stop, as it simply stopped walking and thus ended their forward progress for the night.

"I think your horse is broken," Chamise said, the hint of a laugh still present in her voice.

"I think we should listen to her. She is trying to tell us it is too dark to ride through here safely."

"Look at you! Talking to animals now, eh? When did you learn that trick?"

Miller dismounted, letting the reins dangle nearly to the ground. He walked around in a circle, studying their new location. "Probably a good idea, stopping. The trail looks like it is going to get narrower, and the trees are getting denser ahead. We could find ourselves in pitch-blackness without much effort. I vote we camp here."

"All right. Just remember you're the one who stopped first."

"Fine. You win the most saddle-proof-rear contest. Let's set up camp."

He began unfastening his bags from the saddle, placing them on a clear patch of ground. A spot of charred wood indicated where previous travelers had set up fires. Chamise was unpacking her gear as well, trying to hurry before the approaching darkness overcame them.

Miller got the hint. Instead of speeding up, he stopped to clear his mind. He felt for the flows of magic and focused on his need for light. He tightened his hands into fists and held them at chest height before him. His two thumbs touched, forming a bridge between his hands. He triggered the soft light with a word of power and released it into the air. It drifted upward just out of reach and hung motionless in the air.

Chamise watched him like a tiger hunting prey. "That was a nice trick. Quick, too."

"Free Mages can't do that?"

"Oh, sure we can." She tied the horse reins to one of her heavy bags, then stepped away from her pile of travel gear. A low song came from her throat, quiet and deep. It gave Miller a vision of moonlit water and a lonely coast. A gentle light spread slowly out from Chamise slowly, in all directions. It filled the trail, then went into the grass until it barely touched the surrounding bushes. There was no single point of light, yet Miller could see clearly in the area. It was as if there was a light there, but without a source.

"Oh, nicely done. I like it."

"You? The enchanter? You like this petty thing?"

"Oh, yes. I like it quite a lot. It's a different way of creating light. No, you created the effect of light, not light itself. And you did it with song? Do the Free Mages use songs for a lot of their magic?"

"Sadly, no. This is one of the only ones I know of. I'm just a good singer, so it's easier for me to cast."

Miller's light continued to float, uninterrupted by this new ambient light. The two kinds of light interacted, making a small area seem as light as day, without the shadows that would normally accompany Miller's source alone.

Chamise opened up one of her leather bags and pulled out a wool blanket. She spread it on the ground, taking care to remove any rocks she felt beneath its surface. Miller copied her, pulling out his own travel blanket along with a dirty, wadded-up roll of old padding. He smiled at Chamise, holding it up. "This used to be my armor a few years ago. Now it's only fit for a pillow."

"It's nasty."

"No, I cleaned it. It's just picked up a few new colors over the years."

She looked back at him, feigning disgust. She looked down again and kicked at her blanket, defeating the last few struggling mounds of dirt beneath it. Then she sat down and began untying her vambraces, freeing her arms for the more serious work of removing her leg armor, breastplate, and leather throat gorget.

Miller simply removed his sword belt and set it aside. He had no heavy armor to encumber him. He pulled his boots off, inspecting them for tears and damage.

"Did you really like my spell?"

He smiled at her. "Yes. I liked it. I love to find new spells. I really love to find new methods. I haven't seen the song method used before. It was lovely and elegant."

"One of the Free Mages came up with that. It was about two

hundred years ago. He only left one book at the house, though. It wasn't written very well, either. It's the only spell that I could reproduce from the whole book."

"I like it. It has style, and the flows are very small. It minimizes energy output, so it has to be efficient."

She thought for a moment. "Huh. I remember reading something about minimizing breath when using this. I wonder if that is what the book was talking about."

"Don't you know?"

"Know what?"

"You knew the spell method, right? I saw you use it. Can't you tell how much flow, or what channels will be needed when you cast it?"

"Flow? Channels? What are you talking about?"

Miller gestured toward his floating light. Pinching his fingers together, the light responded by growing dimmer. Chamise didn't try to replicate this effect. She simply dismissed her light. They were left with a tiny candle-sized light drifting about their camp.

Miller continued looking at her. "You couldn't dim the light, could you?"

"Mind your own business, Necromancer." Her response was terse and cold. She lay on the blanket, pulling half of it over her shoulder to keep her warm in the cooling night.

"I'm not trying to be sharp-witted. I need to know some of what you know if I'm going to give you enchanting lessons. Right now, I'm not sure what you know. Everyone learns the craft differently. People start different, they have different teachers, and different circumstances. I need to know how you send your essence out to interact with the world."

"What are you going on about? I've studied loads of spells. We have books, and sometimes I've even had a live teacher. I've memorized more than twenty spells to mastery. I know every word, every move, every breath."

"That isn't what I need to know. Anyone with talent can learn the motions or the words. It's the method that I care about. There are so many different methods to focus magic, and to use that focus to change the world. I need to know about yours, so I can tailor what I teach you. I want it to make sense to you. It won't be that useful if you are just repeating what I do."

Her reply was weak, as if she was admitting some sort of defeat. "We don't have a method in the Free Mages. We learn by memorization. It works. You saw it."

Miller could feel her sadness. She wanted to know more. She wanted to know why it all worked. She had no idea.

Miller lay down on his own blanket, facing the stars. "Let me give you the first lesson tonight, then. I can't think of a better time."

"Really?" Chamise sat up, suddenly alert.

"I'm going to teach you some basics, things that are not protected by the White Hand. Most experienced crafters know these things. The trick is figuring out how to use them."

"Er, all right."

"Look up. Look at the stars."

Chamise looked up. She sat there for a long time, gazing up before she turned back to him.

Miller continued looking up. "How many stars did you see?"

"I was supposed to count them? I can't count that many stars; I'll be here all night."

He sighed. "Lie on your back, then take your hands and form a rectangle, like this." Miller connected his thumbs to his forefingers, showing her the resulting rectangular gap between them. "Count the stars in this simple shape. I count three."

"Five."

He began moving his hands from side to side. "Now, guess how many rectangles cover the night's sky."

"It must be at least two hundred. What do you think?"

"It doesn't matter what I think. If you have two hundred rectangles of five, you just counted the stars, and you came up with a thousand stars. I came up with nine hundred and fifty-seven. We are very close, yet we used two different sets of numbers."

"So?"

"So, we used different assumptions, the number of stars in a square, the number of squares, and came up with almost the same answer. Magic is like that. There is no pure and true method of interacting with magic. We all interact with a something we think is magic, and we use our innate ability to use it with the hope of changing the world. There are differences in the effectiveness, the speed, or the beauty of spells and their crafting, but their essences are nearly identical. If you'd discovered or adapted a general method to your crafting, I would use it. If you are using memorization, then be prepared to memorize a lot of things."

"How hard can that be?"

"How hard was it to count the stars one at a time?"

She rolled over, turning toward him. Starlight shone down on them, mixing with the light from Miller's floating light source. "This isn't going to be easy, is it?"

"It gets easy when you find your method. I can't tell you what it will be. I know some abstractions that others have used. It might guide you. Until then, I'll just show you how to make the moves and say the words. The rest will be up to you."

BEHIND THE SCENES

The cave maw stood open before them. Decayed, stone ruins stood guard, protecting the cliff face from enemies that time had long ago conquered. Short, broken walls of gray stone surrounded the entrance. Moss jutted out from what were once mortared seams. The binding mortar had eroded long ago, but the powerful enchantments kept the place intact, defying time and fate in one fell swoop.

Six people stood inside the ancient walls. Master Easter was dressed in a dark, luxurious cloak. He wore a gold necklace. A gold emblem hung from it. It was the size of a man's palm. The emblem of a bird stood out on its surface, beaten into the metal by a craftsman gone from this world long ago.

"I never thought you were a follower of the gods."

Easter shook his head, showing her a pained grimace. "I'm not a follower; I'm more of an avoider."

The symbol on Easter's pendant showed a raven. While ravens could be found anywhere in this land, they were never used as symbols or family seals. The raven was only carved to represent the Raven God.

The First Gods were animal spirits. Their essence was born at the beginning of the world. She guessed that as long as animals roamed free, the First Gods would as well. Worshiping them never worked. Asking them for favors was rarely successful. Asking the Raven God for anything was suicidal. The Raven was tied to murder, revenge, and darkness in every story she had ever heard of. Easter was right to be careful. But wearing a symbol of the Raven? Was that wise in a place like this?

She pointed at the raven pendant. "Care to tell the story?"

Easter looked at the other four men in the courtyard. "Not right now. But the First Gods are still with us. You know that better than most people. You have seen what they can do, first hand. Permit me these old habits. When I come to a place like this, I want to appease any of the ancient forces that we might encounter."

She nodded back. Years ago, she had encountered the Stag God, far in the north in the wilds of Jarlsland. Not much later, the shamans of that Old God had come to Ingalls, destroying almost half of it, and drawing the White Hand's interest.

They continued their wait in silence. The day stretched on, and the air began to heat up, making both Aileen and Easter uncomfortable in their warm cloaks. Easter didn't want to remove his. Appearances were important.

A small, light-haired boy, no more than six years old, climbed out of the cave. He wore a dark-red shirt that was patched with mud. Only the silver apprentice ring he wore on his left hand gave any indication he was an apprentice to the White Hand.

His high voice squeaked as he called out. "Master Easter? I've been sent to fetch you. I'm Stevin." The boy offered a clumsy bow. It looked like he had practiced it maybe three times in his life and forgotten most of it.

Aileen offered the boy a small smile as he tried to continue.

"Master Hermagon commands that you follow me to your parley." The boy was nervous, and he had every reason to be.

Easter responded coldly. "Master Hermagon commands? Rather presumptuous, don't you think?"

Aileen didn't wait for the battle of wills between immortal masters to begin. She simply walked into the cave. "Come on then, Stevin. We have business to discuss. I'm sure the Master of this hole-in-the-ground is impatient to be done with it."

The boy smiled back, gratefully. "Yes mum. Er, I mean Master. No, Mistress."

Aileen shook her head and kept walking. It was going to be one of those meetings she always dreaded. Hermagon was always particularly difficult.

Stevin led her down a long tunnel. Stairs had been cut into the floor, each two paces in length. She could see where cracks had formed in the walls, and the steps had been chipped and worn. This cave was a thousand years old if it was a day. Aileen could feel the cave hum with magical power; it was a reservoir of energy, and perhaps a fortress, a fortress she was naively walking into with only one other person. Of course, that one other person was Easter. That gave her a little comfort; Easter didn't like to do things that resulted in getting killed, he was particular in that way.

The light faded as they traveled deeper into the cave. Dim lights began to glow from the walls where spells had been sewn into the rock. Stevin knew when to stop, say words of invocation, and bring forth soft light from the stone. They could have conjured their own light, but this was Hermagon's location, not theirs. After ten minutes of walking down stairs, they arrived in a cavern that had glowing designs carved across all of it's forty-pace length. The designs gave more illumination. The soft lights they had found in the hallway stone was present throughout the entire cavern, bathing all of them in its bright color.

Hermagon stood at the center of the cavern, looking down at

an oak trunk covered in papers. He wasn't a tall man, barely taller than Aileen, but he stood with proud dignity. Hermagon had a way with dominating the room no matter who stood in it with him. His pointed, salt-and-pepper beard jutted out in a well-trimmed assault on the lesser elegance of those around him. His robes were silken red, embroidered with gold thread, and untouched by the cave's dirt. In a nod to practicality, he wore short ankle boots of the finest doe-skin. They too were unblemished.

Another person stood next to him, a woman. Aileen recognized her and felt her nerves shoot cold shivers through her spine. Mistress Sword stood next to Hermagon, looking at her and Easter as if they were vermin meant to be exterminated. Her fire sword was sheathed. Its tip danced playfully on the floor's surface as she played with the blade.

Aileen had seen her burn hundreds of people to death with that sword, in less than three heartbeats. The sword's presence wasn't a good sign. She glanced sideways at Easter. His eyebrows were raised, and he was slowly nodding up and down. Did he predict this? What else was coming?

Easter strode confidently forward, taking long steps and forcing Aileen to move quickly lest she be left behind. Hermagon was a Great Master, one of the most influential of all Masters. Aileen would not be left to a servant's position. She rushed forward, back to Easter's side.

Approaching the Great Master, Easter offered a deep bow. "Hermagon."

"Easter."

The greeting was tersely functional and yet conveyed a wealth of information. These two had known each other, dealt with each other, and even opposed each other more than once.

Easter glanced at Mistress Sword, offering her a slightly less-deep bow. She returned a poorly executed attempt at a lady-like curtsy. The broad smile she sent toward Aileen indicated how poorly she viewed meetings such as this.

"And Mistress Shield herself, Aileen, lately of the temple,

welcome. I'm glad Master Easter could find someone to escort him here. The roads are peaceful, but one never knows."

Aileen could see the deftly delivered cut for what it was, a first shot at Easter's position. Was he so desperate that he needed such a new Master to travel with him? Was there some other reason for Aileen to be present? All of these unasked questions hovered in the air.

Easter didn't take the bait. "I've asked Mistress Aileen to represent the interests of Master December, who is away right now, serving the Order, as is his duty."

Hermagon snapped back. "Are we no longer following the naming traditions in your cabal? Or do we now object to the name the Conclave offered to her?" He gestured at Aileen.

"Protocol dictates she has seven years to change her name. There is precedence in the Order for someone to take their time with the naming process."

Hermagon replied with sarcasm. "I'm so glad that our new Master has the time to wade into the pool so slowly. Given the speed of her apprenticeship, I had predicted a much quicker ascension into the Order."

Easter began to reply, but Aileen cut him off. "My name is what I choose it to be. Some committee chose the name Shield, I didn't. I'll use the name, but when and where I choose. Let's just concentrate on why we are here, shall we?"

"That is what I am trying to do. Names are important, my dear. The ancient magics tied names to fates, and if you have kept your old name, you are already tied. Those who craft with elder magics can have you at their command, and you would not even know it. Plus, it is such a lovely name. You have spent a lot of time shielding the people from harm, and your healing magics have shielded many from grief. Can you think of a better name? It's beautiful, if you ask me."

Aileen looked into Mistress Sword's eyes. They were locked on hers, as if seeking to read her intentions, her plans, her very soul. It was unsettling how easily the other Masters could use their channels to truly know someone. Sword was reading her like a book. Judging by the inviting smile on her face, Sword was enjoying what she was reading.

"We've come here to talk about Master December. If it pleases you, I'd like to skip past the usual verbal maneuvering and go right to horse-trading."

Aileen looked sideways at Easter. Easter never skipped the horse-trading. That was his favorite part. Aileen didn't like the sound of that. Easter seemed to want to get this done with quickly. His face betrayed no emotion. His arms and hands remained still. He looked relaxed, but she knew him, he was always dead calm when he was under stress.

"I've spoken to other cabal leaders. The Conclave will meet in six months. At that time, I will propose that December be exiled beyond the edge of the world for a period not to exceed two hundred years. His multiple crimes of murdering the apprentices of other Masters will not be unpunished. I don't know if there is any need to negotiate. The deals are done, all that remains is the Conclave."

Easter's response was relaxed, as if he had expected this opening position. "There is more at stake than December. While December is valued in our cabal, we don't condone his reckless behavior. Indeed, our newest member had recent experience with this when one of her followers slayed four of your very own apprentices while they tried to hold her captive. As you all know, Mistress Shield—Aileen—did the proper thing and killed that follower."

"Yes, she did the proper thing. Let's all celebrate, but that has nothing to do with December. December used those murders in an effort to affect our cabal, and the votes within the Conclave as a whole. There are a lot of other Masters who are concerned with this. I use the word 'concerned' lightly, you see."

Aileen interrupted their conversation. This wasn't going anywhere. "That isn't the point. Our cabal has always been at the forefront in the battle with the enemy-between-worlds. Master December might be the strongest caster we have. He has proved himself in countless battles against this dark threat." Aileen decided to make a leap, telling them a little more than they might know, and adding a little hint of threat in the process. Sometimes fear makes people do things that they would normally never consider. "We have observed new threatening activities by the Takers. They have managed to gain possession of a few dozen highly skilled bowmen. My apprentice is engaged with them now, running for his life."

"Miller? Sounds like he should have kept his previous Mistress. It would have been safer."

Aileen offered her a dark look. "Perhaps if someone had treated him a little better, he would have."

"Ouch." Sword wasn't offended. She was merely playing with her.

"Early evidence indicates another incursion is taking place right now. Master December has been sent out to support Miller and gather information on how widespread this is. The threat is real. We don't have the luxury of a two-hundred-year gap in his service."

"That's a real shame. I've been fighting the enemy-between-the-worlds for a thousand years. Two hundred years will pass quickly, and we have the Masters available to continue the fight in his absence. What we don't have is a rich set of apprentices who can become Masters themselves, and thus perhaps win it. That is why we need to put December where he can't hurt anyone."

Aileen responded to Hermagon's argument. "It isn't that easy."

Hermagon continued. "I know. December has made many journeys back from the Crooked Gate. I can tell, given his instability. This is going to grow worse and worse. In a few hundred years, he will have gone completely insane. I've seen this before. Trust me, you don't want a Master like December free in the world when it finally claims him."

Aileen held her hands forward, as if to stop them. "His mind won't survive two hundred years outside of the world. You're right, his spirit is damaged. What you're talking is a death sentence."

Sword spoke up. "Yes, sadly. If he falls to madness while beyond the world's curtain, we will never retrieve him. He will stay there for eternity."

"But we need him!"

Hermagon only shook his head. "No, you need him. The Order doesn't. The Order of the White Hand needs apprentices."

Easter looked at Hermagon. His voice sounded defeated as he made his final gambit. "There are other issues that could be included in this discussion, other forces in play. Let's talk about those, if you please. I have long opposed your god ascension project. I've never liked the idea of a Master trying to become a god. But for this, I'm am willing to negotiate. You'll never get approval from the Conclave without my support."

Now it was Hermagon's turn to look surprised. "You would negotiate that? Here?"

"Yes."

"Well, it's a weak ticket, that one. I'll tell you honestly, I've already found a way around the Conclave's cowardly decision to limit that effort. Things are mostly on track."

"Mostly?"

"Mostly. That's why you and I are going to talk further, and if it doesn't offend the others"—he gestured to both Aileen and Sword—"I would like to have this conversation privately."

Almost on cue, Sword walked forward to Aileen's side. She offered her arm. "Shall we, sister?"

Sister? Was that an insult? Did it question her commitment? Or did she simply want another person she could connect to, another female Master? This could be as interesting as the negotiations themselves.

Aileen hooked her elbow in hers. They stood there, arm-in-arm, like they were preparing to dance. At its essence, they were. They walked from the chamber out the entrance, and into the sunlight.

24

DANGEROUS LANDS

Sleep kept Miller in its embrace until morning. He awoke to find Chamise tight behind him, yet again. She had stayed awake as long as she could, and then surrendered to fatigue. Miller lay there for a long moment, enjoying the feel against his back. Finally, he pulled back his blanket. Chamise continued to sleep as he fed small branches into the dwindling fire. She must have just gotten to sleep. He checked on the horses, and then began cooking.

She woke just as he finished making breakfast. She sat up, grabbed the hard bread and scooped fried eggs from his small iron pan. Their conversation that morning focused on the trail ahead, and the prospect of finding a traveler's inn a few days up the road.

"It will be four days until we reach the Shepherd Inn. It's the closest," she said.

Miller remembered an old stone inn nearby. "The Stone Inn is next. It's only two days."

"The Stone Inn burned down."

"When? How long has it been since you were there? Plus, it was made of stone." Miller had wanted to stay at the Stone Inn. It brought back memories of happier days traveling with Mistress Aileen and the rest of the old group.

"No idea. I heard it at the LaDeeDah. Some merchants were upset they had to sleep outside an extra night, so they spent a lot of time complaining. And the support beams were made of wood, fool."

Miller cracked a grin. He had been trying to bait her into a debate, it hadn't worked. "Life is hard all around, eh?"

They continued their playful banter as they saddled the horses and broke camp. The skies had darkened even more since yesterday. A low ceiling of dark clouds obscured the skies.

"Are you ready to talk yet?"

Miller looked over his shoulder. "Talk?"

"We've been riding for days, and you haven't said a word about what we will be dealing with once we arrive in Home's Hearth. Do you even know?"

"Sure. I've been there before. We'll go to the temple, then ask to see whatever sister is in charge now. Phyllicitus picks different sisters to act as her lieutenant. She can be lazy like that sometimes. The goddess probably won't bother with seeing us, but she might instruct her lieutenant to house us at the temple, so she can keep her eyes on us. After that, I expect to be given a space in the spirit hall. Then we go to work."

Chamise didn't look convinced. "You expect us to simply walk up to the front door, announce our presence, and they will walk us into their inner sanctum of magical studies? Why do I think it might be more difficult than that?"

"I told you. I've done this before. The priestesses who study magic can be talented, and some are quite advanced, but they don't share the same level of knowledge the White Hand possesses. I'm sure we will be given a few priestesses as helpers, and they will report our activities as needed. Last time I went to the temple, I stayed for three months. I made good friends with one of the priestesses who was assigned to help me. She wasn't very useful in the research, but she had a fine eye for symbology and that turned out to be handy for other tasks."

She rode on a little farther, struggling with how to phrase her next question. Miller began fidgeting with his saddle canteen, freeing it from its tie-downs. He uncorked the seal and began to drink the warm water. It tasted like leather and dirt.

"I can't think of a gentle way to ask this, so I'm just going to ask it. Is Phyllicitus in some kind of alliance with the White Hand?"

A mouthful of water erupted from Miller's face, coating his Mare's head with wet spittle. The mare was surprised and came to a stop, turning its head to discover what had just given it an early afternoon shower.

"What? An alliance? No. Are you insane?"

"Well, this sure looks like an alliance. Showing up out of nowhere, demanding internal resources, access to high-level priestesses. What else would you call this? It's pretty clear to me that the White Hand has their grubby little white hands into a deep pool of influence here."

He chuckled back at her remark. "The Order of the White Hand doesn't have much to do with this. Mistress Aileen set all this up. Remember, she used to be one of Phyllicitus' most trusted priestesses. That carries a lot of weight. Phyllicitus remembers Aileen from earlier days, and personally, I think she would like to recruit her back into the temple."

It was Chamise's turn to laugh. "Can that even be done? I don't know a lot about the White Hand, but I've never heard of one retiring, or leaving for that matter. Besides, isn't there some sort of cabal that Aileen belongs to? Wouldn't that get her murdered, then raised from the dead, then murdered again? I imagine penalties for violating the will of her cabal could be dire."

"No, not really. It doesn't work that way. Masters don't see much use in killing each other. They just come back from the dead by themselves anyway. They don't need any help from the other Masters to do that. If someone tried, they would just anger Aileen, then they would have a nasty inter-order fight on their hands for the next thousand years. No, Masters only kill each other when they're trying to make a point."

"So how does the cabal govern its members?"

Miller thought a moment before he answered. His words were chosen carefully as to not give secrets away. He wanted to avoid any chance that the White Hand would remove Chamise from this world to keep their secrets. Necromancers were serious about secrets.

"I think you have the wrong idea about what a cabal is. To start with, a cabal is just a group of masters who have made an alliance of common cause. The cabals come and go based on what is happening in the Conclaves, who is exerting control, or what emergencies they are reacting to. Some of them seem permanent, but that is just because the masters live so long."

"Aileen doesn't have a Master she obeys?"

"There is someone who gives her advice, but she rarely listens to it. There is a Master named Easter. He is the one who brought Aileen into the Order. She listens to him most often, but there are others. Darjeeling, December, and Gates probably have the most influence over her."

"December? I've heard that name. A real evil villain. He's the one that raised all the dead in Ingalls."

"Yes. That's him. Aileen has some sort of alliance with him. I gather he doesn't just terrify the gentle country folk. The other masters give him a wide berth. Master December has found a way to keep masters in check."

"In check? How does one do that? I'd like to know."

"It isn't a secret. Just murder all the apprentices of another Master. The apprentices aren't powerful by themselves, but they are critical to helping a Master get their own goals accomplished. Killing apprentices has an odd effect on a Master's ability to get things done. They don't like it. Also, even worse, an apprentice usually becomes an ally to the Master that trained them. Apprentices become Masters, after all. When the Conclave meets, it's always good to have allies. Killing an apprentice right now is like killing an allied Master in the future. It's evil, but effective."

"December is killing the apprentices of other Masters? They put up with that? I'm amazed there hasn't been a war."

Miller grimaced. "So am I. But that's what we have the Conclave for. Master December will be penalized severely if Aileen and Master Easter don't find a way to buy off some votes."

"Conclave? What is that? How would it penalize someone who can't die? Take away his apprentices?"

"The Conclave is a big council-of-councils that meets every so often. It makes decisions when cabals conflict with each other. I've never been allowed to attend. Mistress Aileen attends all she can. I guess she is involved with something across the cabals. I'm not sure what it is. Last I heard, they were trying to hang him outside of the wall for a few hundred years."

"There's a lot of new stuff here. What wall? Like outside a city?"

"No, not that kind of wall. We're talking about necromancers here. They believe there is a wall that separates all of this"—he motioned toward the trail, the forest, the sky—"from another place riddled with monsters. They believe the Takers come from there. It's supposed to be a pretty bad place. Most people simply go insane if they're left there more than a month. Some of the other cabals want to put him there for two centuries. There's a lot at stake for Master December. Oddly, he doesn't seem to care that much."

Chamise shook her head. "I'll never understand how your group of necromancers even functions."

"Good. If you understood, then you would be in the Order.

I'm an apprentice and I don't understand it all. The entire structure is based traditions that date back thousands of years. I guess, long ago, spell-crafters and tradesmen had a lot in common. When the Order started just before steel was discovered, it chose the crafting hall as a model of how they would organize. Back then, there were no big nations, or powerful kings, nor did the Order want any sort of oaths or formality. They just liked the freedom that craft-halls possessed, so they based their Order on it."

"They couldn't come up with something new? Besides, I thought necromancers just liked to become dark kings, and rule the lands of the dead."

Miller shook his head again. He wasn't liking where this was going.

"The land of the dead is filled with madness. Nobody rules there, and it's a good thing, too. It's bad enough Takers are seeping into our world? Can you imagine an army of the dead?"

Chamise shivered. "Thousands of walking corpses marching from graveyards into towns, devouring children, blighting crops, carrying disease and pestilence. That vision is much worse than a Taker infestation. And you wanted to join them? What kind of monster are you, then?"

"You don't find these things out before you join. They tell you after it's too late. These are necromancers, not morons."

"And you stayed after you found out?"

Miller looked down at his ring. Its silver, thumb-sized surface showed a skeletal hand. Etch-marks decorated the surrounding surface where he had applied his own enchantments. It offered a future where he was a Master, where he might never die. It was a future full of horror.

"Truthfully, if I could find a way to leave, I would. The Masters have a single-minded goal of sealing the wall that protects our world. They want to eliminate the demon threat forever. They just don't seem to mind crushing everyone around them to get it done. They don't care about their methods, only about their results. I've been trying to make myself feel that way, but it just doesn't work for me. There needs to be a reason to do this, someone to defend, to care about. The Masters don't seem to care about anything other than the fact that if the wall between worlds should fail, then their immortality would suddenly end."

"So why don't we just break that wall and let them feel the joy of mortality."

"It isn't like that. If the wall comes down everyone dies, everyone in the world."

"There wouldn't be anyone left to care. I see the dilemma. Be evil or be dead. It's kind of an easy decision."

"Not to me, it isn't. Like I said, there needs to be a reason why we are alive in the first place."

"I don't know what to say. It's just too much. Logically, I should support such a cause. The way the White Hand treats the world, though, it's just wrong. No matter how far I am from Home's Hearth, I am still a child of the Eisenvard. My father was an Eisenvard knight; he proved that by allowing my mother to be executed—but I am sure there must be more to this tale. It's just too horrible. And you're just an apprentice. How confident are you that you have the entire story?"

Miller nodded back. A snarky grin decorated his face. "Now you are getting the hand of this game. It isn't about what they tell you, it's about what they don't tell you. Either way, I'm just one little apprentice. What am I going to do?"

"You fight That's what you do. If needed, you die fighting. That's what the Eisenvard has done for centuries!"

She dug her heels into her horse's flank and sped ahead of him

Miller watched her go. She didn't understand how big the problem was, and how weak the Order was compared to it. The Masters talked about cracks forming through the entire world. It wasn't a local phenomenon that could be sealed or repaired. The entire wall was cracking. Chamise wanted to fight the noble fight. Who would he fight? The Takers? Fight the cracks? How did one even do that? With all the magic in the world, and all of the crafting art known to its practitioners, they had no idea how to fight this. Most outside of the Order didn't even believe it was happening. He hoped they were right, but knew they were wrong.

They moved on, using the same traveling process as before. Odd hours would find Miller leading the line, riding a minute ahead of Chamise. The even hours would be Chamise's turn to become the vanguard of their small caravan.

It began to rain as evening arrived. Small droplets fell, cooling their horses and leaving small puddles on their skin. The skies continued to darken.

Miller called to Chamise, "This will do. It's going to get muddy soon. Let's not risk the horses."

They set up camp. Miller dug through old leaves to find enough dry tinder to start a cooking fire. He hung his sentry bells in case they had any visitors. They dined on a soup of old vegetables, dried meat, and an odd spice he'd managed to purchase from the LaDeeDah. Chamise became very talkative, describing her studies among the Free Mages, and the level of talent she'd had to demonstrate to join them. The Free Mages had a test to join, then an initiation. The White Hand had none of that. They simply came to the parents and took the talented children, hopefully paying them for their trouble. The other option was far worse.

The evening passed to full night. Miller gazed up at the stars shining down from the early night's sky. Chamise had just finished a particularly engaging tale describing an initiation ritual that had resulted in her wandering through Ingalls muddy and naked, knocking on doors in an effort to find a Goddess Lamp that had never existed. Is that a test or an initiation? He would never understand Free Mages.

"You should get some rest. Your watch isn't going to get easier."

Chamise replied tartly, "There hasn't been a threat at all. I think you're overstating your danger, sir. Were you trying to get me out here, all alone?" She blinked her eyes coyly, while at the same time, lowering herself to enter the tent.

"Just be ready," Miller said with an amused tone.

Miller spread out his small tarp and sat awaiting the night's watch. The clouds began to break up soon afterward. Stars emerged from gaps within the clouds. By midnight, only half the sky was covered, and the rest was alight with stars.

Miller sat there, lost in his thoughts about Mistress Aileen back at the small house they dared call headquarters. She used to stop by his workhouse and spend hours with him while he crafted a new enchantment. They were inseparable for two years. Now he was without her, her wisdom, her guidance, and her laugh. He imagined rejoining that relationship, but part of him feared that would never happen. If Drane was right, and this was a journeyman's task, then his Master's trial would not be far in the future. It was a trial that not even Aileen would speak of. When he pressed her, she merely grasped at her Master's ring and whispered the same thing the other Masters did:

"You'll know when it's your time. The Masters will know when your time has come. If you haven't prepared enough by the time it comes, then you won't have to worry about any future problems."

A dark forecast. How does one prepare? They would not say.

Mistress Aileen insisted that her business with Master Easter was more important than this journey. Master Easter was dealing with December's defense at the next Conclave. If December didn't fare well, the most feared member of their cabal could be removed from the Order for some time. It could be a year, it could be a thousand.

Miller hoped for something closer to the thousand-year penalty.

He didn't pretend to understand the workings of the Conclave. He was, after all, merely an apprentice. Aileen had never fully described it, either. She did let slip small comments that allowed him to imagine what it could be. It seemed to be some sort of a week-long gathering where each of the Masters who attended could speak to the others, and perhaps vote on some sort of future course.

It didn't sound like much. Aileen seemed quite serious about it. She followed news of every Master who would either present business in front of the Conclave, or merely attend. The cabal would meet for hours to discuss strategies and counter-strategies that could defend against the political moves of other cabals, or to attack those same cabals.

Madness. None of the Masters seemed to grasp the simple fact that if they cooperated, there'd be no need for these strategies.

Aileen had merely laughed at him when he suggested it. "That's what I used to think," was her only reply. She was lovely that night. She had just acquired a new black dress, where different fabric types had been woven together into a grand design. But the seamstress had maintained the all-black color as Mistress Aileen had instructed. Her time serving in the temple had given her an appreciation for how clothing looked, and how a woman looked while wearing it.

Miller attempted to recall exactly how Mistress Aileen had looked that night. Her shoulder-length blonde hair hung onto the black silk and brocade, giving her an air of royalty. Her tight bodice had a slight split, buttoned near the neck but showing just a bit of her small chest. He remembered one of the flirtations she'd said, word for word. She was teasing him, but that one sentence had struck him in the heart. "When are you taking me to the ball?"

There would never be a ball. She played with his emotions sometimes, and it left him hurt, alone, and yearning desperately for more. Miller had hoped the journey would at least put some distance between his thoughts and her, but it hadn't. It merely added to them.

And now Chamise was here. Shoulder-length hair, so similar,

but strong, athletic, accessible.
 Then Miller heard the bell.

ALARM

A single chime split the quiet of the night. Miller slowly began to draw his sword. Another chime rang, then another, then another. Not good. He crawled into the tent and whispered to Chamise. She was already up, quietly buckling on her boiled-leather breastplate.

Miller stood up, and crept behind a tree, hoping the shadow would hide him from these invaders. The small fire continued to dance. Even more stars had emerged, showing the surrounding trees but hiding everyone who lurked beneath their canopy.

Miller tried to find the invaders. He channeled some of his spirit to hone the blade in his hand. It was small, crafting magic. Such spells came easily to him.

He didn't know where the strangers were, nor even if they were enemies. It was late, though, late enough that only enemies would have business with him. Chamise left the tent to release the horses, giving them a chance to escape. Good plan. He and Chamise could recover them later, if they lived.

Two shadows emerged from the woods. Each of them had longbows drawn and ready. They moved silently toward the camp, side by side; they had clearly done this before.

They emerged into the firelight with their drawn weapons and their black tabards catching reflections of the starlight. Before Miller could come up with a plan, Chamise stood up from behind a bush and let fly from her crossbow. The bolt sailed straight into one invader, burying itself in his chest. The bowman loosed his arrow at Chamise but it flew wide as he collapsed onto the ground.

The second man let his arrow fly and its aim was true. Miller was just coming out from behind the tree when he saw it launch, speeding its way toward Chamise. He rushed forward and thrust his blade deep into the attacker's abdomen. The spell-hardened edge slid through his leathers and into the man's intestines. Blood poured out of the wound, decorating both the victim and Miller with its hot, sticky substance. Miller spun to check on Chamise but could not find her, but there was noise from the ground near where she had stood. He pulled the blade from the bleeding man and ran to her.

"Chamise! Oh, Goddess! No!"

Chamise lay on the ground, kicking her feet and holding tight to the arrow that had penetrated her throat. Blood covered her hands and her chest as she kept pressure on the wound. Any loosing would mean a quick death.

"I'm here! I'm here! Don't let go, please don't let go," Miller said as he reached down to help her control the bleeding. Her eyes were alert. They wouldn't be for long; she'd be unconscious soon.

He reached beneath his cloak and pulled up his shirt, leaving it on while he used the ends to soak the blood in a frenzied attempt to save her life. Miller cursed himself. He should have been quicker. He should not have waited to be sure. Now he might have killed her.

"Don't worry, I've got you." He tried to sound confident, but he was terrified. He wasn't very good at lying.

She coughed blood in reply, spraying the sticky red fluid across his upper arm and shoulder. He could hear the buttons and laces rip from his shirt as he tried to get a better seal on the wound. There was nothing his magic could do; he simply didn't have the skill. If Mistress Aileen were here, she could save Chamise. Aileen's healing skills were amazing. If Miller hadn't been working on the forges instead of learning something useful, he might have learned those skills.

He looked at the tent where his pack lay. The last potion was packed snuggly in its contents. If he went to get it, she could bleed out in the few seconds he was gone. "Stay with me, Chamise, just a bit longer," he urged her, but had no idea how to fetch that vial.

More shadows emerged from the forest. Two bowmen stepped into the campfire light. They saw their prey, and the bodies of their fallen companions. These newer two killers were more cautious than their dying friends. They stood side-by-side, one with a notched bow and the other with a short, well-honed knife.

Miller knew he was about to die. If he ran, he might survive. Chamise would surely die. Miller could not will himself to run. He stared helplessly at the approaching raiders, holding onto Chemise's neck, trying to keep her life's blood from leaking onto the ground.

A third stranger came out of the woods. He wore a hooded black cloak that was difficult to see. Miller recognized it as a crafting at once. Such a cloak could completely hide you in this type of night. How long had that hidden one been following them?

This just got worse. He didn't think he needed to worry about the Master's test any longer.

The knife-wielding man began to approach, guarded by his bowman friend. Any move on Miller's part would simply cause him to get shot. The new arrival walked up behind the bowman as the knifeman said to the bowman, "You were right, they're alone. Go ahead and shoot."

The bowman adjusted his aim, pulled back a little farther on the string, then jerked. The arrow flew wide as he fell onto the ground. The third arrival pulled a long, thin, silvery knife from his back and continued his silent approach.

Knifeman called out, "You missed, idiot!" Turned, saw the reason and his approaching doom.

He charged toward the dark shadowy stranger with his blade outstretched but he only managed to get three steps before he came to a stop. Miller felt the energy of the spell as it came into being, holding Knifeman's attention immobile, enmeshed in a fascination that only he could see.

Miller recognized the signs and shivered.

The dark stranger walked up to the frozen raider and calmly slid his own thin, silvered blade between his ribs, holding the dying man gently as he slowly lay him on the ground.

He added another entry to his doom list: murder by sorcery, then knife.

There was no romantic dual or heroic fight. The newly arrived man simply distracted the knifeman with a spell, and then ended his life with a surgical stroke of his blade. Quick, clean, efficient.

Dangerous. This one was especially cold-hearted.

Miller began to shake with fear. He had no idea if the new arrival intended harm or not, and either way, he had only one choice: hold onto Chamise and try to keep her alive. As useless as he knew it was, Miller prayed to the goddess, begging her to save Chamise. He didn't even know how that could happen, but he was desperate. Gods never answered prayers.

The stranger knelt at the side of the dead man and spent several heartbeats whispering in his ear. When the dark stranger finished, he moved to the body of the bowman and did the same. The stranger then gently grasped the bowman by the shoulder and pulled him up. The bowman stood under his own power. He began to meander around the camp.

Miller wondered if he was drunk? How was he alive? That knife had gone directly into his lungs and probably his heart as well.

Miller kept his grip as Knifeman began to stand up. He, too, began to wander the camp, listless, moving with a dazed gait. Miller had seen the knife strike. He had seen the blood, and the murder weapon. There was no way to live through that. His mind sped through all the healing arts and magics he knew, but none of it would cure someone from such wounds so quickly. His analytical mind, trained by the White Hand, solved the puzzle within three seconds. First Principles showed an answer: Neither of these two bowmen still lived. They were in fact, quite dead. A spirit animated their corpses and now served the bidding of the dark stranger. Necromancy was controlling them.

Miller felt the terror beginning to grow inside his heart. He had seen necromancy in the Order, but never felt in danger from it. Those had been safe, well-controlled events where Mistress Aileen stood close by to ensure his safety. These rambling corpses entering the forest were a different matter. They would soon leave the range and control of their dark master and begin to do what their nature demanded: feast on the living.

He didn't know how to stop them. Strangers would be killed. Farms would be destroyed. His hands were covered in Chamise's blood as he cursed himself a fool. They were both doomed and all he could think about was rescuing others.

The dark stranger walked forward, pulling his hood back. He was tall and thin, with long black hair speckled with gray. A short, pointy beard grew only on his chin, partially covering the cruel smirk on the mouth above it. Miller's heart fell as the stranger emerged into the firelight. This might be a rescue, but it might also be worse than simply dying.

Master December stared back at Miller, his cold gaze taking in the camp, the tents, and Chamise's struggling form.

"Are you going to lie there all night? Just let the poor girl die already so we can get out of here."

26

TO SAVE A LIFE

Miller was momentarily stunned, then he regrouped, trying to get some form of help out of that cruel man. "Come on! Help out, curse it all!"

December walked forward, shaking his head and looking sadly down on the pair. Miller sprawled on top of Chamise, desperately trying to hold in her life's blood. Miller thought he heard a soft whisper. "It's a tragedy really. She was so young."

Then December pulled up his gaze to rest squarely on Miller's face. "I assume from the level of blood that your Mistress," he said, pronouncing Mistress with unfiltered disdain, "has yet to instruct you in the arts of the body."

Who had time? There was so much to do, so much to craft, so much to investigate. "Assume that my training had not reached that point yet. How about a little help?"

"It looks like you have things well in hand. Time has a way of solving this sort of dilemma."

Miller's hands were coated in blood. Chamise struggled to breathe as he held to her on with all his strength. He didn't know how long he could hold, how long he could he keep her alive. "Please just fetch a small parcel for me from my pack." Miller shrugged toward the tent. "It is small, wrapped in red leather. It has a goddess symbol branded into it."

"A goddess symbol, eh?" December sneered as he went to the tent. He reached in and pulled out the satchel bag, opened it, rummaged through Miller's clothing, crafting tools, and travel gear until he retrieved the packet. He stood there, staring at the packet until he reached some sort of decision, then he opened it. The two empty vials were fastened next to the last full one. December stared at them a moment then withdrew the last vial, whistling in appreciation.

"What a treasure you have, little apprentice. Mistress Aileen seems to have expected trouble. I suspect that her confidence might be less than you expected."

A pinprick of anger grew in Miller's heart. December could be such an ass, even when it was unwarranted, especially when it was unwarranted.

"Please, Master December. That vial can solve this and see us back on the trail quickly. Please." He urged December forward, toward Chamise's gasping body. December took a step toward him, then another, and then stopped. He glanced again at the vial, its goddess seal glinting in the firelight.

"This is a king's ransom. It heals almost everything." He shook his head slowly and placed the vial beneath his own cloak. "This woman isn't worthy of it. Let the poor thing pass on, and let's get out of here."

Miller was struck with disbelief, and then anger flared. "Give me that vial, you bastard!"

December stood unmoved, a slight grin starting on his face.

Miller struggled to keep Chamise alive in his grasp. Her eyes were wide and panicked. Chamise was going to die tonight. The only question was how he was going to die, fighting or begging.

Not begging.

Miller's voice grew cold and calm as he accepted an imminent demise. December was powerful, and challenge would be useless. Miller resolved not to give into him without a fight. "I swear on the five channels, Master December," he swore, "I will carry revenge in my heart for eternity."

December paused. He no longer looked so smug. "Be careful of oaths like that, boy. We live a very long time. They have a way of striking back at you."

"Be careful with that vial, then. Both our fates might rely on it."

Chamise began to tighten her hands on his wrist. She was terrified. She knew that she was less than a pawn in this game, and her life depended on its outcome.

"So be it, then." December announced, throwing up his hands in mock surrender. "I won't sacrifice the vial. Aileen gave it to you, not to this girl. She meant it to save your life, not hers. I can't imagine the bargain she made to get this, but I promise you that it was far more expensive to her than the life of this lovely young lady.

"So here is a new bargain that I will make with you, Apprentice: You will stop crying about this vial, and I will teach you some quick lessons of the body. That way we get to keep Mistress Aileen's investment, and I get to train her wayward, lazy, uneducated, apprentice. You get to save this girl."

"What? I don't know much of body magic, at all. I can't do that. Surely you have the skill, can't you just heal her yourself?"

"I surely could, if I wasn't distracted with our new roving patrol." December gestured toward the walking corpses. "I prefer that our time here be uninterrupted. So I am going to keep our new minions from doing their job. I suggest you perform your own. Might I remind you that I don't care whether this girl lives or dies? I care only for the good opinion of Mistress Aileen."

"But—!"

"No buts. It is your only option, take it or let her die. I tire of our game," December replied crisply, anger beginning to emerge.

Miller looked down at Chamise. She was close to losing consciousness. Her eyes pleaded with Miller to take any path to save her, any path.

"I am going to regret this."

"We both will. Either way, life is simply full of regrets. Best to get over it now and lend our attention to the task at hand."

Miller nodded in defeat.

December walked closer to Miller and Chamise, uncomfortably close. He leaned in to inspect the wound, touching where the arrow impaled her neck. Chamise winced in pain. December gave her no relief as his exploration continued.

"Careful! The arrow! Don't kill her," Miller gasped.

December pulled his hands away from the wound and examined his bloody hands. "That is what I was checking for. It would have been so much easier if she had simply expired. But no, the apprentice might have called it right. Her main blood flow is uninterrupted, so she has a good chance. So here is the first lesson in the body: Don't waste your energy healing the near dead. You won't save them in any case, but you will tire yourself in the process."

"Tired? Are you mad? I think I can put up with a little 'tired' for any chance of saving a life."

December moved behind Miller now, leaning down to whisper. "There is never only one life at stake. Always plan on more, no matter what your condition is. Just hope that one of them isn't yours. Now stop talking and start listening."

Miller resumed his focus on the wound, keeping his bloody hands tight against the arrow. "Now comes the art. Remember the five channels. The elements, the binding, the harmonics, the fates, and the essence. You know how to channel binding, elements, and harmonics. Right now, we are going to channel essence."

"I don't know how."

"You don't get to pick. You want the deal or not? You have

at least studied essence? Most regard it as one of the basic lessons."

"Yes, I have read of it, but not practiced it." Essence, the grounding of necromancy, was not his favorite area of study.

"Look around, this isn't practice." December mixed a small amount of anger into his whisper. "You need to concentrate on her. Feel her resonance. Listen for her harmonies. Use your mage's eye to see it. Use your heart to feel it."

December waited for a score of heartbeats until he continued, transforming his bitter reproach into a softer-edged lecture. "The body has few core fates, but the primary one is to become whole. It will always try to heal, given enough time. This woman does not seem to have enough time, so we need to encourage the body to work faster.

"The first part of the task is to find the wound and understand it. The body has limited resources to heal, so we will need to give it what it needs to grow new tissue and sew the wound together. You will use element channels to create blood and flesh, then use fate channeling to move it toward where healing is needed."

The secret seemed easy enough in theory. There was going to be something else, some form of trick, when it came time to put it into practice. There always was.

"It will get difficult after that. The body's second fate is to resist invasion. That means you. You are invading her body with your powers and your elements. The body will fight you. It will reject the healing as an attack. Your job is to convince the body that these new things are not dangerous."

"How do I do that?"

"Same as every other conversation, lie to it."

"What?" Miller had begun whispering at the same low volume that December used.

"It's quite simple, really. Open your channels slowly. Allow some of your essence to mix with hers. You need to feel her harmonics and adapt yours to hers. Your harmonics should be supportive. You need to make her feel safe and loved. Once she trusts you, the healing will progress. Slowly is the key, no rushing. Once the healing begins, guide the essence to the right place and allow her body to determine how to do the healing. Keep her calm, and that's it."

"Sounds fairly straightforward. I thought it would be harder."

"You've never seduced anyone, have you? I'll just let you learn that one on your own."

"Seduced?"

"Yes, you've heard of the concept, haven't you?"

Miller struggled with the idea of it. His hands were covered in her blood. Now December wanted him to romance her? "I don't think that's going to work."

"Then she's going to die."

A PURPOSE FOR LIES

"That would make this entire affair easier, unless of course you would like to quiet your mouth and listen. Your other option is to tell a little fib, and to feel it. Send the emotions through your channels, toward her harmonics, her fate, and her essence. Let her know that you are here for her. Don't use words, just send the feelings. Use the harmonics as your guide. You will know when she is ready to receive some spirit energy."

Miller calmed his angry mind with yet more mental exercises. After a few short heart beats, he was ready. He tried to remember their close encounter on his last visit. He felt overpowered, out of breath, and panicked. He had been unsure and continued to be. He tried to pass some of the spirit to her, but the body did not willingly accept it.

"Remember," December interrupted to provide what some might call encouragement, "you don't have to tell the truth, you can lie a little."

"I can't."

"Try."

Miller began searching for some sort of emotion that he could share. He remembered his family, his parents, and his brothers. He had been apprenticed since the age of twelve. The memories were faded and did not strike the emotional harmonics that he needed. He thought about Mistress Sword, and her strange sadistic ways. The only emotion he could find was fear, and a little bit of loathing, and sadness. Sword had never cared about anyone, especially her apprentices. His thoughts finally found memories of Mistress Aileen. He remembered when Aileen had crafted the bargain to bring him into her service. He remembered the long evenings they had spent at the forges, building blades and experimenting with cures of the blood curse. He remembered her laugh, her wit, her gentle guidance. Those were the feelings he had been searching for.

Miller slowly opened the three channels, and let his emotions fill them. Chamise smiled upward at him as she held onto his hand, to the blood-filled rag, and to the arrow jutting from her neck. December leaned down, reaching into his sleeve to extract the long silver knife. It was close. Miller could see small runes etched along its length, and a spirit crystal set into its hilt, still filled with mystic energy. He didn't know what game December was playing at, but he possessed reserve magical powers, and he wasn't using them.

December's whisper caught his attention. "That's right, you are doing well. Now slowly allow her body to access spirit energy. Let her drink from it. The body should do its own healing. Feed the spirit to her slowly."

"What are you doing with that knife?"

"Watch and learn."

December slowly and gently reached under Chamise's head, cradled it in his left hand, and then raised it up by the length of a finger. Chamise jerked as he slid the knife beneath her neck.

Miller channeled more feelings, more memories. Aileen had awoken early to feed the fire. Aileen had called him aside to instruct him on dealing with Northerners. She had touched his hands, oh so gently, showing him spells to guard his thoughts. "Stay calm, Chamise, stay calm. I've got you."

December finished his task and retrieved his knife along with a newly cut arrow shaft. Dirt coated the tip of the bloody shaft from where Chamise had fallen onto the ground. "You are doing well enough, Apprentice. Don't change your pace now."

The bleeding had slowed to a more controlled pace. He watched as December fetched a new cloth and wiped the tops of his hands off. Then he cleaned off the arrow shaft that still impaled Chamise's neck.

"This is where the tricky part occurs."

Tricky part? What part of this isn't tricky? He was holding her life in his hands, and December just called this TRICKY? Miller nodded, not wanting to show his aggravation.

"First, you need to relax your hands just a little bit. Shortly, I am going to say the word 'now,' and then I am going to pull the arrow from her neck. You will surge spirit energy to her then, but not before. If you are too early, the flesh will close up around the arrow, and probably grow into it a bit. It would a mess, and ruin all of our excellent work this evening. Nod again if you understand."

Miller nodded.

"I am going to say 'now.' I am going to remove the arrow. You are then going to provide spirit into all five channels. You are not going to worry about any final bleeding that will occur. You are not going to panic. You are not going to try to do anything that her body does not guide you to. You are definitely not going to try to be efficient or crafty. Don't be a show off. Just send spirit, don't try to guide anything. Don't try to engineer anything. Nod if you understand."

Miller nodded again.

"All right, keep your head. Remember, the most important part is that the arrow comes out first."

December replaced his dagger within his black sleeve and grasped the arrow shaft with both hands. He began taking calm, thoughtful breaths. Miller began repeating the process in his head. Listen for the signal, make sure the arrow is clear, channel spirit, don't get crafty. Listen for the signal, make sure—

December snatched the arrow shaft from her neck.

Chamise jerked up, grabbing for the wound as blood sprayed across Miller's arms, chest, and began leaking onto the ground.

He went early. This wasn't how it was supposed to happen.

December watched Miller struggle to hold in the leaking blood. Once Miller's newly cleaned hands were coated in hot red blood, December calmly spoke the word. "Now."

Miller began to panic. Events were not occurring as predicted. Chamise began to kick and buck on the ground. Were these death throws? Games! The Masters are always playing games!

Miller could not think what to do. He channeled spirit, more and more spirit. He brought in every good emotion that he had inventoried just a moment ago, and tapped his spirit until it was depleted. He reached into his own elemental channel, converting his body energy to give Chamise more. It hurt. It felt like hard frostbite mixed with a heart attack.

Miller's head had begun to spin when December reached down and took his hands from Chamise's throat.

"What are you doing?" Miller shouted at December.

Chamise coughed deeply and sat up. She quickly turned to vomit.

"Trying to stop you from choking her to death. Fool."

"You pulled the arrow early!"

"You looked like you were going to panic and go early, so I went first. The arrow had to come out before the channeling, no matter what."

"She could have died!"

"We are all going to die. It's best to get used to that idea in this guild. She isn't that special. She gets to die, too. We were merely trying to postpone it."

Miller's hands trembled. "You are insane."

December's reply was not what Miller had expected. December's voice became thoughtful. "Sooner or later, we all are. That is the price of long life. It is the price demanded of us. The world is cracked."

Miller didn't know how to respond. Instead, he focused on Chamise. "Is she going to be all right?"

December went to Chamise, and gently moved her head, exposing her face and throat. Her throat was red where the wound had been, but it was sealed over with fresh skin. A small spider web of dark black veins had formed on her neck, reaching its tendrils up onto her jaw line. "I think she needs a little more mending." December chuckled before continuing. "She needs healing to recover from your healing. Your first body mending did work, but you did a butcher's job of it."

He was smirking! Why did December think this was funny?

"I can't do it. I have nothing left. Use your spirit crystal."

"You saw that, eh? Well, that's in reserve. Right now we are vulnerable to any enemy who might find us. I'm keeping that for later. No, I'm afraid you have a few more lessons to go."

"I'm empty."

"I know. I also know who your Master is, and I know she gave you all the right tools. You can recover enough to do this. Use your disciplines to make yourself ready. After that, I will guide you through some small mending crafts that will require a much steadier and more accurate casting, but much less spirit."

There was no use arguing. December was going to do this his way, damn the consequences. "All right, I'll try."

"You will do more than try; you are going to do it. You just brought her back from near the edge, but you left her with broken blood vessels that have scabbed up. Those scabs are inside her body. That means that as she moves around, those small scabs will break loose. The bloodstreams will take them into places that cannot tolerate them. Within a few days, she will lose the use of a couple of her limbs, and then she might go to sleep and never awaken. No, you need to clean this mess up now, while it's still fresh."

December sat next to Chamise over the next hour. Miller performed the meditations he'd learned from his newest master. Mistress Aileen had always insisted that the most important spell was simply to be ready for whatever insanity would occur next. He was starting to think Aileen might not have been as paranoid as he had initially thought.

December began his discussions on how small wounds are healed, and how to use the elements to trigger healing in localized areas. He told Miller how to identify locations that need crafting, and how to do it in a way that did not jeopardize the rest of the body. December was a skilled teacher, even if short-tempered and impatient. Removing the danger from Chamise's blood required six more hours and three more meditations.

Noon had arrived before December pronounced her well enough not to die on the first day of travel. "Rest for two hours. Then we leave."

"Can we rest longer? She still doesn't look recovered."

They had spent the entire day trying to save her life. The thought of roving dead, meandering around the countryside, somehow failed to stir him. It was too much. Even with December here, he just couldn't handle everything by himself. Hunting down the next risen dead would likely get them both killed.

It was bad enough he had to deal with the Takers and their taken victims. Hunting down December's risen dead was just too much. Now Chamise was wounded. Would it ever end?

The black spider webs within Chamise's neck had faded to a soft pink. The pink color stood out against her paper-white skin. She didn't look like she had the energy to get on a horse, let alone travel all day.

The stain of death was on her.

"I can't stay longer," December stated. "We have company out in the woods. My scouts have stumbled across some trouble. I don't know what kind, but I'm willing to bet it's the kind of trouble that carries swords and other pointy things. We need to move on."

"We need to go back to Ingalls. These woods are too dangerous."

"I doubt we have that luxury. I don't know how you stirred up this bee's nest, but there are a lot of raiders out there, and they all seem to want to sting you."

They left camp two hours later. Chamise rode atop the mare. Miller tried to keep control of the black war horse. December urged them to make quick progress as he went back for his own horse. "I will catch up today, tonight, or tomorrow at the latest. You won't travel fast enough to outpace me. Just concentrate on keeping in front of the raiders."

28

BLOOD ENEMY

The weather had stayed clear, but clouds began to dot the sky. Rain showers far to the west threatened to delay their journey. By unspoken agreement, they decided to continue, hoping to avoid detection beneath the dimming skies.

They stopped for a rest after mid-day. Miller cooked a meal while Chamise used her knife to clean out the horseshoes. She had not left his side since they'd broken camp in the morning. They'd done no scouting, nor any heavy riding. Their words were rare, but it seemed like each one now carried a larger meaning.

"Are you ready to ride more this afternoon?"

She looked up from the hoof, smiling. "Sure." Her stare lingered on him for a few moments before returning to its previous task.

"You're being quiet today," Miller said, concern in his voice.

"I can't help it. Sorry. That was a close call last night. Now I can't stop thinking about the most trivial things. It's all small, but much more important to me, right now."

Miller nodded, giving way to the silence. He dumped the beans and carrots into his iron pan, then added two small slices of meat. The smell filled his senses as he relaxed. He thought about Drane, and his philosophy of life. He was living in the moment. Drane would be so proud.

"What are you going to do when you get to Home's Hearth? Do you have a place to stay?" Her words came as a surprise. "I mean, well, I mean, do we have a place to study?"

"Study? That is what you are worried about? After last night, I mean."

"You owe me. You are not going to back out." An anger had crept into her voice he did not recognize. Aileen's words came back to him: Chamise was an Eisensvard witch; he should be careful. But still, he could not imagine her turning on him.

"No, I'm standing by my word. You will have a month of my time, but we need to get to Home's Hearth first."

"I'm going to hold you to every minute of that promise."

Miller served the stew into two metal bowls, serving Chamise, then sitting at the fire with his own. She slid across the ground until she was within an arm's reach. She didn't want to be alone, not even for a moment. Miller couldn't blame her.

They ate together, staring at the campfire smoke, yet giving it no mind. The smoke drifted up toward the green canopy until it was captured by the wind and taken away.

The silence was starting to become uncomfortable.

Miller broke it first. "What do you want me to teach you now?"

"I don't know."

"All right, what projects are you working on now?"

"Nothing, really." Her reply seemed vague, and unfocused.

"So tell me you have a reason to be out here." He showed her a smile that was one part laughter, and another part feigned concern.

Chamise balled up her fist and punched him in the arm. "Ouch!"

"I had a plan. It's just that, well, I think my plans changed last night. I just don't know what the new ones are yet."

"We have two weeks until we arrive, so there is plenty of time."

The meal continued, silence becoming the third participant at the fire.

"Guard tonight?" Miller proposed.

"I'm shot. I won't be of any use tonight. I think we should just trust the bells." After a few moments, she gestured to her neck. "My throat hurts more than it should, I think. It hurts when I breathe. Just eating this stew is difficult."

A little sadness crept into Miller's voice. He had bungled that, too, hadn't he? He spent a little time in silence, hoping that he hadn't permanently damaged her with his poor spell-crafting. "Sorry."

She reached out to grasp his leg and stared directly into his eyes. "Don't be. I'm thankful just to be alive. I was so close. I mean. It was. You were. There for me."

Miller wished a master healer had been there. Then it dawned on him, a master healer had been there. December was just too much of an ass to help. "It was lucky Master December wandered by."

"Luck? Oh, I doubt that."

She was paying attention. Good.

"He had a word with me when you were in the woods taking care of things." She struggled with the wording. Miller had gone into the forest to relieve himself. He was gone ten minutes.

She began to wrap strands of hair about her long, thin finger. "It was strange."

Miller instantly felt the cold spike along his spine. "What did he want?"

"Just to give me some advice. He is oddly protective for, well, who he is."

"You need to be careful of him. I mean it."

"I am fully aware of who I am dealing with. That was Master December, one of the leaders of the White Hand. A right bastard if there ever was one. I lived in Ingalls when he came before; that town will never be the same." She paused to remember what had happened before, the dead, the carnage. "If Ingalls had to choose between joining with the North and worshiping their elder Stag God, or align with December, well, we would all be speaking Northerner right now. I would be first in line."

"So, what did he say to you?"

"He told me you'd ask what he said, and I should think very carefully before telling you."

Not good. Miller let the silence stretch out a few more moments before Chamise exhaled a long breath.

"He told me you were only drawn to me because I remind you of Mistress Aileen. He said you had deep feelings for her, and that you were doomed to never leave the White Hand. He said you would die there, and that you had no time for happiness."

"December is a lying bastard. Never believe a thing he says. Plus, you don't even look like her."

"You have a weakness for strong women."

"I know." Miller didn't know what to say.

Chamise continued. "He could have healed me last night, but he lied to you and forced you to do it. But I'm actually grateful for that. If December had healed me, then I'd owe him. I don't think I'd be happy with a debt like that. I think at heart he's a bit of a monster."

"I think it's more than a bit. He did know his body-crafting, though."

Silence stretched out for a long uncomfortable moment. "Miller, I've been hurt before. I've been healed before. It didn't feel the same. This time, when you did it, it wasn't like the body art I had seen before. It was different. It didn't feel very good."

Miller quickly arrived at the unwelcome conclusion. Damn. It dawned on him that he had just had his first December necromancy lesson. A skill he had purposefully avoided. Damn! Damn! Damn! The Order kept pulling him in deeper and deeper.

"I don't know what that was. I was just trying to keep you alive."

She smiled broadly, her eyes alight with unfeigned joy. She moved closer and took his arm in her hands, hugging it tightly. Her soft voice cut through the night. "I heard things from the other side. I heard them. I smelled them. Thank you for not letting me go. Never there, never."

Her tears began there, at that moment. She tightened her grip and pulled her face toward Miller's arms. She cried, cried again, then cried more. Miller sat there holding her for a long time, waiting in silence as the clouds passed overhead. They grew darker as time stretched on.

"Chamise, I hate to say this, but we need to keep moving. Are you ready to travel or should we find a place to hide tonight?"

She sniffled, pulling herself out of his arms. "I'm sorry, I'm so sorry. Yes, give me a moment and I'll be ready to ride. I'm sorry."

She should not be sorry. He felt guilty for failing her. He'd known he wasn't ready, and he had tried anyway. He was failing everything. He had failed Chamise. Now he saw that he was going to fail Aileen.

Miller spent a few moments thinking about December's words. Chamise did share some features in common with Aileen. Her build was athletic like Aileen's, and she had an impressive intellect, much like Aileen. Chamise was a force of nature, strong, wild in its course.

But Aileen was more, so much more. She seemed to command the place in the world she occupied, simply by being there. Miller had always been drawn to that. She made him feel a sense that someone out there knew exactly what was happening and how to deal with it. It gave him a feeling of safety he hadn't had in years. Maybe it was her priestess training? Maybe it was simply the reason that Master Easter had spent those years enticing her to join his cabal and leave the temple.

They resumed their journey at a quicker pace, trying to make up for their break. They rode at a brisk pace as the gray clouds continued to grow until they covered the entire sky. Miller had begun to think he was lost until he finally spied the Stone Inn.

The Stone Inn had indeed been burned. The walls continued to stand, though. Their masterfully crafted block-and-mortar construction had weathered the fire. The roof and interior had been gutted through the entire structure. Weeds grew between charred timbers and ash. Miller remembered the grand fireplace fondly. The innkeeper had made a good meal for him on many occasions. He remembered being new in Aileen's service, and listening to the excited chatter from other members of their small company. He remembered Faust with his dour voice, warning caution over all else. He remembered Hugo returning various comical curses on the idea. Hugo lived in Home's Hearth now. Faust didn't really live anymore.

"I see a body," Chamise announced to Miller while pointing just to the left of the grand fireplace. Miller scanned the area carefully until he saw it. It wasn't burned. The failing light made the body difficult to recognize until he walked up to it, leaving footprints across the ash floor. It was a man wearing local peasant garb, but he had a leather archer's brace on his left arm. His cloth shirt had been ripped in three places, leaving his torn skin exposed. His throat had been crushed. It must have taken ages to die. His traveling gear lay sprawled about his body. A thick canvas bag spilled out its contents on to the floor. A hunting bow lay discarded nearby, along with its arrows.

"I don't think we should stay here. I don't like this." Chamise's quavering voice almost begged to leave.

"There is no way we're staying here tonight, but I need to do something before we go." Miller glanced around the floor and rummaged within the ruins. He recovered a cup, its clay cracked top to bottom. "I am going to need some light. Can you help?"

"Sure. I've got it." Chamise began chanting in the Free Mage way, calling on the channels to redirect and implement her will. A small light sprang into being, a point of light that floated just above head level, just above the corpse.

"This body is fresh. It hasn't been here more than a day."

"Is the killer still here?" Chamise redirected her stare outward, toward the dimly lit clearing that surrounded the Stone Inn.

"Oh, the killer is still here. I think we can count on it." Miller walked across the floor again, pausing when he felt the supports shift. Then he changed direction and walked back to his pack, keeping close to the outer wall the entire time. "We need to find whoever choked the life out of him, but I've got something to do first."

"Do? What is there to do? Let's get out of here."

Miller went to the mare, patted her head. "Stay alert, things just got worse," he said to both Chamise and the mare. He opened his travel bag and pulled out his artificing roll. He laid it on the clean grass and unrolled it, removing a shining white cloth, a glass lens, and a small journal. He returned to the body.

"Can I get more light?"

"Won't that give away that someone is here? Shouldn't we be hiding?"

"We don't need to hide. We've already been seen. Just give me some more light, please, and then stay alert. This is going to get frightening. Prepare for it."

Chamise uttered more words, strings of words that moved her channeled energy. Each syllable layered power atop the other. The words moved the channels, and the channels moved power. The light doubled in intensity before she stopped growing it. "How is that? Can I stop? I don't feel very good."

Miller reflected on what he was seeing. That was a lot of work, and a lot of words, to do such a simple thing. How far behind were the Free Mages?

"It will do fine." He started planning the lessons he'd teach her. Her first would be the recovery discipline. These Free

Mages just didn't have the supporting practices. They had the spells, but no understanding of them. He could use another White Hand right now.

Miller thought of Master December for a moment.

Well, maybe not.

DARK WORK

Miller spread out the smooth cloth. Its white surface reflected the light and began to gather it in. The light shone from the cloth, softer, much like a cloudy mirror.

Miller took out the journal, turned the pages until he found a set of small drawings depicting insect-like things, each with six legs, and a curved spiked tail. He put on thin, finely crafted gloves. Small runes stood out, branded into the fine leather. Spells had been sewn in, using crafted thread. The gloves were nearly elbow-length. The fit was exact. Miller had made them himself.

Drawing his knife, He looked down at the wrecked body. "You might want to start a small fire. We are going to need it."

"I don't want to go out there to get wood."

"I have oil in my bag. Use one of these charred beams. Knock the ash off, then pour the oil onto it. Wait for the count of twenty, and then light it. It should be enough for what we need."

Chamise began her task as Miller returned his attention to the body. He retrieved his long belt knife. It was an excellent blade for everyday use, but now he wished for a longer, thinner blade. He needed a knife that could keep him just a little safer, just a little farther away.

He thought of December's knife, and shivered.

"Do you think the guy was a raider?" He resumed the conversation as he turned the head to the correct angle. He was careful to avoid touching the blood. He needed to keep it off his gear, or they would end up cleaning all night.

"He doesn't have the tabard. He's got a bow, though, and a long knife. Could be, but I'm not sure." The raiders had kept whatever uniforms they'd worn in the early days before they had been taken. He was grateful, as it made them easier to identify.

Miller set the cup near the base of the man's throat. Then he pulled his knife and set it against his neck, just above the cup.

"How is the fire coming?"

More light leaped up from the clearing. As the fire started, Miller stabbed the blade into the neck, then pulled it out quickly. He set it on the white cloth, staining it. He picked up the cup and attempted to scoop the blood. It oozed out of the wound in thick globs, collecting in the cup. He continued until it had just covered the bottom of the cup. Setting the cup on the cloth, he pulled the cloth from the body.

He picked up the lens and began to look through it, to the blood in the cup, on the knife. "Can I get more light? I can't see."

"I think I'm going to vomit."

"I know, but this is really important."

"It better be." Chamise began her chanting. Crafting the spell took longer this time and used a more complex structure, but the floating point of light began to shine like a beacon. The entire area lit up with an intensity brighter than daylight. Every charred plank, destroyed table, and collapsed beam stood out in stark relief. Shadows jutted outward like spokes, splaying across the outer clearing and the tree line.

She could have just put more wood on the fire. Was she trying to show off?

Miller pulled up the lens again and knelt over the pool of blood. He saw nothing unusual. There must be something. Or did December's scouts simply kill the first hunter they encountered?

Miller snatched up the knife again, being careful not to splash the thick blood. He began carving power symbols into the bloody pool at the bottom of the cup. He tied each one to a channel, then back to his personal spirit.

"Do you see what I'm doing?"

Chamise leaned in to view his crafting. The glyphs showed how channel aspects tied together. "Heat and spirit purity?"

"The Takers have a spirit that is out of harmony. The crafting will generate heat when faced with disharmony. That way we can spot them. They have grown harder to detect."

"Simple, but smart. I'd call that elegant."

As the last arcs of the glyphs were finished, the blood began to bubble in three locations. Moments later the number of bubbles had grown to nine locations, and soon the entire pool had reached an angry boil.

"Found them. The new Takers are smaller. It helps them hide. But they are not impervious to magic."

The liquid blood became a thick brown paste, then a solid stain on the white cloth. "Sometimes it's easier to use indirect methods. Channeling won't detect the Takers, but that doesn't mean they aren't there. The key is to use their environment. The blood doesn't recognize them, so let the blood guide you."

"Blood?" Her face showed how the idea sickened her.

"Blood. That is the environment the Takers have invaded. That is how we find them. Blood holds secrets. All we need to do is encourage it to tell us a few."

"You've been in this Order too long. You are starting to sound like December. So if you know blood, why is healing so different?"

"It is, believe me. Less talking, more light."

He stooped down and pulled the corners of his white cloth together, trapping the bloody contents within. The packet came together in an envelope of white cloth. Miller walked to the fire and laid the cloth packet within it. He motioned to Chamise to stand back, and then he took three steps backward as he connected the elemental channel to the fire. A column of flame poured up, overcoming the nearby inn walls in its height.

"I think the men from that last village had been taken. That explains their odd behaviors. You can't see the Takers, and our defensive spells don't work very well against them, either. The Takers have changed enough to avoid the defense we came up with a few years ago. I've been testing infected blood whenever we could find some, I know."

"By defenses, do you mean the potions that could protect us? I remember being desperate to get my hands on them."

"That, and some specialized channeling to detect the Taken. It was mostly nature magic that focused on insects."

"Insects?"

"Yes. I discovered it by accident. I was trying to clean out some cockroaches while one of the prisoners was in the room. One vermin-killing spell interfered with that prisoner's ability to speak. It was odd, but it worked. None of it works anymore."

"Sweet goddess. We all thought they were gone. You're saying that the Takers have come back?"

"That's why we are going to Home's Hearth. I need to talk to the priestesses, especially those with a talent for channeling. We need to act early, or we will face that chaos all over again."

The fire tower sputtered and extinguished itself, leaving a perfect, clean white cloth that contained a glass lens and a dagger in its folds. He stooped to collect his tools and repack them. Chamise brought the light back to its original dim illumination. She didn't look well.

The skies had closed overhead, blocking the stars. Miller knew he needed to find a new campsite, sooner rather than later. She wasn't going to hold up much longer.

"Come on. I don't want to be here." He picked up the oil then dripped it across the corpse. Then he lit it on fire, as well. The flame quickly spread across it.

Chamise nodded and took the mare's reins, walking clumsily forward. "Miller, if the Takers have returned, doesn't that mean they will begin to spread again?"

"Yes. These new ones seem to spread more slowly than the old ones, but they are harder to detect. Don't worry, the temple will find a way to beat them." Hopefully.

"What? Me worry? Why would I worry? December just animated two dead men and sent them shambling around the forest looking for random people to either eat, or pass their newly improved curse to. What could ever harm me?"

He realized she was right, those men had been taken. They didn't act mindless; they still had their own identities. Somehow the Takers had them under their power. This was the new world, the new Takers. All the rules had changed. Now Miller just needed to figure out what the new rules were. They had to find the duo to stop them. They needed to get back to December and let him know about these taken. If the new strategy was to subvert the Taken instead of completely subsuming them, he had some insight into that kind of thing.

"And what about the zombies? December left a real mess with those things."

"Yes. We need to discuss that issue, as well."

Miller was lost in thought. What had that maniac done? Or, more likely, December had intentionally set these things loose on the local populace.

"What about him?" Chamise asked, pointing at the corpse.

Miller wished he knew what had happened to the dead man, but he wasn't ready to try necromancy just to satisfy his curiosity. "Let's at least bury him to keep the body safely away from wandering necromancers."

They toiled for an hour digging a grave for the stranger. It was a shallow hole in the ground, unmarked except for the fresh dirt.

"We need another camp. I say we move away from here, then stand guard tonight. We'll switch off at midnight. The bells are lovely, but they might not be quick enough."

"That sounds good to me," Miller replied.

Despite her wounds, Chamise stood the entire evening watch, staying awake until midnight. She woke Miller as the moon was fully overhead, then curled into her blankets.

He spent a moment to gaze at her thoughtfully. Only a short while ago she had been shot in the neck, nearly passing through the final black door. Now she was alive, energetic, and seemingly untiring. Her healing came from December's strange art of necromancy, not from a priestess. The nature of it seemed different. It wasn't twisted, nor evil, only different.

Miller stood guard the rest of the night. He stared at the forest, at the trails, and at Chamise's sleeping until the sun began to rise.

She looked tired in the morning but could at least walk in a straight line without much effort. Miller gazed at her determined face. She looked like she was ready for war.

Miller had seen a similar look before. Mistress Aileen had such a look after her all-to-frequent nightmares. She would stay awake all night, pacing, thinking, and planning. After what Chamise has been though, she would have nightmares too. Necromancy leaves a bad stain, and it didn't wash off easily.

A WALKING CURSE

"I've got to do something about the two risen-dead December unleashed. If they are hunting through the lands under their own will, people will be killed, devastating the people living nearby, then spreading. Their bodies could be infected. They could pass the Taker's curse along to anyone they encountered. It will spread. It will spread."

"What can we do?" Chamise reached for her heavy leathers and her weapon. "You don't plan on fighting these things, do you?"

"That would be my last choice. I could try to hunt one down. Then, well, maybe neutralize it somehow."

Miller was at a loss for words. He didn't even know how to approach fighting something that was already dead. How would he do it? Light it aflame? Would it even notice pain? Hand-to-hand combat would be the worst option. Even if he won, he'd be covered with infected blood—not a good plan.

He only had the beginnings of an approach, and not a very good one. "We could start by tracking one of them down. At least we'd be able to warn people away. Mistress Aileen will reach out to me in a few days. I can ask her advice. She's been dealing with December's little tricks for years."

"Little tricks? Is that what you call this? I would hate to see what you'd call a serious problem."

He thought about some of Mistress Aileen's past battles, the ones she had brought him into. The battle beneath Castle Tweed, the ground dwellers, the infected, swords, blood, darkness, and necromancy. They had always won the day, but the aftermath was terrible. They might just as well have simply killed everyone within a half-day's walk and moved on. "I've seen a serious problem. Trust me. You don't want to have anything to do with those."

She continued to make herself ready, buckling on the breastplate, tying the braces, and setting the sword at her belt. Her next words came out slowly, as if she were deliberating each syllable before she uttered it. "How is this journey going to end, then? Phyllicitus is a pacifist. She even dismissed her own guard. She despises violence and cruelty. How are you and your Order even going to get an audience with her?"

Miller grimaced. He wasn't sure, either, if the goddess would see him. He sort of doubted it. But he had his instructions. "Mistress Aileen says she will see me. I've got to go by her word. I have no other plan."

"What? Why are you special? All right, you're easy for a lady to look on, but that isn't enough to get an audience with her, even if she is the goddess of love."

"She and Mistress Aileen share some kind of understanding. They aren't formal allies, but I don't think it's really that easy to just leave Phyllicitus' service. She is a goddess, after all."

"Aileen was her priestess, her servant. That isn't enough to overcome the stain of what she has become. If anything, it should be harder."

Miller waited a moment before he responded coldly. "Stain?"

"Don't play stupid. I know what your Order gets up to in the dark corners of the world. You aren't fooling me, and you won't fool her."

Miller snapped back, a hint of anger in his voice. "You don't know what you're talking about. Mistress Aileen and Phyllicitus have a deep history together. I won't explain it to you, so just accept it. Phyllicitus might talk to me because I represent the Order, but she absolutely will talk to me because I am sent by Mistress Aileen. We are dedicated to removing the Takers from the world. If anything, we are her ally in this. But even if I showed up at the Temple door, with no gifts or even promises of help, she would still see me. There is no way she'd keep me away. Mistress Aileen promised it would be so."

The look that Chamise gave him asked for details. It wanted to know why this mysterious White Hand Master could send her apprentice to an audience with the goddess herself. Miller ignored it. Telling her would simply make it more confusing.

"If you want to know the details, ask Mistress Aileen."

"Oh, I intend to."

Chamise finished readying herself, and then brought the saddle to the mare. It stood peacefully still as she put the saddle on and buckled it tight. Miller prepared the warhorse, buckling on the larger saddle, packing it with his storage bags and travel gear.

They rode out toward the southwest. The sky had cleared, but a chill wind had begun to blow from the north. Miller pushed the pace faster, making it difficult to talk to her. It seemed to be the best way forward. He didn't know how to deal with Chamise right now.

They stopped for an afternoon meal. Chamise took on the duties of preparing food. Miller scouted the area immediately around the camp. He looked for signs of violence, of walking dead, but he mostly looked for time to be alone. He returned an hour later to find a cold meal of salt ham and a raw apple on top of a piece of dried travel bread.

Chamise looked up as he approached. "My cooking isn't that bad. You didn't have to run away." She looked apprehensive, as if she didn't want to frighten him away. "I'm sorry I upset you. I didn't know that, well, you had a thing with Aileen." She looked away from Miller when she said it, keeping her gaze focused far down the road.

"There isn't a thing. It's just, well, Aileen and I have become closer than most Masters and apprentices. We work together a lot, and closely."

The conversation paused while Chamise waited for more.

"She tells me things about her feelings, and how people have treated her in the past. I guess I'm used to being one of her defenders. The other Masters can be cruel. She is young for her position, and she didn't arrive by way of a normal apprenticeship. But she is in the fight. She is giving it her all. I don't think most people give her enough credit."

"Are you and her, well, coupled?"

Miller spat out a laugh that was part denial, and part wish. "No, not me. Never me."

"Why not? Doesn't your Order live a longer life? Soon, you will be practically the same age."

Masters. Growing old together. Loving together. It's only happened once in the history of the Order, and it didn't end well. Plus. Aileen has. Complications.

"It wouldn't work. It never has. No matter what anyone wishes, it never will. The White Hand is everything. The Order, the cause, it's just too big for anyone to run away from. It demands too much, and the penalty for failure is too high."

"Why do you do it, then?"

"It sounded like a good idea in the early days. It isn't so appealing lately."

Chamise stood and moved away from her resting area. She walked up to Miller. He stared at her, not knowing what she would do. Chamise reached out, embracing him, hugging him. They stood there for a few seconds, Chamise holding him tightly, and Miller too stunned to react. Finally, she placed a single kiss on his cheek and backed away.

"Not everything is doomed. You still have me here."

"If you could just figure out a way to stop two rampaging corpses from spreading curses all over the county, that would be helpful." He smiled, trying to show good cheer.

"Now that you bring it up, I finally got some time to think the problem through. I've got something you just might like."

Their mid-day break grew by two hours as Chamise called on her Free Mage spell craft. Her casting was like a dance, mixed with a song. She called to birds in the forest, asking them to search for December's walking corpses. Afterward, she spent an hour recovering her spirit energy by eating sweets, reciting chants, and finally taking a short nap.

She was awoken by returning birds.

The birds began to fly into the camp and land near her. Their bird speech was unintelligible to him, but Chamise's spell craft was sufficient to understand what the small creature was trying to say. Miller got excited when the first bird scout returned and reported to her. But two hours later they still did not have an accurate idea of where the corpses were.

Eventually, long after Miller had given up the entire effort as fruitless, Chamise announced that she had found one of the dead.

"This raven found one of the walking corpses. It is farther east, about an hour away as a raven flies."

"What about the second one?"

"I've only heard of the one. Perhaps they separated, or one is hiding."

There was no use delaying. He hoped Chamise knew what she was doing. "Let's go."

They rode urgently through the late afternoon. After leaving the main road, they took to old farmer trails that crossed open fields and passed through patches of thick trees. Small hamlets lay near enough to the farmlands to be useful, yet near enough from the trees so their passage remained stealthy.

"What are we looking for?" Chamise asked between the jarring footsteps of the trotting mare.

"Believe me, we will know it when we see it."

In a few moments, they had found it. An exhausted-looking man walked down the two-track road, pulling a cart that held a woman and her newborn child.

"That's not one of the corpses."

Just wait, it will be along soon enough. "Let's talk to him. Maybe he's seen something."

Chamise nodded and they slowed their pace.

The man pulling the cart saw them moving toward him. He stopped his labor of pulling the heavy thing, and then walked back to the cart. He returned holding a wood cutter's ax in his two hands. Its heavy iron blade wasn't shaped for war, or to rend armor, but its weight would break bones and tear any unprotected flesh in its way. Miller pulled his horse to a stop. It tried to go forward, sensing an imminent battle. This was a warhorse, not the best for talking with strangers. It wanted a fight. He wondered where Chamise got this beast.

"That's far enough!" the cart man roared at them, hefting the ax to reinforce the sense of threat that he posed.

31

STRANGERS

Miller pulled back on his reins. The horse tried to continue forward, lowering its head and readying for action. Miller pulled the reins harder to the side, forcing the warhorse to move from its path, turning him sharply around in a circle until he stood calm, pointing at the cart man again.

"Nice horsemanship." Chamise commented sarcastically, wielding a smile like a shield.

Miller ignored her. "Good travels to you!" he cried out in the custom of the north counties. "We are on an grave task! Have you seen a man, a monstrosity, walking these roads? We need to find him before he causes harm."

The cart man relaxed, lowering his ax until it rested near his chest. "Aye! Come forward! I have news for ye!" His voice was tinged with the peasant lands, marked with a history of hard work and toil.

Chamise didn't wait for Miller, she simply advanced, the mare making its own way toward this stranger and his family. Miller urged the warhorse forward, and it took a position behind the mare. He hoped he would get his horse back tomorrow. Chamise looked well enough; she could have her blood-thirsty beast back.

They approached closer, so they no longer needed to shout. Chamise gestured Miller forward. He dismounted then walked to the cart. "This man we are seeking was wounded. He might not be thinking clearly."

"If it's what we've seen, he's right gone mad. Me and the family, we live in the village of Burgess. 'Tis less than an hour back, just beyond this hill." He gestured toward the road his cart occupied. It sloped down a gentle hill where a copse of trees grew on its peak. "Your madman came to our village just after mid-day meals. He set on us! Why would he do that? He seemed crazed with the blood lust. And he wouldn't stop. I tried to stop him," he said while he gestured with his ax, "but there was nothing to it. He would not fall. So, we fled."

"Aye, 'twas like a Taker had him in its grip!" the wife interjected, as she held her baby close.

The man replied with warning. "You need to be wary. I've seen things like this years ago. It's the White Hand. I was at the battle of the asylum. It's the same. Your man is already dead. He's been cursed."

Miller knew he had better calm him down. People could get overly-dangerous when they thought they were dealing with necromancers.

"The White Hand has been gone for years. This might be something left over, though. We ride on the Temple's business. We will take a look at the madman and see what is to be done. The goddess will be with us, I have no doubt."

The man pulling the cart did not look like he believed the lie, at least in its entirety. "Well, luck to you, then. But don't get too close, he might just try to kill you, goddess or not."

Chamise sounded nervous as she interrupted. "Good man,

you saw him, right? You didn't see him, well, eat, did you? If this is a devil from the White Hand"—she paused, drawing the symbol of protection over her heart with her fingers—"you would have seen him feed."

"Nay, I saw that not. But mark my words, it is the same as before."

"Then we better not stand here talking. I wish you a safe journey." Miller walked back to the warhorse and carefully mounted it. They rode around the cart and its family. They accelerated up the hill, toward December's walking corpse riddled with Takers.

They traveled to the top of the hill and through a wide span of tall pine trees. The dead needles made their ride quiet, and the ground was clear of bushes and obstructions. The local inhabitants must keep this place cleaned out regularly. Miller wondered how many people lived there; more than fifty to clean out this much forest.

They exited the wooded area just after cresting the hill. A broad valley lay sprawled below them. Green grass countered the tan wheat fields to sew a mosaic of rural life. A set of thirty or more homes lay at the base of the valley where three sizeable buildings surrounded a sparkling, blue pond. The town looked empty. The only motion came from three dogs busy running about its edge.

Chamise dismounted. "I don't like it." She went to her pack and removed a long, wooden-handled item with a spike-studded cylindrical piece of iron fastened to the far end. A flanged mace, a brutal weapon. He hadn't seen that one with her before. He had to remember who she was, and not be surprised when these things happened.

"Where do you get these things? Warhorse? Sword? Mace? Who has these things just lying around?"

"My skills made me valuable to a local lord. Baron Volder had a need for someone who could keep roads dry. I got recruited by my father to help out. At first, I was just supposed to ride along and help. It got complicated. I'm done with all of that, but I still have the toys."

Miller understood. She had weapons left over. But why hadn't she sold them? Simple: She expected to need them.

Chamise began walking back to the gray mare, but it pulled away from her. The mare looked like it was going to panic.

"I don't think the horse wants to play with you today."

She grabbed for the reins again. The mare simply galloped away, stopping when it was safely beyond her ability to assail it. She advanced slowly but the mare continued to keep its distance.

"Let's just switch horses. I've been missing my horse for a while now, and it doesn't look like she fits your plans anyway." Miller dismounted and began removing his bags and equipment from the saddle. As they fell to the ground, the mare trotted around Chamise and stopped at Miller's side.

"That horse is so smart, it's scary. Can you train warhorses like that?" Chamise watched it as Miller began removing her gear from the mare's saddle, then loaded his own back. He held his short sword, thinking hard about what was coming, and then slid it into one of the bags.

"It isn't trained. It's just smart. We have people in the Order who train horses, but none of them end up this way."

Chamise stared back as she walked up to the black warhorse. It reached out its neck, hoping for a scratch and quickly receiving one. "So where do you get them?"

"This one was given to me by Mistress Aileen. It was just one among a herd of young horses the locals were raising. She didn't know she was special. I don't think the rancher did, either. You can't breed these. Mistress Aileen has tried. You don't get one of these horses; they get you."

"A goddess gift?"

"Hardly." Miller chortled at the idea. He finished tying the last of his bags to the rear of the saddle, and then mounted it. "The truth is, none of us know where these horses come from. Mistress Aileen thinks there are simply a lot more of them than we realize, and they've been hiding in plain sight for centuries.

Master Easter, well, he's a bit farther out. He thinks that one of the First Gods is aiding us, a Horse God, if you will."

"First Gods? That's terrifying. Every tale of the First Gods ends in pain. You should leave that well enough alone."

"That's what Aileen said. She seems to have a healthy respect for the old ways, even though she doesn't follow them herself. The only time I have ever seen her angry with me was when I ridiculed a villager for dedicating food to the Bear God. That village was near starvation after a hard winter. I thought she was going to beat me right there, on the spot."

"Why would she do that?"

"Truthfully, I think the First Gods scare the wits out of her, which is saying a lot. She is a White Hand Master, after all." He pulled himself up into the saddle.

Chamise mounted her warhorse and adjusted her grip on the mace. They turned toward the village. "I can't believe we're going to do this."

"Neither can I."

Chamise spurred the warhorse forward. Miller followed closely behind, allowing the mare freedom to choose its own path. Miller saw that she understood what they were about here, and how bad this was likely to get.

They arrived at the bottom of the hill. The village lay before them. Five small houses stood decorated with flowers in small window gardens. A woman's body lay on bloody grass, just a few feet from an open door. Chamise saw it and spurred the warhorse onward, assaulting the streets of the village as if it were the ramparts of some castle.

They moved into the depths of the village. The outer houses were closer together, narrowing the muddy street. They rode around two carts that had attempted to block the way, although poorly. He wondered where the villagers had gone.

The center of the village consisted of a pond small enough that a man could throw a rock across it. The three significant buildings stood twenty paces from the pond, flanking it on three sides. The cooper's yard stood empty, the tools abandoned by the workers. The granary was abandoned as well.

The last building stood two stories tall. It was painted dark red with an emblem of a tree and mug illustrated with great care on a sign nailed to the front. Narrow windows stood protected by thick shutters painted black. The walking corpse stood in front of the inn, beating on the door in an effort to gain entrance. Five arrows jutted from its torso and arms.

Two bodies lay in the muddy road near it.

FURY

Chamise screamed out in fury and the warhorse bolted forward toward the dead thing. Her mace crushed into its skull, caving a fist-sized dent into it. She rode quickly by it, attempting to avoid the spray of blood. The spray didn't come. Instead, blood seeped out of the cracked skull in thick, syrupy brown globs, slowly oozing down the side of its head. It looked up toward Chamise, then returned to its task at the door, redoubling its efforts to gain the interior. It clawed the entry door, prying apart the wooden planks by inches as its fingers became a bloody mess from the task.

Chamise began to turn her horse for another pass. She had abandoned all intentions of subduing the thing with magic and guile. It was easy to think about fighting the dead when they are just an idea. When they stand in front of you, their hunger close to your throat, it's a completely different thing. He needed to get Chamise back on plan.

"Chamise! It isn't counter-attacking! The thing isn't following you! Stay with the plan!"

Chamise pulled back on the warhorse, stopping its eager charge. She swung her leg around and climbed down from the saddle, keeping her mace ready for any danger. Miller calmed his breathing and patted the mare, mentally pleading with it to be still, and began his part of Chamise's strategy. First, he focused on her spirit energy, her harmony. Once he had a feel for its flow, he altered his own, so they were synchronized. Finally, he allowed a small amount of spirit energy to travel along that newly formed channel between them, empowering Chamise to draw on his own magical spirit.

Chamise gasped, recognizing the feeling and the spirit that it gave her. She was unprepared for the depth of the flow, and immediately dropped onto her knees. Throwing the leather fighting gloves from her hands, she shoved them into the mud. She quickly began the hand dances beneath the mud, calling nature's power to her Free Mage's will.

All the plants in the front of the inn began to grow. The short, ankle-high grass became knee-high within ten heartbeats. The small decorative tree grew higher and thicker, too, as nature drank in the energy Chamise fed it. The corpse stopped its effort to gain entrance to the inn and turned on her.

Chamise called out, "Are you sure you can do this? Do you have enough left?" Her words were strained as she grew the garden.

"I'm fine! Keep going!"

The energy flow began as a trickle then grew in intensity. Miller felt it being pulled from his grasp like a slithering eel.

The dead thing leaped down from the front porch and landed in the grass. It turned to sprint at Chamise, hissing like a snake. Before it took a second step, the garden erupted. Long grasses, roots, and other living plants animated, wrapping themselves around its feet, around its legs, around its knees until it was pulled to the ground. It struggled against them, but every time it broke free, twice as many plants would wrap around it. Soon it was imprisoned in a cocoon of nature, and nature was squeezing it, hard.

Miller dismounted. He calmed himself with the disciplines before he walked up to the thing. He looked at the gelatinous blood staining the grass, then retrieved his glass lens and looked again. "Interesting, the blood is different."

"Just check the cursed thing, will you? Then maybe kill it, permanently? I can't hold it much longer!"

He checked his curiosity. Then he spread out the white cloth and put out the bowl. He scraped a few portions of the blood into the sample bowl and heated it with crafter's oil. The blood boiled, but slower and less violent than the other samples had. The corpse continued to fight the living grass holding it.

"Something is different. I need to check it. Can you hold it?"

"You better check fast!" Chamise screamed, moving her hands in the intricate Free Mage spell motions, trying to channel spirit and harmonics, and maybe something else into the weave.

He moved closer to the dead thing trying to claw and bite its way out of the trap. He brought up the lens again, looking closer at the blood. He considered the problem from the First Principles' point of view. He had solved plenty of problems based on the First Principles of magic. Blood leads to life, life is movement, movement is the action of potential. Potential is all fates. But the blood wasn't moving as it should. The mystery was: Why was it slow?

Miller examined the writhing corpse more thoroughly. He looked at the head wound. He traced the blood flow down the thing's grass constrained torso.

"I'm losing it!"

He heard her cry and jerked back. The corpse began ripping off the grasses and roots that constrained its far arm. It quickly freed that arm and began to rip off the rest. Chamise was at her limit and could not focus any more strength onto the garden.

Miller used his disciplines to move spirit into the five channels of fire, then connected the channels to the beast. He poured all the spirit that he could fit through the channels and the corpse thing lit up with fire like an oil-soaked torch.

"Is it supposed to do that?" Chamise called out in fear.

The flaming corpse stood up, pulling the burning plants from the ground, letting them fall away from it. Its skull shriveled up and glowed with heat. The face cooked away right in front of them. It took a step toward Miller, then another, then fell down. Charred limbs crumbled away from the burning mess.

"Yes," he replied, his heart beating against his chest. "That's about right." But it wasn't. That thing was much stronger than expected.

Miller retrieved his sword from the packs. He drew its arm-length blade. Its intricate runes stood in black contrast to the metal. Walking up to the charred corpse carefully, he slowly reached forward and stabbed the blade into the charred body until it passed entirely through it. Miller retrieved his lens and began inspecting the wound.

"Will you leave that thing alone?"

"I've got to make sure it's not still bleeding."

"All right, then, I will go check the inn." Chamise picked up her mace and retrieved her gloves, pulling them onto her hands and readying the mace. Getting away from the cursed thing.

Miller turned his attention to the burned body. It was cooked into a man-shaped charred rock. The oozing blood had cooked away. Multiple probes with his sword verified that the center was fully charred as well as the skin.

His stabbing blade struck one of the remaining arrow shafts. Miller grew curious. He had expected the shafts to have burned away. He drew his dagger and began extracting an arrow.

Chamise began walking up the porch stairs toward the main door to the inn.

He withdrew the remaining arrow shaft. The fletching had been destroyed, but the wood buried within the charred body remained mostly intact. He gazed at the arrow as he reached down with gloved hands to clear away the blackened ash from its tip.

A broad arrowhead lay fastened on the end of the arrow. Its metal gleamed after the charred ash was cleared off, exposing an engraving. A maze of angles that folded back on themselves stood in stark relief. Another Mage Arrow?

He reached down and grabbed a second shaft. He moved quickly, pulling the arrow out of the charred remains with brute force. It came clear easily. Same arrowhead. Not good.

"Chamise! Don't go in there!" Miller called out.

Chamise stopped just before she reached the door, hooking the mace to her belt loops. The door swung open, revealing two men. One held the door open wide, kneeling to stay out of the way. The other held a hunting bow with a Mage Arrow drawn and let fly.

33

FINDING TROUBLE

Chamise jerked back as the hunter released his deadly arrow. The arrow struck her boiled leather chest piece at an angle, deflecting off the thick, wax-covered leather into the overgrown vegetation. She slammed her mace down, striking the hand keeping the door open. The man screamed as his hand, along with the handle he had been holding, were reduced to wreckage. The door started to close under its own weight when the bowman kicked his assistant in the shoulder, forcing him out onto the landing and blocking the door from closing.

Was she going to get killed in there? Miller altered the channel between Chamise and himself. Instead of funneling spirit directly to her, he began to flow it toward her elemental harmonies. Chamise screamed a battle cry as she charged the bowman, swinging brutally around her. She struck the door frame and splintered it. The bowman backed into the building as the frame broke apart around him. Each of her blows forced wooden shrapnel to fly toward the bowman, spoiling his aim. This woman can fight!

The channeling began to find his new focus, Chamise's skin. Miller opened an identity channel, then weaved the spirit to Chamise herself. Energy began binding her skin and bones to protect them from being crushed, split, or impaled.

"It won't hold long! Get out of there!" Miller cried out as Chamise charged into the doorway. She rammed the bowman with her shoulder, knocking him backward onto the floor. She didn't retreat; instead, she dashed into the building. Cries erupted from the interior. Miller couldn't see what was happening as she had left his line of sight. The flow began to come unfocused. Miller saw it coming. Now was the time to choose. Was he in or out?

Miller charged into the doorway, narrowly avoiding the wounded man. He entered the main room to see a half-dozen armed combatants facing Chamise. She held a chair in one hand as a makeshift shield. The body of an old woman lay on the floor, her chainmail-covered skull was crushed in and bleeding out onto the wooden planks. The old woman had obviously met Chamise's mace.

The armed men were getting organized for a push, a final charge that would overwhelm her. Chamise didn't seem to notice their tactic. They planned to lure her out and then charge as a mass. Miller didn't like it at all. Where was December when he needed him? What good was it to have the most feared cabal member assigned to him when he didn't even show up? He darkly assumed that this kind of behavior accompanies the act of giving up all sense of honor.

Welcome to the White Hand leadership ranks.

"First Principles, First Principles," he muttered, thinking fast, searching for some way out of this mess.

Chamise launched herself into the right side of the group, seeking to keep at least one side free from attacks as she pressed forward.

A thrown dagger hit his shoulder. The enchanted cloak absorbed most of the impact and deflected the steel blade, sending it tumbling to the floor. He was out of time and he didn't want to do this. Five channels would bring fire. Tying them together could heat it further and grow its ferocity. Miller called fire and fed it, constraining the fire into a small layer that stretched along the length of his sword.

He began to channel and form the fire along the blade.

A short, greasy-haired man screamed out "Sorcery!" He rushed around Chamise, gesturing with a sharp falchion, its blade pointing the way. Another man, dressed in townsman garb and wielding a short spear, charged beside him.

"Back off!" Chamise yelled as she struggled to intersect the two. If she succeeded, then she would be at risk of being flanked. The fight would be done at that point. Miller advanced to come alongside her and prevent a rear attack. They were not aiming for a flank, they were aiming at him.

The spearman thrust his weapon toward his face. Miller parried in a blur of red fire. As he deflected the weapon, the short man rushed forward with a wide, ugly-looking blade, its weighted end looking like an oversized cleaver. Miller stepped back just as the blade smashed into his arm. It missed the cloak and cut directly into his muscle, piercing clothing easily.

Miller screamed in pain. Chamise used her left hand to thrust her makeshift shield chair into the side of the spearman, pushing him away. Miller struggled to keep the fire channels open but the attacker closed again and began a flurry of blows. Each blow knocked his blade aside a little wider and exposed a little more flesh.

The flames went out. Miller's concentration was focused entirely on surviving this fight. It was not looking good, not looking good at all. He had the inescapable feeling that the short guy would kill him in the next five minutes, then December would bring him back as a walking sack of meat, gloating over his ghost for a week.

Chamise saw the danger as well. Another war scream erupted

from her lungs, each foreign syllable bringing dread into his heart. He knew the scream well, from long ago. He still had nightmares after all these years.

"In der Gott des Krieges! Ich bin fur dein Leben gekommen!" Eisenvard's war cry erupted from her lips.

Their attackers knew the phrase, too. They began turning toward her. Chamise rushed forward recklessly and brought her mace down on one attacker. The man tried to parry with his sword but she'd put all of her might behind the blow. The sword was knocked aside, bending oddly in the middle as the mace impacted his shoulder. Bones sprang through his wool shirt and sprayed blood across the floor.

She continued the mad charge, kicking the second foe in the knee as she neared him. Murder shone in her eyes. The Taken man knew what was coming for him; the final door awaited him. Being a Taken would not stave off death.

Miller saw how the battle magic wasn't working. He needed another plan fast. He tried to think of a tactic from First Principles, gave up, and thought about elemental magics, without result. There wasn't enough time.

Chamise screamed again as her enemy fell to one knee. The mace crushed down, leaving a fist-sized dent in his forehead. He fell back, bleeding out of his nose and eyes.

The spearman thrust toward her and scored a clean hit into her chest. The tip slid off her breastplate and knocked her back.

The short man closed on Miller again, seeking to remove him from the combat, permanently.

Miller scrambled back again. The wall was directly behind him. There was no more room to retreat. He tried not to panic. Elements, like fire, were not going to help him here. Chamise screamed again, swinging wildly at the spearman, who wouldn't come within range. A man wielding a short sword sprang forward and Miller reacted out of instinct. He reached out with a tendril of energy and aimed it into the man's psyche. Blunt, not usually effective, but quick.

Miller lost track of Chamise as his attacker stumbled to the side. He wasn't out of the fight, but that small tendril had an effect. It would take a few moments for him to recover. A thought struck him. They didn't seem have defenses against White Hand magics. He might have been fighting the wrong fight.

Chamise screamed from his side. He had lost track of her fight in the last second. "I'm hit!"

Miller seized the magical channels surrounding him, pouring energy into channels, hoping that brute force would create an effect. He pushed the waves of energy through the room and beyond into the town, tuning the channels, finding their target within each of their enemy's essences. He remembered December's words: Every human or animal born of this world shares one desire, they all want to live. Their base inner self constantly reminds them with urges to flee or fight when threats arise. Miller channeled fear into that inner self. Screams erupted as the Taken stepped back, trying to regroup. He poured more spirit in, emptying his reserves.

The attackers broke. The spearman turned and fled, leaving four feet of spear jutting out of Chamise's side. The short man with the sword threw his blade at Miller and ran away. Miller turned so it hit his cloak and tumbled onto the floor.

Chamise grabbed a table, her legs shaking. "I'm not doing so good."

Miller took a step forward and held her steady. He smiled at her as she grimaced in pain. He saw this Eisenvard clearly now; how had he not seen this? He wondered if it would be better to just let her die. Would she kill him in his sleep?

"Don't be like that. I know what you're thinking." Chamise struggled to pull a chair out and take a seat. "I'm not one of them. I never was. My father was, though, and he taught me a lot."

"Eisenvard? And a Free Mage?" Miller kept the conversation going as he grabbed a cloth from the bar and began wrapping it around her, trying to staunch the bleeding.

"It makes no sense. I know. My father, well, he was a

believer. But he was conflicted. My mother had the talent, and he had hoped to purge it from me. He tried to make me good; it just didn't stick."

Miller pulled out his small dagger and began carving small cutting runes into the spear. "I thought they burned all crafters."

Miller sent a small tendril of energy into the runes and the spear shaft split, dropping the extruding four-foot section onto the floor.

"No, not the ones dedicated to the cause—but it required a lot of dedication."

Chamise grabbed his forearm and pulled herself unsteadily to her feet. "Look, I would love to catch you up on my family history, but right now I suggest we get out of here." She began slowly moving toward the entrance, holding her hand on the bloody rag to keep it at her side.

Miller stepped up next to her to help but she waved him forward. "Be a dear and open the door for me." Miller pulled the body from the doorway. Chamise slowly moved out of the inn. Miller could see the pain in her face with every step she took.

The outer area was completely empty. The surrounding buildings were deserted as well.

"You cleared the whole village. Where did you get that trick? Are the townsfolk all right?"

"They will recover soon enough. Just another one of the guild tricks. But you knew that, didn't you?"

She offered a brave smile as she walked on. The horses were gone, as well as every single animal within three hundred yards. "Yes. I knew. I never thought you would show it to me, though." Miller let the silence stretch between them for a minute. Chamise lost her patience first. "We need a horse. They will be back."

"Don't worry. I'm pretty sure that my horse will return soon enough. The mare is pretty smart like that."

"Yes, probably."

He changed the subject while they were waiting. "So, Eisenvard, we have time. What happened with your father?"

"Oh, you know, the same thing that happened to the rest of them. They exiled themselves up north after Phyllicitus released them from service. He tried to stay on, but she wouldn't take him. By that time, he had lost his belief in their ways."

"Lost belief? I've never heard of that before."

"I don't want to talk about it. Let's just say when a maniac order of knights burns your lover at the stake for witchery, then you can have a crisis of faith."

Miller couldn't think of a reply. He simply took her hand and held it, along with the bloody cloth staunching her wound. A few minutes went by before they heard the sound of approaching hoof beats. The mare cantered from around a barn, leading the black warhorse back to them.

"You really need to name that mare."

"I know, but I don't want bad luck. She will tell me her name when she wants me to know it. Names are funny things. Smart people, or horses, don't give them away easily."

"Yeah. So the White Hand believes. I've never known it to matter much."

Chamise scowled and pressed her hand tighter to the wound as she climbed up into the saddle. The mare was gentle to her, keeping still as she gained the saddle. Chamise looked forward, toward an unseen thing, lost in thought and pain.

Miller didn't know where to go. He simply rejoined the road and followed it forward, away from the village. The black war horse seemed agitated, ready for some kind of fight. The mare kept a smooth and steady pace. The road climbed up a long, gently sloping hill. Stalks of wheat filled the fields left of the road while the fields on the right had gone fallow. They continued up the hill until it entered a copse of thin trees. There would be no hiding there, either. It would be too easy to be spotted.

34

RAIDING FORCE

Brita had arrived at the campsite without fanfare or notice, but none was needed. When she encountered the first of the sentries, she was recognized as their own. The Friends were the only pass she needed. She hadn't needed to speak with the young man who guarded the entrance to the camp, she simply knew where to go.

She was thankful they were communicating again. The Friends had been quiet since the farm. Not good. She knew what happened when the taken didn't obey. Not good. Ebber was difficult to understand with them, and almost impossible to understand without them. The Friends had shown their annoyance with her by cutting her off from the others. When she arrived at the camp, they began to communicate again.

The camp was spread across the clearing. It was organized and functioning perfectly. Tents made the clearing feel crowded.

Campfires decorated the spaces between tents, spewing their smoke into the air. Horse lines were set up just outside the clearing among the trees. Latrines had been dug away from the camp, yet conveniently near to a stream. Cook fires were small, but each fire had an ample supply of wood, and at least six of them had cooking cauldrons hanging over them. They were each black iron and large enough to cook stew for twenty people. They hung by dark chains above a wooden tripod.

She took her time entering the camp, trying to count how many people were here. It was difficult. Ebber simply walked into the crowd, searching out where the cooking tents were. "How do you like that? The Friends have this whole encampment running like clockwork."

"Yes. Let's go see if we can avoid breaking it."

Ebber smiled back at her small retort. "I think we can manage it. If not, well, there are worse ways to spend our time than trying to fix an army camp."

It was an army camp. Men worked at cleaning armor and setting it up on stands. Others sharpened swords or cut arrows from straight branches. Men, horses, and weapons were evident everywhere.

"Where's the war?"

She didn't expect an answer. Ebber closed his eyes for a moment, then pointed out beyond the camp. "That way, not sure how far. I guess we should get some details."

He paused again, searching the crowd for something, someone. Brita didn't know how to do this, but she had learned to pay attention when Ebber showed her things, no matter how crazy those things seemed.

"At least I found Gardin and Terp. They are on the other side of the clearing. Let's go meet with them."

That was quick. The Friends were being handy again.

"Sure."

They dismounted and walked their horses through the busy camp. She had expected a lively crowd, but this crowd was manageable. Foot traffic moved smoothly. They knew when to stop, when to start, when to get out of the way. Moments after entering the camp, she gave up trying to navigate it and merely let her feelings, her Friends, guide her.

There was no need to talk, she simply paid attention to her instincts, and used those feelings as a guide. It was like she was thinking with only her intuition. It felt so odd, but it worked.

Terp soon arrived to meet them. He stepped forward and then paused, staring at them without uttering any words. She wondered if he was using the Friends to check on her. Could she do the same?

She stopped and looked at Terp. After a few moments of silence, she began to "feel" Terp. He seemed strong and healthy. He had just eaten an hour ago, but the food hadn't tasted very good.

Terp broke the silence between them. "The journey went well?"

She guessed that some things are easier to say with words instead of using the Friends. Taken could only communicate so well.

"Well enough. We made good time."

"There was an issue with a young boy you left behind at the farm."

She was surprised at Ebber; why did he need to mention that?

Terp's eyebrows shot up as if he had heard her thoughts. "Boy?"

"Yes. There was a boy hiding in the wheat. He saw the entire event. Did you really need to kill his mother in front of him, then let him live?"

"I didn't kill anyone. You can talk to Gardin about that kind of thing."

"Won't do any good, and you know it. Gardin isn't the careful sort. But there are no problems, we found the boy, and the Friends were there as well. That little problem is over."

Terp nodded. His face scowled with unhappiness, then it relaxed with a small level of relief.

She started to worry about what he would say. What would happen when they discovered that she had let that boy go?

"Can we go see Gardin now? I only want to tell these stories once."

Ebber glanced at her. She understood without words: Terp would know it eventually, best to frame it in their own way first. They had taken care of the boy, they just hadn't killed him.

They walked to the far edge of the camp, avoiding the deep trails carved into the muddy ground. It was organized, but it was unplanned. The people in the camp had their places, and the equipment and supplies were stockpiled and distributed. But who determined what they would need? How would all this work when supplies start running low? She thought of the trouble she had when serving at Durmitt's Inn; supplies always spoiled or went missing. Someone needed to plan for this. Someone needed to have an idea what they were getting into.

Brita could not identify anyone truly in charge. People walked by her on their own tasks, intent on their immediate goals. No one shouted directions. No one tried to organize it.

A tall, older man walked by her. Before he passed, he reached out his liver-spotted hand to touch her shoulder. Instantly, she was aware of how the camp worked. She knew where the seven basins of supplies were stored, and how they accumulated and distributed their wares. She knew where the horses were cared for, who had the duty to feed them, and what to do if she needed new shoes.

These Friends were serious about organization. Old Durmitt would have loved this trick. The camp was alive and full of energy, almost all of it focused on accomplishing work, or resting for future efforts.

"Did you feel that?"

Ebber looked back. "I found someone earlier. That touch was for you. Let's go see Gardin; maybe we can get fresh mounts."

Terp led them through the camp to the edge where they found a group of unsaddled horses grazing in a meadow.

Gardin stood off to the side, overlooking the horses, making sure none of them walked off. Three other men stood near him, each wearing thick leathers and carrying weapons.

It looked to Brita like they had just gotten back from patrol. She wondered what they were guarding against. One of the horses was limping. It looked like a wolf bite, a big wolf bite.

"Brita!" Gardin's voice cut through the camp noise. "You took long enough. All of your parts still connected?"

What did he expect? A bucket of Brita parts to walk into camp? Well, Taken and all, maybe that could happen.

"Ebber and I survived the trip. We just followed in your wake. No issues."

He looked at Ebber who was busy hunting down wildflowers, then scowled. "Did Ebber give you any information on what we are doing here?"

"Not really, but he did teach me some nice dancing moves. I wondered what all this was about, but the Friends, well, they told me it wasn't time to care yet."

"Aye. It's probably time now, though."

"All right, I'm game. Why are we chasing Miller all over the countryside with an army? How dangerous can an apprentice be?"

Frowning, Gardin came closer to her. He removed his glove then reached up to touch her cheek.

She instantly felt the connection. Friends shared feeling and thoughts between them. She wondered if Gardin was concerned that she still had feelings for Miller. Would that be possible? Would the Friends permit that?

"Something is troubling you, Brita. What happened?"

She took a calming breath and regrouped before answering. She decided to borrow a trick from Ebber, to distract. "We rode through the farm; we had to clean up some things you left behind."

"Behind?"

"Yeah. There were witnesses."

She tried to remember the look on the boy's face, and how it made her feel, especially when she realized she should kill him. The Friends came to her aid and sent the emotion to Gardin.

Gardin took her hand in his. This time it wasn't to use the Friends, it was simply to offer some level of comfort. "No issues, can't blame you. But maybe not worth worrying about. Nobody is trying to be secret here."

"We don't care if we are discovered? Miller is that dangerous?"

He shook his head. "That boy isn't dangerous. He already had his victory a few years ago. He was one of the White Hand necromancers who pushed back the old Friends. These newer Friends already know his tricks and do not feel threatened."

She shook her head in disbelief, even though she could feel the truth of his words through their touch. "Then why all this? Why an army? Why come out of hiding for an apprentice? It doesn't make sense."

"That's what I thought at first. It took me a while to figure it out. We aren't trying to kill your young friend, we really need to bring him into the family and make him one of us. What the Friends would really like is to bring in one of the Masters. The Masters can't be taken, though."

"Why? The Eisenvard fought them before. Why can't the Friends?"

"The Eisenvard fought them with swords and spears. They can be killed, but killing a White Hand Master doesn't do much except annoy them. A few days or weeks later, they cross back through the final door and fight again."

The thought stunned her. All the stories about the White Hand, all the dark tales, they were true?

"The Friends have tried to take Masters in the past. It never worked. The Masters have some kind of defense. I think it is based on their rings. The apprentices have a different kind of ring, though. The Friends think they can take one and learn many of their secrets. Perhaps enough to finally win the war."

"Why haven't the Friends allied with the nobility? I'm sure they would join against the White Hand."

Gardin shook his head. "Think about it. How would you convince someone to join us willingly? People out there don't understand what it is to be part of this."

She nodded. She hadn't been given a choice, either.

"That makes it clear why the Friends wanted me. They want me to bring him in with honey, nice and sweet."

He nodded. "It shouldn't be long, though. Once we are all together, we will seize young Miller, and you will be reunited with your old friend. We have over two hundred people. He can't run anywhere; our scouts are already ahead of him. We know where he is going to be, and with these numbers, it will be over quickly. He's obviously heading for Home's Hearth. He isn't going to make it."

She looked back at the main camp. There were a lot of people here, much more than necessary to capture one apprentice. But Miller had helped stop the last wave of Taken. Converting him could remove a major threat to the Friends.

She thought about Durmitt's Inn, and about the bodies that had decorated its floor. Someone who could stop the Friends from taking more people, that didn't sound like an apprentice. It sounded like a powerful caster.

What was she doing here? The people needed help, she needed help. She needed to get out of here.

Brita instantly became calm again. She wondered for a moment why she had been so upset. Odd, she couldn't even remember what she had been thinking.

He watched Chamise as they rode. They traveled about ten minutes before she began wavering in her saddle. Sweat began beading up on her forehead, dripping down across her pale face.

He thought about that last healing draft. Taking it now might be the best plan. He tried to believe that if he could find a safe place to hide, they would be fine. It was getting harder and harder to think that way. He looked across the fields and found nothing within an easy ride. Rolling hills decorated the horizon in every direction.

They arrived atop a hill that afforded a good view back toward the village. Looking back, he saw a group of about fifty or seventy-five people had gathered on the road. He saw horses, and dogs. It looked like a second attack was underway. He didn't know what to do.

If he gave Chamise the healing draft, she would be fast asleep right here next to the road. If he waited until later, he might expose her to battle when it wasn't necessary. Either choice was bleak and had bad outcomes.

He looked down at his apprentice ring. It was useless. It wasn't even a Master's ring—if he were a Master he could return from the final door. He wished Aileen was here with him. She always had a plan, a spell, a tactic. He could feel a sense of doom descending on him.

Miller tried to push the horses faster, but the mare didn't cooperate. She kept to her steady gait as Chamise's grip became weaker.

"What's that?" Chamise croaked in a weak voice. She released a hand from her saddle and pointed up, slightly left of the road. Then she quickly returned the hand back to the saddle. "It doesn't look good."

Miller looked up over the treetops that crowned the hill. A black cloud stood alone in the sky. The darkness was beyond rain, or weather. As he looked at it, he saw a flock of birds, or maybe bats, flying in and out of it. Fear began to well up within his heart. At once, he knew that if he traveled under that thing it would mean his doom.

"It's not good, but it is probably good for us. I think Master December is out there. That looks like something he would create. We need to find him. We definitely need the help."

"Ah, no. I don't think that is one of your best ideas, just ride far away from all of this. That cloud is just a portent. Whatever lives beneath it is evil, pure evil. I'm willing to chance the gut wound. I can make it an entire day if I have to. I don't want to go in there."

"Sorry, you aren't healthy enough to ride for another hour, let alone a day. Let's find somewhere we can be safe for just a bit. I have something that can help with that stab wound you're so fond of clutching."

As Chamise began her angry retort, Miller dipped his hand into the saddlebag and pulled out the box. The seal of Phyllicitus stood out proudly from its walnut surface. "I just need a half hour, an hour at most."

"December won't—"

"December will need you for the fight. If there is one thing you can always count on with December, it's self-interest. But that means we need to arrive quickly. You need enough time to recover from the effects of the healing."

"That's a king's ransom, you know that."

"Quiet. Ride. You are worth three ransoms to me, especially just before a fight."

She answered with a weakened smile. She urged the mare forward, slightly off the road and toward the dark cloud.

Miller glanced back toward the village again. The gathering crowd had seen their movement and had begun leaving the town. They had draft horses from the fields, riding horses from the wealthier families, and a few war horses from times gone by. He could not use channeling to disrupt them, they were too far away.

They started riding over dead plants and weeds that decorated the fallow field. Their hoof prints left a trail that led directly toward their goal. Chamise was struggling to hold on within minutes. The jarring ride sent fresh ripples of pain across her face with every step the mare took.

Behind them, the villagers were gaining. They rode as fast as their mounts could take them. Their dense crowd had transformed into a stream of mounted men, with slower horses at the rear, faster mounts speeding to intercept them.

Miller looked at Chamise. Her wound had begun bleeding again, and the red stain covered her left arm, and dripped down onto her legs. "Hold on! We are almost there!" Miller cried has they entered the trees.

The trees were tall enough that they rode easily beneath their lower leaves. This might just work.

Chamise had begun to grunt in pain as they sped through. Two minutes later they crested the hill and then emerged on the other side. Wild grass filled the downward slope. The dark cloud stood motionless in the sky. A single tower stood on the land below, its ancient rectangular form jutting up, defying the rolling hills about it. The cloud's shadow lay across the tower, darkening it, and filling the air the shapes of huge bats that flew erratically around the tower, shrieking fury, hate, and death.

Chamise pulled back on the reins. The mare slowed. "Sweet goddess. We aren't going there. There's no way."

She saw people, or what had once been people, walking around the perimeter of the tower. Two dozen villagers worked the field with their farm implements, but they did so clumsily. They dragged spades across the ground without breaking the surface. They stabbed pitchforks into bushes with no purpose. One villager had decided to simply crawl down the trail toward them. It had little choice, as it had no legs. It pulled its rotting remains forward toward them.

"They're dead. They're all dead!"

When the truth is worse than a lie, it's time to lie. That's what Aileen had said so long ago. Miller had never understood it until now.

"Don't fear, be brave. This is Master December's work. I can tell. You won't come to any harm. Right now, we need a place to heal up. I think we just found it. No one will lay a hand on us in there."

Her voice rose an octave. "Don't fear? Are you looking at the same thing I am?"

He reached down and pulled the mare's bridle forward. The horse quivered under his touch. He sympathized with the mare. He wondered if December would just kill them to make his task easier. After all, he could just bring them back and add them to his little peasant army.

"Today isn't our day for the final door. This is mostly theater. It's there to frighten away the locals." He saw the disbelieving look on Chamise's face. "This is how the White Hand uses a light touch. Think of it as mercy. If the peasants see this, they won't even try. We just need to be brave enough to wade through it. December has it all under control."

"You're a worse liar than December is." She grabbed onto the mare's saddle tightly as it began its cautious approach. "That isn't theater. That is death, and it has decided to walk free across the land."

They approached the village, avoiding the crawling horror that had taken up a position and the very edge of the cloud's shadow. Its maggot-ridden face turned to stare at them as they passed by. As they neared the tower, the sense of fear became palpable. This wasn't a conjured fear, it was his body's reaction to being so near to the home of death. Every feeling he had screamed at him to flee. Chamise had started shaking as she recited her Eisenvard mantras in a foreign tongue.

Having an Eisenvard at his side was making him feel safer right now. He hadn't expected that.

Two of the risen dead stood in their way. In life they had been simple peasants. In death they became animated corpses bound to the will of whatever dark force had recalled them. Right now, that will had little use for them. It bent its attention to greater deeds, leaving the moving soulless husks to their own devices. Their last orders were to kill, to maim, to destroy. Nothing was close enough so they battled each other in a strange dance of death. One of the dead had a hoe, recently used for gardening now re-purposed for murder. The other had a scythe, ready to harvest the body parts of it's neighbor. The first peasant chopped into the other, burying the hoe into its chest. The other swung back the the scythe, cutting an ear off. The first pulled out the hoe and struck again. In turn, the second cut with its scyth. They continued back and forth, each taking a turn striking with their make-shift weapon, receiving a blow, recovering, then attacking again. Their heads swiveled toward Miller and Chamise as they rode past, giving the dueling corpses a wide berth.

Three other dead things stood in their way. These poor souls had died years ago. The flesh had mostly left the bodies, and parts of skeletons jutted from their torn clothing and rotting body parts. The dead shambled out of the way, showing a path to a shadow-covered door.

"Well, I guess it's now or never."

Reaching out, he grasped the door handle, and pulled.

THE MASTERS

"Relax, everything is going to be fine. Miller is a bright one and he has good instincts."

Aileen continued her pacing across the old wooden floor. Her apprentice was out there, alone. She knew how it felt, fleeing for her life, hordes of taken chasing her. She remembered when her master had sent her out into the unprotected world, all by herself. She stared across the room at Easter. He had put her through hell, literally. Easter would do worse to Miller. Sadly, he was the best Master she could have hoped for.

Easter lounged in a wide chair on the other side of the room, utterly relaxed. His smile, which used to disarm her, brought fear. She knew what could happen to a White Hand apprentice traveling alone. She knew that Easter always kept a hopeful and positive face, even when things were going badly.

And here he was, telling her to relax.

"You were always confident in everyone. Even those of us who never made it back."

He looked up, a slight frown appearing on his face. He met her eyes, then brushed his hand through his short black hair. He was dressed meticulously, as usual. At first glance, Easter presented as a somewhat successful merchant, a master scribe, or some other educated freeman. He tried to show himself as educated, cunning, and wise. He was all of these things, and much more. He always knew just a little more than you thought he did. Dangerous, shrewd.

He always talked to her, never shutting her out. But sometimes he didn't speak truth.

"Ouch, you wound me. I'm not uncaring. I just understand, well, the way the world works. It tends to discover which of us are survivors, and which aren't."

"Miller isn't like us. He is a gentler soul." She paused to think about what she was about to say, unconsciously fidgeting with the sleeves of her long black dress. "Even if Miller did nothing else for the Order, right now, he does something for me. I need his crafting skills. He is mine. I don't like this entire idea. Why did we send him out alone? We could have sent a little help."

Her voice started to grow, to gain a biting edge. Anger started flowing into her body. "Damn it, Easter! Haven't you taken enough from me? Miller is mine!"

Easter's smile shone back at her. "And who do you belong to now? Are you rethinking your allegiance?"

He simply gazed at her. He was calm and filled with purpose. Dark eyes looked into her own, searching for some clue, some leverage.

Her voice was filled with bitterness. She felt deflated. "No, some decisions can never be revoked. And it had to be done. This land." She swept her arms outward, as if to encompass everything. "This world is just bigger than my own needs; it always has been. No, I am not threatening to leave, and I won't be looking for a new cabal. We have a lot of work left to do together, you and I."

Easter slowly stood from his chair, then reached down for a scroll tube. His voice remained on edge, but his body showed relief. He was the same height as Aileen, so their eyes quickly met. "I'm glad to hear it."

So was she. A slight twinge of fear passed through her chest. She had almost ruined everything. She couldn't help herself, she thanked the goddess in her secret heart.

She copied Easter's previous motion, running her hands through her blonde hair. Easter was more than another Master, he was the key to the entire cabal. He kept the other cabals at bay through a combination of favors, fear, schemes, and things only the goddess might know.

Walking forward to approach an empty table, he unwrapped the scroll case and pulled a long, thick parchment from it, laying the contents on its surface. A map now rested there, showing coastlines, cities, forests, and the boundaries of kingdoms.

The map immediately piqued her interest. Aileen hadn't seen this map before. She walked over to stare at it. It was an unusually accurate map, showing features across many lands. "Tricky. How did you get this? How did you get all the detail in there?"

She didn't get a response. Instead, Easter went back to his coat and retrieved three small leather bags that fit into his palm. A smile emerged from his face, and he began untying the bags. "We were talking about Miller, weren't we?"

She wondered what the old fox was up to. "We were. Do you have word? My latest is three days old."

"My news is older than that, so let's go with what you heard last." He picked up a bag, and reached two fingers into it, emerging with a pinch of brightly colored green sand held between the thumb and forefinger. He moved his hand over the map, sprinkling the green sand and whispering an evocation.

Aileen felt the magic move. It wasn't like her spells, it wasn't an elemental force, it wasn't a spiritual calling. It felt familiar. It reminded her of Miller when he worked on the forge. It was the magic of crafting.

Small, bright-green areas began to emerge from the map. Each position marked a location along with a note detailing a date along with an event. She bent down to inspect it closely.

"I like it. Where did you get this map?"

"You aren't the only one who gets a talented apprentice, you know."

She gazed down, studying the new marks intently. "These are the raids." Easter had been tracking raids by outlaws and by soldiers for the past year. He knew these events better than she did. She looked at the map, tracking their locations and times. Some were missing. "These aren't all of them. What about the massacre at Reynolds' Field?" She pointed at a blank spot on the map. "What about the banditry on the Long River Road?" She swept her hand over the curved line that represented Long River.

"I spent a lot of time looking for a pattern. Why were the raids happening? Why were they getting closer to our encampment in the north?"

He sounded a little proud of himself. She wondered what he'd found.

"There was just too much going on. The unrest with the raiders questing Eisenvard stragglers, normal criminals, it was all getting mixed together. I had to simplify it. So, I had my apprentices go through the reports and remove those that didn't have anything to do with the Order or its members. Then once they'd narrowed it down, I had them sort the reports based on who was involved. And this is what we found."

He removed a pinch of blue sand from another bag and sprinkled it on the map. A new set of locations, notes, and times emerged. She bent over to read the new information, then grew cold.

"They are tracking Miller? Why didn't you tell me?"

"I'm telling you now. The obvious bad news is that the Taken have discovered who invented our ability to detect and defeat them."

"The good news? We need to get him back, now."

"The good news is that I am getting word of raiders, bandits, and a variety of other ill-reputed sorts heading toward Miller's location. The enemy sees an opportunity to end our troublesome apprentice."

"Enough of the tricky plots, all right? You need to bring him back."

"What's one more apprentice to the Order, eh? But there is one problem with your plan. Miller is probably the closest to finding a cure to this next wave of infected. These new Takers are different than the first ones. We will need a sharp, dedicated mind to solve it. Miller will find all the tools he needs at the temple, plus a few helping hands."

"Don't worry. I agree that Miller has too much talent to be used as bait. I sent some support to help out if he got into any trouble."

"Support?" A shiver began to run up her spine. This wasn't going to be good.

He sprinkled sand from the final bag. Five images of dogs emerged on the map. Each appeared as a ferocious mastiff attacking its prey. "I've sent dogs to each of these areas. If Miller is threatened by a force large enough to seize him, they will help, and then call me forward."

"You will take the field? That seems risky."

"I need to do it. Not only is Miller a very useful apprentice, but he nears his final test. His Master's ring is close, and you know how much we need more Masters."

The enemy grew bolder. They invaded through the cracks in the world. Easter was right again, but Miller? She doubted that he could be hard enough, or cruel enough, to take his Master's ring. She remembered the terror when she gained her ring. She knew that Miller wasn't ready. The ring would consume him. She hadn't done a good job making him hard, making him a Master. Instead, she had made him into a friend. That simple kindness might cost him his life.

She looked down at her own ring. The simple black band lay

on her middle finger. It smelled of disruption, broken worlds, and fear. It came from a place outside of this reality, and she never wanted to return there. But she had to, didn't she? That's where the war was fought.

She noticed Easter staring at her, concern showing in his eyes. She looked at his ring, much older, imbued with powers beyond even her understanding. He was right, if they didn't have more Masters, none of this would matter. She knew that everything would pass away if they lost, everything.

"The dogs will be helpful. They can clear paths, and they will find him quickly. But they won't be enough to ensure his survival."

She raised her eyebrows in surprise. That was a lot of raw power. These were not just any dogs. These were Easter's dogs. He'd spent years training, enchanting, and honing these beasts. Why would he send them out? To simply screen and protect Miller? She was thankful, but it seemed like it too much muscle for the job. What was Easter up to? Memories of the beasts attacking villages came flooding back. Visions of an armored man being torn apart awoke in her memory.

Why would he send just dogs? It didn't make sense to her.

The truth struck her. A familiar cold streak ran from her neck down her back. When Easter was involved, look behind every plan to find the secret plan, then look behind that one, too.

"Who did you send along? Dogs won't be enough to guard him closely. They will be too far away. What are you planning?"

He waved her concern aside. "Yes, yes. You have discovered my plan. Point to you, my dear. I sent someone to follow along earlier, just in case this occurred. Don't worry, he'd be strong enough to handle a few dozen bowmen, or rabble, even without the dogs."

She didn't want to ask what his plan really was, but the cold chill in the pit of her stomach would not be denied. Her voice grew cold. "You need to tell me. Tell me while you look me in the eyes."

OBLIVION

He stopped moving, then placed his hands on his lap. His dark eyes stared back at her, so full of secrets. He was always confident, but now she had something important she could lose. She was afraid of losing anything more. She had lost so much, so many people. Very soon, it would break her heart. She knew the grief would kill her.

"Shall we play this game? Really? You know who I sent. I needed to solve two problems, and young Miller provided an excellent opportunity to do so."

Her words came out slowly. "You sent December?"

"Yes. It was logical."

"You sent December?" She repeated, her voice rising to an angry shout. "You sent the cold-hearted lunatic that has killed more of our own apprentices in the last three years than all of our enemies combined! To guard Miller? My Miller!"

Easter smiled back calmly. "What are you so angry about? Didn't you have an informal agreement with Master December? You and he are so close lately. I never imagined this would distress you."

There it was. Her alliance with December had been a thing of necessity. It gave her temporary protection from the worst of the other Masters. But it might have separated her from the rest of the cabal. December had never been popular. Unless he was needed, then he suddenly gained in popularity. She hoped his stain hadn't rubbed off on her.

"December should be preparing for the inquest. Everything is at stake for him. If the Conclave rules against him. We could lose him."

"That is precisely why Master December needed to be busy, and somewhere else. He isn't very good at being idle. We don't need any more incidents, and the other cabals could see this as an opportunity to settle old grudges, to weaken us. December also needs to do something useful for the Order. He needs to demonstrate why he continues to be valuable."

She turned and began pacing. Her steps emerged quick, and angry. Her heels struck the wooden floor with angry force.

She kept her voice calm. "So, let me understand: You sent a Master who is so hated in the Order that he is at risk of final oblivion? They want to take him and hang him outside of the skin of the world. They want the invaders to eat what is left of his mind. Even the High Masters consider his murder of apprentices to be too offensive for the Order. And you paired him up with the person who discovered how to stop the Takers last time? Forgive me, and please remember that I hold you in the highest esteem, but this sounds like you are trying to kill him."

He shook his head, denying the charges. "I think you underestimate how much Master December values your alliance. You are the only one of any cabal, including our own, who would publicly ally with him. He knows your apprentice and has spent time with him. I believe that Master December needs an opportunity to show his good will and show others that he doesn't mindlessly kill every apprentice he meets. Surely you can give him that?"

"My temple days are over. I don't need to give anyone an opportunity to cut my throat."

"What is it the goddess is so fond of saying? 'Reach a hand to those in need, and do not ask for a price.' Your apprentice was in need. I sent him help. Our brother is in need, I sent him on a journey to find his way. I think we both need to have a little faith."

Aileen paused, deflating. She wondered why the words of the goddess continued to speak to her heart. She had long since allied with the White Hand. It was too late to turn back. But maybe it wasn't Phyllicitus speaking to her heart. Maybe it was her heart crying out to Phyllicitus. But it was too late now. She turned toward her wine cup. It was empty. She walked back to the table and picked up a bottle, then poured a generous measure into her cup. It was a dark wine. It's rich peppery aroma drifted upward as she poured. Aileen lifted the cup and took in a deep breath of its rich aroma. She paused to enjoy the sensation.

Just a moment of sanity, that's all she asked. She had been doing this long enough. She knew better. There was another piece to this puzzle that she needed to find. Easter might give her clues, but he would never take her by the hand and lead her to those puzzle pieces. Sometimes, it was about the fun of the game for him.

She paused again, then took her first sip.

Easter walked over and picked up the bottle, then refilled his own glass with a meager portion.

"The wine. Isn't it from the south? Amorsi, isn't it? How did you get it this far north? I didn't see any of it in our baggage."

"Oh, I know some people. They picked up a bottle from the vintner's market when they had an opportunity, then sent it my way. Sometimes the extravagances are worth the bother, don't you agree?"

Then the last puzzle piece fit. She saw how Easter was maneuvering her, and Miller. She saw it all, the entire scheme. Miller was moving unprotected in the land. The new Takers had grown in power, and now had hidden forces on the move. The Order had beaten them once, and the Takers hesitated to show themselves.

The Order needed them delivered somewhere out in the open, away from the commoners. The Order needed to kill them, but first they needed to find them. Miller was known, and "only" an apprentice. If the taken discover him unprotected by the Order, they'd be sorely tempted to kill him. Or perhaps try to take him and gain his conversion. Easter hadn't sent the dogs to protect Miller. He'd sent them to prevent the taken from escaping. Miller would draw them out, exposing them to attack.

If December could prepare, there wouldn't be much left of the Taken. He would burn them, and everyone around them, into ash. December wouldn't hesitate, he'd simply destroy everything in his path.

She looked up from her wine. Easter stared across the table, aware of her sudden revelation. She couldn't help admiring such a beautiful plan. If it worked, the Order would reveal how the Takers had grown in the past few years. If it didn't, then she'd lose someone she valued, and Easter would be untouched. She met his eyes. Even as her heart ached within her chest, she nodded in understanding.

"Why didn't you just tell me? Why this whole wine thing?"

"I didn't need you to know the information. I needed you to understand it."

He reached out and set his hand on her shoulder. "I would never risk what is yours, if our need wasn't so dire. You know that, don't you?"

She placed her empty hand over his. With a simple nod of acceptance, she stepped back, breaking their connection. "I think I need to see a few people. If you will pardon me, I must depart." She set the wine glass down, then walked out as Easter was trying to form words. She needed allies that could travel quickly. She thought about the problem a moment longer: Easter was thinking about this in the wrong way. The enemy had already fought The White Hand once. They had learned lessons and most probably changed tactics. This time wouldn't be so easy.

Now she knew the plan. Easter had told her, but in his normal wheels-within-wheels manner. Easter's plan was good, but it didn't factor in what they didn't know.

"I want you to be careful. Miller is valuable to me. I have plans for him. I don't want to lose him."

She knew she needed help. She needed someone Easter couldn't control. After a moment's thought, she thought of that person.

THE FORTRESS

Miller pulled the weathered tower door open. The action was smooth, as if it had been freshly oiled. Was someone expecting company? Dust hung in the air. Beams of light crossed randomly through the room. Dozens of mirror shards stood arrayed against the wall, along with wooden furniture, and roof beams. Each shard was hung by a single string, forming a mosaic of broken mirrors and shifting light.

But he didn't see the any windows. There wasn't a light source to be seen, other than the narrow beams. Confused, he put his hands out, trying to touch one of those beams of light.

The mare snorted loudly, then began to back away. Miller reached back to stroke her mane, pulling his hand away from the appealing light shaft. "It's fine. I know. Something is wrong here. You don't have to come." Now that he wasn't looking directly at the lights, he could think clearly. Touching that light would have been a grave mistake.

He looked up at Chamise; she was holding up well. The fear was in her eyes, but her body sat calmly without a tremor. "It looks like December left us a little puzzle."

"A puzzle? Is this a good time for puzzles?"

He sighed wearily. "For Masters, it is always a good time for puzzles."

Chamise slowly dismounted, placing each foot on the ground, then walking a few steps. She moved unsteadily, but she moved. Miller reached over and pulled his saddle pouch from its place and then removed the arrowhead within. He didn't want to leave it for anyone else to find. He retrieved the case with the healing potions.

Finally, he pushed the mare back. "Go find safety. Come get us when this is done."

The horses turned and walked away, keeping clear of the walking corpses.

Chamise peered into the room. "The light, the mirrors are sending it, and reflecting it at the same time. What is this even for? It looks wonderful, but why?"

"It's definitely a trap. If you guessed at the worst possible ending that you could ever experience, you might be close. Welcome to December-land."

"But it's just light. It's actually kind of peaceful, almost artistic."

Chamise reached out into the room. Her hand moved toward a beam as she stumbled forward. Miller reached out and gently held her shoulder. "That would be a mistake. The first idea is always the one that usually gets you killed."

She looked back at him. "How about smashing the mirrors?"

Spoken like an Eisenvard. "Let's assume that the mirrors are placed here for a reason, and then try to figure out what it might be."

"I don't like puzzles." She growled back.

"Believe me, I don't either. I've done a lot of them."

"So how do we solve it? Is there a key?"

Miller stared at the mirror puzzle for a full minute. His vision traced how the light beams traveled between the dozens of mirrors. Each beam was a potential trap, and a lethal one at that. He grew frustrated. Why did December have to do things like this?

Chamise made the first comment. "We could almost slip between them. I think I could do it without armor, and without the wound." She pointed at three areas where the beams were farther apart from each other. "Once we got through, we would be trapped in another tangle of beams, though."

"First principles." Miller spoke out loud while still exploring the idea in his head. "This riddle is about first principles. Look at the mirrors. Each one is positioned at exactly the right place to send the light to the next mirror. The light shines between them even though its source is gone. The mirrors are perfect reflectors, but they don't create light. They only reflect it. Reflection is their nature, their fate. Every potential of a mirror exists to reflect the light. If one light beam breaks, then the potential is destabilized."

"Destabilized? What are you talking about?"

Now was not the best time for her enchantment lesson. He explained quickly, skipping some of the details. "Channels can be connected to potentials. If a potential is fulfilled, or denied, then channels can be activated. This entire thing could be the prettiest death curse you could ever see." Miller could see that she was only understanding some of his explanation, and not the important parts. "I will explain more when we get some time."

"That enchanting craft of yours, well, remember our deal. I want some."

"Sure, but let me solve this puzzle first, eh? These sorts of puzzles never have a direct solution. The answer is usually, no, always something outside of its construction. Who would put the key in the lock?"

"What is outside of light beams? Dark beams?"

"I think you are being too literal. Give me a minute."

"I don't think I have minutes. I'm starting to get dizzy. We had better get through this soon, unless you can spare a vial of Phyllicitus' draft for me?" Miller nodded then pulled out the case. He opened its shell and pulled out a single vial, placing it into Chamise's hand.

She stood there, momentarily surprised.

"Use it when you need it. You will have about ten heartbeats before you fall asleep. It would probably be a good idea to lie down first."

She stared at it for a long moment before she looked up, giving him a simple nod. She pulled the vial toward her chest, waiting for the right moment.

He returned his gaze to the light. Dozens of mirrors sent beams of light toward each other. None of the beams crossed. Some mirrors were close together. Some mirrors were placed on opposite sides of the room. The room was designed to hold at least two horses, and probably a half dozen guards. Another door stood closed on the opposite side of the room. The path to the other door was defended by a labyrinth of light beams. He thought of the First Principles. Looking harder, he tried to find what wasn't there. What did he expect to find, yet was missing?

He looked across the floor, hoping to see something to climb on, perhaps to climb over a beam or two. Furniture, old opened barrels and splintered crates decorated the floor. A small pathway wound snakelike through the room, wrapping between obstacles almost randomly until it arrived at the door. The light beams appeared to cross over the path in more than ten places. Miller stared again, following the path, until he saw it.

"I think I found a way through. The crooked path. Leave it to December, it's the crooked path. There is a way to move through that only intersects three of the beams, and the intersection points have a nice gap between them."

Chamise nodded, but her hands were beginning to tremble. Her face had turned sickly pale in the last few minutes.

Miller pulled out his satchel and retrieved the mirror from it.

He looked at the gaps between the beams, then at the dozen mirrors that did not have light shining from them. When finished, he walked up behind Chamise and reached his hand around her waist. The blood had already begun to dry on her dress. There was a lot of it. He pulled her body tight. "Stay close. I think I've got a way through. Just don't leave the trail."

"Trail?"

Miller began slowly walking forward, then turned onto the crooked path. It didn't look like a path, merely like a section of floor that was randomly less obstructed than the others. He urged Chamise on calmly, like he was trying to charm a wild horse. Chamise had discipline, though, and she kept to the path. They passed between clusters of light beams, each holding a potentially deadly secret in its glow.

They moved around a narrow turn. A light beam stood before them, blocking the path. Miller slowly reached out with his mirror until it cut into the beam, reflecting it onto one of the unused mirrors. From there, it reflected to another, and then another, until the light had completed its path and the entire structure stood whole.

"That was tricky. You've got good eyes."

"Let's not get confident yet. Two more to go."

They continued the dance down the makeshift path. They squeezed together tightly to avoid an upended table and a knot of light beams that imprisoned it. They continued their slow pace until another light beam cut across their path.

He stood there concentrating on the light beams. "I think we have a problem. My original plan didn't have the new light pattern right. Now I've got to come up with another solution."

"How about there?" Chamise gestured at a polished glass that stood alone on a small bookshelf. It looked clean, yet worn. It wasn't something that would be common in a tower like this. He guessed that it was not from here. Instead, it was December's next riddle.

"Now you have the good eyes. That's going to work."

Miller spotted one of the random mirror shards to use, then

used his hand mirror to redirect the beam toward the glass, and then to the shard. The way opened for them, and they continued down the twisted way. They approached the door, its black surface worn, and oddly welcoming . . . it might lead to safety but might simply be set up to look that way. The way through the light beams shrank to its narrowest yet. The dust had become thick, lending a sour smell to the air.

Chamise began to cough. Her body trembled as she fought to control it. "I can't breathe," she sputtered between spasms. Miller felt the discomfort then, and knew that soon he would be as bad off as she was.

Miller watched her waver, her chest wracked with coughs. It seemed like she was going to leave the path. The stupid coughs might just kill them both.

There was no time. Miller thrust the mirror out, reflecting the last beam, hoping that whatever mirror it struck, it would be enough to get them out. He steered Chamise by grabbing her armor and forcing her forward, keeping her on the path by raw physical force. "Get through the door!"

She fumbled with a brass latch, then raised it. The door opened, and she stumbled through without looking back, coughing and spasming as she went.

Then Miller began to cough. The mirror was unsteady, it diverted into an unsteady mess. Thinking time was over, now it was time for running, he sprinted into the open door, slamming it behind him. He stumbled and fell on the floor. He looked at Chamise. Her chin and throat were covered in her own blood. She had been bleeding through the mouth. Miller hadn't noticed when that had that started. He looked closer. Her skin was pale. Her face was covered in sweat. He didn't understand how she could even be walking. She was getting closer to the Crooked Gate with every step.

"It's all right. Drink the vial. We're in. It's safe. Drink it."

She struggled with bringing the vial to her lips. She pulled the seal off with her teeth and greedily lapped up the lifesaving fluid. Her breathing soon relaxed, and she went in search of

dreams.
    But they weren't safe.

38

BEING PREPARED

The sound of clapping filled the room. It was slow and unenthusiastic. Miller looked up toward it. Master December stood to the right of them at the foot of a wooden staircase. His wide smirk greeted Miller like a long-lost enemy.

"Oh, well done, well done, dear boy. I'm so glad you've finally joined me in my little vacation home."

"How? What? Why didn't you open the way?"

December stood at the bottom of the narrow wooden stairwell, smirking as if he owned the day. December looked tired, like he had been channeling a lot in the past few days. Miller calculated the amount of magic that would be required to build the corpse army, build the mirror defense, and predict when he and Chamise would emerge from the town. It was impressive under any circumstances.

"How did you know?"

"I guessed how this would go when I discovered the raiders were in the town. This town has been completely infected by the new Takers. All the villagers need to be cleansed. I would have done it myself, but I thought I'd leave that task to you. Think of it as a learning experience."

"That isn't going to happen. We can find a way to save them. I've done it before on the old Takers. I have to believe we can do it again."

December shook his head and sighed in resignation. "You mistake my intent." He turned and began walking up the stairs. "Follow me, I have something to show you. Leave the Free Mage, she will need to be rested soon enough."

Chamise had already curled up on the floor. She groggily waved Miller forward. The healing draft was taking effect. Miller turned and followed December up three flights of stairs before he caught up with him. He stood on the edge of large square room in front of a narrow window, looking down at the fields.

"There they are. You've brought the whole village here."

The line of villagers and riders had arrived at the tower. Skirmishes had begun between the walking corpses and the host of locals. Their arrows did no good against the dead, and they'd been forced to enter into a melee. Miller looked on with an odd detachment, analyzing the small battle and looking at how the villagers and raiders worked together almost seamlessly.

"They must have been practicing together for a while. They look fairly disciplined."

"Indeed," December replied, "but how could this be? We would have detected such a thing."

Miller looked at the battle with new interest. How could they hide an armed force this size? Villagers could not simply disappear for weeks or months at a time. Raiders would have been tracked by the White Hand if they'd gathered in great numbers, arming, drilling. Now more than two hundred villagers and armed raiders had gathered and joined battle immediately below him.

The risen corpses seemed immune from the variety of

makeshift weapons that the villagers brought with them. Wood cutter axes crushed bones, but the dead did not feel pain. Spears impaled vital organs that had not been used for years. There were a hundred villagers engaged with less than fifty of December's army, yet the dead were holding them at bay.

"It's the Takers. They are coordinating all of it," December said after a few minutes watching the battle. "Normal villagers always flee from the dead. They are smart enough not to try fighting them. Running is the best option for them and they always take it. Even if they won, the villagers would pay a terrible price. By the time they get to the gates, I will have recovered enough power to counter attack. It doesn't make sense. Humans would never try it, but the Taken are no longer thinking like a human."

"Are you going to butcher the entire village?"

"Don't be a fool. That village died months ago, these are just the Taken who have moved in. I can't save those poor people, and neither can you. They're already gone."

They continued to watch the battle from the tower. The villagers had lost a dozen people, while only three of the dead had fallen, dismembered.

Miller saw motion on the hill. A group, perhaps fifty strong, had crested the hill. "More Taken." He pointed.

December peered up to the top of the hill. "That's unexpected. They look like raiders and militia mixed together. Do you see the ones in brown robes, though? Who are they?"

A group of mounted bowmen had begun lining up on the hill, preparing to descend into the battle. Their bows had been stored, and swords, axes, and short spears had emerged. A small group of four people wore robes the dark color of brown earth and dried blood. They gathered in the back of the line and spoke among themselves.

Miller looked at them critically. They covered themselves in robes, but each one of them stood a head taller than the rest of the raiders. "I think they are foreigners. They don't dress the same. They don't even have the same height. Northerners perhaps? Do you think the Jarl has joined with the Takers?"

He continued to gaze at the invaders. Something seemed familiar about one of them. With a start, Miller recognized her.

"I know one of them: Brita. She was a serving girl in Clockshire. She has lived there her entire life. Why is she here?"

"She's been taken. Strengthen your heart, boy. It's too late for her."

"No, it can't be like that. There has to be a way."

December ignored Miller. His lips moved in silent chanting as he moved the channels to his will. He turned toward Miller after a few moments. "Not Northerners. Crafters of some sort, though. My powers are weak thanks to my little project." He gestured toward the dead engaged in the battle. "What do your senses tell you? Are they summoning?"

Miller cleared his mind, focusing on the exercises that Mistress Aileen had taught him. He opened his mage sight to the channels, following the streams of essence toward the group of four casters. They were building something large. A tangled knot of channeled power floated about the group, it's whip-like tendrils stretched out to form a circle around the tower, the village, the battle, and everything within.

"I think they are casting some sort of—"

Abruptly, Miller's mage sight deserted him. In one second, he viewed the world as a composite of reality and the flowing streams of magic. The next second, he could not see any magics, or even feel them.

"That wasn't good."

December's was the worst understatement Miller had ever heard. "They have sealed us off from the channels. I can't touch essence or fates."

December pulled him back from the window. "We need to go, now."

"Chamise can't go anywhere," Miller replied in cold realization. The dire truth dawned on him: Someone was going to die in that tower today.

December looked Miller in the face and lied, "Don't worry

about her. They don't want her, they want us."

"I'm not leaving her. Even if I wanted to, where would I go? And we can't let them take a Free Mage. Can you imagine if she went back to Ingalls to collect more of them?"

The dead continued their fight, but the line of mounted raiders had reached them at a full charge. Horses screamed below. The dead clawed and struck. Tons of horse flesh made a difference and the dead were trampled down, then set on. The villagers and raiders tore into them with hand weapons. The villagers had begun dismembering the dead, flinging their separated limbs into the fields.

He watched as the ground collapsed. Then he saw new risen dead begin to crawl from their buried hiding places.

"Didn't see that coming."

"Good. Hopefully they didn't either."

December left the room. He went back down the stairs and returned to the earlier room's entrance. A thick oak door stood alone, trying to keep out any invaders. Its strong locking bar was unfastened though, leaving the way clear for December to open the door, December moved through. and returning to the next floor where his trap lay. December moved nervously as if at any moment the floor would erupt with the Taken or the very curses he had left for them. Miller followed. He didn't want to deal with the traps.. Pausing to check on Chamise, he listened to the screams from outside. "The trap is still functioning. It should slow them down. We might have some time."

"Might?" December didn't sound convinced.

Miller inspected Chamise's wound. It had begun to heal but not quickly enough to be useful. She could be moved. He picked her up by the shoulders gently pulling her from the room. She was a mass of muscle, armor, weapons and gear. Miller struggled before he gave up. Releasing a thread of essence, he channeled world forces to lighten her body. He stopped struggling and easily carried her back up the stairs leaving the trapped room behind.

December walked his pattern within the cluttered room,

pouring more spirit into his trap. He tied the small mirrors together with channels of essence, and set fate barriers in hidden places between stacks of crates. When he finished, he stepped back into the room, shut the door, and pulled down a crossbar to hold it tight. December returned to the upper room rejoining Miller and Chamise. He closed the heavy door, blocking the entrance to the upper room. He had always expected a blood bath and it looked like he would get one.

A NECROMANCER'S APPRENTICE

Weapons had begun to batter on the door below. The villagers had won past December's risen dead.

"This isn't going to work," December muttered. He sounded tired, spent. He waited a moment until he uttered his next words. "We can't let them take us. We can't let them turn you."

Miller decided that if December was going to murder him after all this, there was no use being polite to him.

Miller shot back in anger, "Yes, and if you could please give us an army to fight back with, I would appreciate it."

Chamise returned to consciousness and pulled back, surprising Miller, grasping her side as if anticipating the end to come. The final black door was close. He could feel it. He didn't want Chamise or himself to go through.

"Yes, an army! Why didn't I think of that?"

"What? Do you have one?"

"No, but I have a cabal."

"One problem, they aren't here. We can't even channel to them. How will they know to come?"

The sounds of battering small weapons paused, then a large boom emerged from below. Miller could hear the cracking of timbers, and the fall of stone. The raiders had gained the entrance and entered. A few seconds later, the screams began

December smirked, then pulled Miller away from Chamise, leading him to the center of the room. He kicked an old broken chair and bucket out of the way before he gently pushed Miller toward the floor. "Sit, be comfortable. I have a task for you."

Chamise looked desperately across the room. Her eyes were lost in a fog of sleep, but she kept trying to fight the potion.

"What am I supposed to do?" Miller asked. "It's the end."

"There are other magics than the channels we teach apprentices." December took out a small leather wrap and began unrolling it. It contained a long white cloth similar to Miller's own, and three blue stones, whose edges were rounded as if they had lain within a river for a millennium.

"I have something I need you to do." December edged close to Miller. He reached out with his left hand and held Miller's shoulder reassuringly.

The white cloth bunched up between them. It was thick, bright-white, unstained cotton. Miller didn't know what the cloth was for, but it was probably bad. He didn't trust this situation at all.

"Don't worry about that. Tell me about Aileen. How do you feel about her?"

"I'm sorry? We are getting ready to get butchered and you want to talk about my Mistress?"

"Can you reach out to her? Does your link still work?"

"I have no channels. How can it work? I'm blocked."

Victory cheers came from below, then pounding began on the inner door.

"I said that I have different magics, close your eyes and try. We can't let the Takers have anyone in the Order. They would gain more than a follower; they would gain our secrets."

Miller nodded and assumed his meditation position. He tried to imagine Mistress Aileen with her blonde hair and black flowing dress. The channels didn't open. His spirit voice was silent.

"I can't."

Then the pain struck. Miller's chest erupted in agony. He fell backward onto the floor as he opened his eyes. Master December knelt beside him, his right hand holding the handle of a thin knife. The same knife he always kept concealed within his sleeve. The blade was buried deep between Miller's ribs. The knife felt cold as it jutted into his chest, just missing his heart.

He felt the final door, its cool breeze caressing him, moving through the flows, through his magical senses. It opened through the Crooked Gate, the place where discarded souls roamed.

December had killed him.

Miller coughed a spray of blood into the air, it rained back down onto his face. His eyes grew wide as his death rattles began. He kicked out randomly, no longer in control of his own body. He felt his bowels loosen and his hands bury his fingernails into his own palms. He tried to speak but it came out a gurgle. December leaned down and spoke into his ear. His quiet voice was comforting, caring, and gave him the feeling that he was not alone in these final moments.

He could see what December was preparing for. He was going to bring Miller back! He would be another walking corpse. He tried to think, to determine how he could foil that plan. He had no channels, no force. He felt himself slipping toward the Crooked Gate, nearing that final place.

December's words were soft but drew his attention as if they were his single reason for existence. Miller didn't understand what December wanted. He was sinking slowly, then falling rapidly. He glanced at Chamise, who had awoken and was staring in shock and horror at his dying form.

Finally, blood covered and betrayed, Miller journeyed through the final door.

CRACKES IN THE WORLD

The darkness was odd, it played across his vision like different shades of dark purple. He wondered if his eyes were even open.

There was no direct light source. Dim, ambient light gave soft outlines to unrecognizable shapes. He stopped and tried to focus until he began to recognize them.

It was like the world had been soaked in a wine stain and smudged with shadows. Broad-leafed plants sprung from a wall that stood an arm's length away. There was no breeze, yet the leaves swung lazily in random directions.

This wasn't what the tomes from the White Hand libraries had described. He paused to take it in. The final door was a black tunnel, surrounded by brown misshapen rock, the kind of rocks that old rivers would carve into strange shapes. This looked more like a tunnel than a gate or a door. He supposed the brown rock could be a Crooked Gate. That explained why the two terms were used almost as the same thing. His analytic mind wanted to know what separated the twisted gate from the final black door. Why were they different?

He didn't have time to think much about it. A moment later, he felt something slam into his head. He flipped backward, the room going dark, spinning. It took a few heartbeats to recover. When he did, he found himself somewhere else new, and almost lightless.

He felt the ground. It was solid beneath his grasp, but then it yielded like a thick dough. He let his hand rest until the texture changed again into an oozing cold slime that enveloped his hand. He pulled his hand up quickly, then stood. The ground held his weight. He had no idea what was happening. He didn't even understand what he was standing on. It was solid, yet pliable, like some kind of wax, if the wax were made of sponge.

His vision was limited to a short distance. He saw the wall. It was close enough to touch. On the other side, he could barely see the faint glow that ran along the edges of the leaves five paces away.

He walked to the other wall and held his hand out. The leaves moved slowly out of the way by their own power, dodging his touch. Other leaves seemed tolerant of it, so Miller reached out to stroke one along the broad surface. It was smooth, but not like a plant, more like a cold pelt of hair. After a few seconds, his hand began to tingle, so he pulled it back.

That was enough of a warning for him. He wasn't going to pet the plants. This place was strange enough without playing with the native forces.

He spent another minute gazing at the shadows and waiting in vain for his eyesight to adjust. He decided to examine himself as well. His hands traveled to where December's long, thin dagger had stabbed into his chest. There was no wound. He explored for a cut in the fabric of his shirt; its tough leather exterior was unharmed.

He noticed the shirt was his workhouse shirt. He normally

used this when he was working at the smelter, or the forge, or doing anything that would ruin his normal clothes. He paused, wondering how the shirt had gotten here, and on his torso at the same time. He hadn't brought it with him. It should still be back at the cabin. He couldn't help but wonder what kind of death this was. Was his eternal reward a favorite shirt? It seemed kind of a weak afterlife.

He continued the inventory. His knife was missing, as well as his short sword. His money pouch was gone. The contents of his pack were nowhere to be found. The only item he kept besides his favorite clothes was the arrowhead with the maze carved onto its broad surface.

But the arrowhead had changed—it had become more solid. It weighed more in his hand now, and it tingled as he touched it with his fingers. He could feel the arrowhead trying to attune itself to him, but failing. He could not feel any spirit energy within himself.

Miller could not sense any spirit within the arrow head either. That absence caused confusion. He wondered how it was possible that the mage-arrow could contain flows of magic one moment, then be empty the next. Were the rules of magic completely different here?

That was probably a good thing given where he was.

His spirit channel was missing. He reached out with his spirit, trying to move the forces through those channels. All he found was pain. His head instantly began to ache like he had been struck with a club.

And why not? He should be bleeding out of his nose and fighting off the mage sickness right now. Here he was without a spirit channel, unharmed and unaffected.

It violated first principles.

"Am I in the lands of the dead? What if things don't work the same here?" Miller spoke out to the empty space, not expecting an answer, but comforted by the sound of his own voice in any case.

The gravity of his situation began to fade as his curiosity

awakened. As an experiment, he reached out to the magical channels, expecting to find some minor trace. He found nothing. There were no channels; there was no magic. He had no spirit. Yet the arrowhead felt heavy with spirit before he came to this place.

He moved a safe distance between the walls, ensuring that none of the plants growing there could reach him. He sat between the walls, resting, seeking his center. Then he entered the meditative state.

The familiar sense of quiet didn't gently descend. Instead, his vision erupted with colors and details. He could now see twice as far as he could when the world was shrouded in purple shades. The plants, ground, and roof above emanated their own internal light. He could see now, but it hurt his eyes. It was like walking out of a dark building into the full summer light. He held the mental state, but his eyes did not adjust to the pain, they just kept hurting. He finally surrendered to the pain and returned to the comfort of the darkness.

"All right, nothing is normal. I guess that sounds right, given that I'm dead and all."

A feeling began to grow within. He was missing something, something important. He tried to remember what December had said. He talked about a different kind of magic. Was this what he meant?

If his mental state could control what he saw, then the rules of reality had changed. The magical channels were gone. There would be no spirit to channel, anyway. What would this mean to the First Principles?

He began casting. He started with the most basic cantrips and minor glyphs he'd learned in his youth. He remembered Mistress Sword teaching him these. She had acted like they were the greatest treasure the world had ever seen. Now he moved through the casting as if they were mere rote exercises. He noticed that magic had become normal. He wondered if it was the magic, or if it was himself, finally arriving at a place where he could see what was always there before, hidden away.

Miller remembered the excitement and joy from years ago. He loved discovering new magic. He loved mastering the arcane skills. He loved it all—except Mistress Sword. He remembered how she had toyed with him. She promised him power and everlasting life, and in the next breath she promised him a burning death.

Sword had made him feel valued one second and despised the next. It all ended that one evening, though, when she asked him to her bed. For days before, she had been kind, oh so kind. It was such a lie. He thought about how foolish he had behaved, believing her. Miller spent a few moments remembering when Sword confessed her love for him and pulled him into her room. He had felt special, lucky, blessed. That all died when he walked into the room. Sword loved many men, and they were all in that room, waiting for him.

His mind was full of questions. Where did that memory come from? Miller shook his head to clear it. The memory blocks had gone from him as well. Aileen had put them here so long ago. The pain didn't attack him like it used to, though. He could feel the pain, all of it, but it was a ghost of what it has been before.

Miller finished his casting. None of the First Principles' charms had worked. But the memories that had come to assault him gave him a clue. Again, he asked himself unanswerable questions. What if this world of death lies outside of a place spells can inhabit? But something else is here. What is it? The arrowhead continues to have its power, but nothing else. Had the arrowhead been forged here? Was its odd maze of lines his clue to understanding this death world? Is this a death world?

Questions began to crowd into his mind. He was contemplating an idea when he heard the leaves move. Something had brushed against the leaves farther down the passageway. Miller was not alone in this new place.

A sharp hiss erupted from beyond his sight. A chill ran up his spine as he imagined what could be there. The hiss was followed by a rasping cough. It sounded like a huge cat coughing up a hair ball, if the hair was still connected to someone's head.

Miller scrambled up. He prepared to enter into his meditation state but only achieved partial success. He had calmed his heartbeats and could see more details, along with muted colors. Part of his mind kept screaming at him, RUN! RUN! He could not run. His curiosity, mixed with his reduced sense of fear, held him in place. He grasped the arrowhead tightly, more as a charm than a weapon.

The thing came into view. It walked on four legs, like a waist-high cat. The head was unlike anything he had ever seen before. Two fist-sized eyes jutted out from each side of its head. It did not appear to have a nose. A wide mouth hung open, hinged from a jawbone that started somewhere in its serpentine neck. And teeth. There are a lot of teeth.

It stopped and stared at Miller.

It could see in the dark just fine.

The thought had barely finished when it leaped. Its sharp scream filled the hall. The dark leaves shrank back away from it, toward their walls. Its mouth opened to expose a maw as large as his forearm. Dozens of teeth decorated the edge of the jaw, and small tendrils danced within its mouth. Each tooth was as long as one of his fingers.

Miller did not flee. His thoughts were controlled, disciplined, well-ordered. The beast was terrifying. It was going to rip him to pieces, yet he was mysteriously unfazed. He stood his ground, holding only the arrowhead.

The monster struck him. He immediately lost his balance as it struck, driving him onto the ground. The ground began to soften, becoming like it had earlier, losing firmness second by second. The nightmare thing ripped its claws into his chest. Pain rippled through his body. Miller brought the arrowhead down, aiming the weapon toward the tooth-coated jaw trying to eat his head.

He grabbed its neck with his right hand but could not get his hand fully around it. It felt like tough leather; it smelled like a sewage pit. It continued to rip its claws across his leather coated torso and began flailing, trying to free its head and continue its mayhem.

He brought up his free hand and jammed the arrowhead into its eye. The eyeball burst and sprayed liquid across his face. Its rage-filled scream was deafening. It pulled away from him. It wasn't steady. It lurched clumsily as it tried to escape.

His channeling senses snapped alert. Something channeled nearby, he could feel the flows. He could feel the remnants of a channeling, but there had been no channeling. It lasted less than two heartbeats, but Miller recognized it. It was fate-crafting. It felt like he had stepped into a pool of cold oil. Fate-crafting was the strangest of magics, it manipulated people's future, or futures. He didn't pretend to understand it, and he had never met anyone who had mastered it. It was unreliable. He didn't know why it should be here of all places.

The thing continued its retreat. Two of its limbs had stopped working, and it used the rear limbs to push itself away. Its screams became weaker, then pathetic as it tried to escape deeper into the passage. He hadn't even hit a limb. It was definitely in pain, though.

The thing crawled slowly away, trying to turn a corner. It moved more slowly, now trying to crawl away on its belly.

He stood and checked his own wounds. His clothing was torn, but the sturdy shop wear had done an acceptable job of protecting him. He had dozens of shallow scars across his chest and shoulders that hadn't penetrated deeply.

Again, curiosity overcame his fear. He walked forward to stand three paces from the miserable beast. The thing was clearly dying. Miller didn't know if things could here, beyond the Crooked Gate. The rules of reality seemed different in this place. In truth, he could be dead and he wouldn't know. Perhaps this was what the world of death really was.

Finally, the thing stopped its attempt to escape. It simply lay down and whimpered. An odd, maze-like design appeared on its body as it began gurgling out of its mouth. He was growing impatient with its death throws. He just wanted the thing to leave him, passing beyond. But where would it pass beyond to?

He paused a moment until the beast stopped moving. The design faded from its skin, and it moved no more. Miller bent down and retrieved the arrowhead.

Stepping away, he began his own retreat back the way he had come. He continued past where he had arrived in this odd place and explored beyond. He didn't want to know what that thing had been crawling toward.

He tried to keep the slightly improved vision that his light meditation gave him. It escaped him, though, slipping away, leaving dark shadows in its wake. The passageway was thickly walled with leaves. In the near-dark, leaves would occasionally reach out toward him, trying to brush against him.

The hallway widened into a broad, open space. The leaf-covered walls gave way to slate gray slabs of stone that radiated a soft blue glow. The dim light highlighted the cracks that occupied its surface. Small worms hung off the wall, twisting wildly as Miller neared them. Their dance cast chaotic shadows on the floor and ceiling.

Someone stood in the center of the space. He was slightly taller than Miller, and heavier set. He had the build of a smith, or warrior, but he wore clothing fit for a merchant. The man turned toward Miller and spoke. "I've been waiting for you."

Miller's blood froze in his veins. He recognized this man. He'd never expected to find this in the lands of the dead. But why wouldn't he? It made complete sense.

Miller stepped forward in trepidation. "How have you been?"

"Well, I've been better, I must say," Faust replied in the same emotionless, factual tone Miller remembered from long ago, back when Faust was alive.

"I didn't expect you to, uh, meet me." He tried to think of what evil he had done to deserve this. If Faust, the eternal torturer and inquisitor, was his guide through the lands of death, he might have some problems ahead of him.

"Don't get excited. It isn't divine providence. Aileen asked me to get into position in case you came over."

"What? The Mistress knew that December was going to kill me?"

"Ah, I see the confusion. Well, if it makes you feel any better, you are not dead, at least not yet."

"December stabbed me."

"He didn't do a good job of it, then. I've been dead for a long time. Believe me, I know the difference between a dead soul and a live one."

Miller took a moment to think this through. It seemed overwhelming. If Faust was here, then it followed that this should be the land of death. Faust told him it wasn't. He wondered if both of those statements could possibly be true.

"Calm down." Faust interrupted. "Stop panicking. Your breathing is getting out of control."

"Breathing? Why does breathing matter here?"

"If you breathe too hard, and too fast, you might lose consciousness. Then I will need to drag you to the exit place. I don't want to do that. Yes, I'm dead, but I'm also feeling lazy."

"Faust? I don't know what to do with this."

"Don't think too hard, then. I found it easiest when I first arrived. Aileen talked to me before I came to this place and described some of what I would see. Didn't she tell you anything?"

"No. She didn't even tell me that you were still alive."

"That's because I'm not. I'm quite dead. If you look at me, focus on the edges, you will see where the spirit bleeds out. It's an imperfect form, but Aileen needed me to scout the cracks, and this form is what she came up with."

"The cracks? The cracks in the world?"

The things the White Hand Masters were devoted to repair. He had always thought that cracks between the worlds was just some madness dreamt up by the masters. If the Masters had been both right and truthful, then all his ideas about the world would have to change. He didn't know if he was in a place near that tower where December and Chamise were fighting off the taken or stuck in those mythical cracks between the worlds.

    He shook his head. It made no sense and as long as he was in the middle of this situation, he wouldn't be able to tell.

MISSING DETAILS

Faust looked at Miller with an expression of resignation. "They didn't tell you about this?"

"Yes, they told me a lot. Most of it is White Hand speak, you know, stories, lies, and occasional deceit. I never expected the story of these cracks-between-the- worlds would be true. Does that mean the creatures that come through is true? Just the idea of other worlds is mind-bending. How was I supposed to believe something I couldn't even envision, let alone understand? Was I supposed to believe whatever the Masters say, even if it made no sense?"

"Of course. What do you think I am doing here?"

"I have no idea what you're doing here. You got killed, remember? It was three years ago. We buried you in a grave outside of Clockshire. So what are you doing here, back from the dead? Is Aileen playing with necromancy now?"

"There was work to do. Things were coming through. Aileen needed me, and apparently, so do you. Someone needs to do this task."

He said it with the same shrug Miller remembered. Miller remembered how Faust was in life. He could never stop working, and there was never a moment when there were no tasks to do. No breaks, no pleasures, there was only the next task. He had been such an icon in the House of Questions. Too bad that wasn't the best skill to have when Phyllicitus returned. She had no room in her house, or in her heart, for torturers. Torturers like Faust.

"I suggest we talk as we walk. We can depend on visitors that will be inconvenient, if we stay here."

Miller gestured for Faust to take the lead. "So you said there was an exit?"

"Yes, less than an hour's walk down this passageway, then a turn to the right at the Golden Lake."

"Golden Lake?" His curiosity rose.

"Don't get worked up about it. You'll see it as we pass by. I was told that if you came through, I needed to send you back to your body. I guess I should ask, why did December send you through?"

"I have no idea. It was right before a battle. We were surrounded by raiders."

Faust cut him off. "You didn't think that was an important detail to tell me?"

"Please, I'm dead, or at least I'm in the land of the dead. What can I do?"

"You can't do anything. I can. Tell me exactly where the battle is. I can fetch help."

"Can you fetch help in just a few minutes? It won't matter either way shortly."

Faust gave Miller an exasperated look. "Look, Miller, I'm a spirit who walks through the cracks of the world, and through the lands of the dead. Just assume I can at least send a message. Now answer my questions."

The last statement hit Miller like an iron bar. It was the voice of Faust the inquisitor, Faust the torturer. It brooked no insolence. He felt like an idiot. He had been dancing through this place as if nothing mattered. Faust probably could help him out. For a moment, he wondered if feeling like an idiot all the time meant that he was an actual idiot, or did it mean that he was getting smart enough to realize when he was being stupid.

Miller quickly described the village and its surroundings to Faust. Faust made hand motions, urging him to speak quicker, or in more detail as he required.

"I have to leave you. Things are crawling around down here. My advice, run before you fight. Also, watch out for these plants. Sometimes they will snatch you away. I will be back as soon as I can. Don't worry, I will find you. And don't do anything stupid. Your powers work differently down here in the cracks. You might accidentally burn yourself to bits."

Before he could respond, Faust simply faded away. One second he was there, standing in front of Miller. The next second he was gone.

Time passed. Miller could not tell how long he stood in the passageway. The leaves began to become more active, and he returned to the open space where he'd discovered Faust.

Miller was still surprised that Mistress Aileen had sent Faust to wait for him here. He hoped that she had some sort of arrangement with December. Or, all of this could be some part of a larger White Hand plot.

There was room to stretch. Miller took a seat on the ground and entered the meditative state, just to pass the time quicker. After a long span of time, he emerged back from his meditation. He grew impatient. All he could think of was how long it was taking for Faust to return. It must have been twelve hours, at least. Then the scariest thought occurred to him. Perhaps time didn't even work the same way here. He might have been here moments, or years. He shook his head. It was best not to think about worst case scenarios.

He wasn't hungry. He had yet to feel hungry, or even sleepy since he arrived. But he did feel weakness. More time passed, and boredom began to creep in.

Growing even more impatient, he started looking around. He thought he might as well investigate this place since he had nothing else to do.

His earlier experiments focused on how his magics failed to work. First Principles were useless. He remembered Faust saying that casting spells could have an effect, but not why. For lack of any better options, he started his investigations with that assumption. Faust had urged him to be careful, but he wasn't a spell-crafter. How does he know?

Miller pulled the arrowhead from his pocket. It glowed with a soft pink aura in the odd light. Miller entered meditation and looked again. Now the maze glowed in a variety of colors, mixing to form a knot of angles and lines. Part of it looked like a knot composed of angled lines. That could be the channel. Then he set about trying to activate it, to open the channels and flow spirit.

The arrowhead had functioned when he had stabbed the beast with it. He didn't want to stab himself just to test it. Miller had years of experience building magical things, attaching channels, fates, and permutations to their essence. But where is the essence here?

Miller stared at the arrowhead for a long time. Finally, he arrived at an experiment. He didn't have any materials and his capability was limited. Instead of attempting to channel spirit, he tried channeling fates, then different elemental calls. There was no reaction.

The pattern didn't react to channeling. Maybe he was going about this wrong. What if it didn't need a crafter, maybe it had its own internal energy. He needed to check what powered it.

He began focusing his attention on crafting, and the lessons he knew from building magical items. He tried to sense its energy scale, then determine its aspects. None of these resulted in any reaction until he used a test to check if any other magics had been connected to an item. Spell-crafters had a habit of protecting their materials and artifacts by laying subtle spells entangled within other spells.

The arrowhead reacted to his test. White light shone from the arrow head, illuminating the space and casting animated shadows against the walls. When the shadows lay across a plant leaf, the leaf reacted wildly, twisting and snapping to escape its obscuration.

He still didn't feel any of the magics. None of the channels were active. But here it was, a reaction. The light was new, and the plants didn't like it.

He sat for a long moment thinking, trying to imagine what would cause this. Out of desperation, he cleared flat a section of ground and began calculating the channel entropy forces. This calculation was difficult and involved multiple steps. There was no stylus or writing surface, so he reached for the arrowhead to draw into the floor.

The floor reacted as the arrowhead touched it. When the bright white arrowhead approached the ground, it transformed. The flat surface churned. Small beads the size of his fingertip began to form, emerging from its surface as if they were bobbing up from far below.

Odd. Miller shut down his channels and ended the test, and the arrowhead's glow returned to it's earlier light pink color. He tested it against the ground again, without the channeling. It had no effect. Even odder. Did color have an effect? Or does the effect have a color?

Miller used the broken wooden shaft behind the arrowhead to complete his calculations. His solution indicated a lot less spirit energy would be released than what he saw. Light energy is normally easy to produce, but movement energy was much more difficult. The entropy forces weren't right. He guessed that there wasn't going to be a solution here, either.

EXPERIMENTS

The experiment had yielded only a small hint to what was happening. His materials were limited, and the experiment suffered because of it. Miller needed time, a variety of materials with these enchantment-mazes forged onto them, and the history of each. He had none. All he had was a single result. The earlier test told him that the item had a distinct magical identity, and that no other spells were encroaching on it. But the arrowhead was an item, not a spell. It should at least have a mage-curse spell on it. That was how a craftsman made such things.

But this was different. He thought about the beast and its dying screams. A mage arrow would not have done that.

A thought struck him. This might be both a spell, and a crafted item at the same time. Could they be, in effect, the same thing? That would satisfy the test. It would explain why channeling didn't affect it. But that would also fundamentally break the first principles of magic. He shook his head in frustration. The first principles were different here. Some seemed to be missing.

He constructed an experiment in his imagination. He visualized the forces at play and tried to imagine them as items as well. It made no sense until he considered the maze patterns. Those patterns could be forged to create interconnections or locking points. Those locking points could interface with energies. But energies didn't exist here, wherever here was.

And he had returned to the original question. Where am I? Everything was different here. All he knew for sure was this arrowhead had a unique identity. The pattern seemed to connect it with other things, probably with identities. He thought about his world, where he'd been just a few hours ago. He pondered what else would have a unique identity.

The answer was obvious. Everything had an identity in its natural state. Identities don't get corrupted with spell craft. That corruption wasn't natural. This place had no spell craft, so identities here were perfectly protected.

Identity was the cornerstone of crafting. It allowed casters to focus channels and direct power. While the arrowhead had no power of its own, or ability to react to power, it did have an identity. He had to assume it could connect to others through its pattern. Would it be any different back home?

He conducted another thought experiment within his imagination. First, he assumed that the identity rule affected the arrowhead and his normal world in the same way. Then he constructed a chain of magical theories, predicting the behavior of both artifacts and spells based on their identities. Then he followed that logical chain backward until he came to the first principles, and then further until he came to the base axioms of crafting and spirit power.

He spent a moment thinking about how magic worked here. The rules weren't different, the place was. The magical environment had changed but magic had not. Channels were not flowing because there were no channels here, not because magic did not exist. But identities must always exist or there would be no reality to cast into, or even observe. But if there was identity, then it followed there must be a non-identity. What was that? And how did the pattern link to it?

He rubbed his face in aggravation. It seemed the secret to this place was almost in reach.

The implications of his thoughts were profound. It meant the actual environment influenced casting beyond anything he had ever learned, or even heard of. This place was a different environment. It had different ways of interpreting the rules of magic, but it did not have different magic.

He thought about the pattern on the arrowhead, then imagined how the identity of this arrowhead could be used to signal others to come to his rescue. He worked the spirit calculations in the ground, using the arrowhead and found he had plenty of energy to do this, as long has his assumptions about the arrowhead and its pattern were correct.

Faust had not returned. He had nothing to do with his time. He prepared his test. If this worked, then Faust should be able to detect him. It didn't seem hard. He entered the meditative state merely to see a little better.

Faust had said to be careful. Miller didn't even know what to be careful of, or how. He suspected this entire experiment might explode in his face at any moment.

He considered the risks that his chain of axioms predicted and found them to be minimal.

But did the axioms even apply here? All the rules seem to have changed.

He used his own identity to forge a connection to the arrowhead. At first, the connection was slippery and refused him. He went deeper into silent meditation, and tried again. The working slid in almost naturally. He felt the connection resonate within the environment. The arrowhead began to vibrate, then the air began to vibrate slightly. He felt it in his ears.

As the reverberations struck the plants, they erupted in

chaotic movement. Small gaps emerged between the leaves, showing absolute darkness beyond.

Only now did he stop to consider a problem in his analysis. This place made him brave. He hoped that he didn't underestimate the danger he was facing.

Creatures began to emerge from the gaps between those dark leaves. They were small, round things that moved on tentacle limbs. Each one was slightly smaller than his chest, and covered in long, bristling hair. The creatures had a gaping mouth that split half of their orb-like bodies. Creatures from the void had come to devour him. He had no idea what to do.

Miller leaped backward and turned to flee. The walls behind him had exploded into motion, waving and slicing with the edges of their leaves. Dozens of these creatures stood on the path blocking the way back. Their angry hisses filled the room with hate and the stink of rotten fruit and vomit.

He bolted toward them. He had to get through them fast! Go! Go! He ran into their midst trying to run past, fleeing one horrific mob only to be engulfed in another. His plan was to use his larger weight to force his way to the exit. The things bit into him. Their jaws locked onto him. Their tentacle limbs wrapped around his legs and arms. Within seconds his progress had been reduced to a slow walk. He used his hands to rip off one beast, while more latched onto him.

What a way to go. He hadn't had this ending on his list of dooms. Hadn't he already passed through the final door? How was this even happening?

He moved forward another three steps. Each step took more effort. He felt the tentacles clutching at his neck and then tangling his legs together. He began to stumble. He still wasn't afraid. He should be terrified. This was the end, and it was as horrible as he could imagine. When he thought about the loss of his fear-senses, he became even more concerned. Fear was a very good tool for staying alive.

The exit was at least ten feet away. The creatures piled on him, dragging him to his knees. Swarms of tentacles lashed and flailed at him. They began to cut his skin and clothing. They drew blood from dozens of small wounds. Ah, there it was, back to the litany. Death by a thousand cuts.

The swarm dragged him down. He moved on his hands and knees now. The pile of horrors pulled him backward, away from his escape. He pushed two from his head so he could see the exit, but could only see the dark shapes of these creatures blocking his vision. He saw an even darker shape ahead. This new shape seemed to float in the midst of the nightmare creatures, untouched by them. It was a ball of pure blackness surrounded with a corona of fog. It floated there, and seemed to call to him. Miller didn't know what to do. His escape was gone, and the beasts were on him. He crawled toward the dark, floating blot, hoping against all logic that it would give him just one more chance.

He felt something sharp dig into his ankle just as he came within reach of the floating stain. He pulled himself forward, dragging something behind him that had begun to devour his leg, one bite at a time. He screamed in pain, calling out to Phyllicitus for aid, however hopeless that might be.

Then he felt something.

Fate magic.

Something was inside that dark blot. Miller reached his hand forward toward the blot, and it dissipated. A small object floated one foot from the ground. It turned in midair like a flipped coin. It wasn't a coin, though. It was a black ring. Its black surface lay decorated with a maze of etched patterns. It called to him, and Miller recognized it as his own. The etchings were connected to its identity, and he knew instinctively that they were his identity as well. Snatching the ring could give him the power to escape this insanity, and maybe preserve his life.

In that instant, he understood why the Masters took their rings. It wasn't for the power. It was for their survival. This ring was forged from his own identity, the part of him that governed all else, even his soul. It was made of the dark fears within. It was forged from his hate, his desperation, and his pure desire to live no matter what the cost. It was no wonder they all went mad in the end.

Miller stopped moving forward. The pain erupted from across his face, and then his leg felt like his foot had been bitten off. He needed to make a choice. It was either live an eternity with a beast within his soul, or a few moments of painful end. He had made his decision long ago. He would not become a monster. That was the price of a ring. Miller began to push back into the swarm of horrors, and away from his Master's ring.

SOMETHING WRONG WITH THE PEOPLE

"Something is wrong."

Ebber looked back. "What?"

"The Friends, they're so, quiet."

He continued a moment toward their goal. The tower jutted up above the trees. Brita felt apprehensive as they neared their goal. Something terrible was going to happen, she was sure of it. She wasn't afraid of what the future held, merely accepting of her fate.

"I know, I might be feeling it, too. They're too quiet. Starting to make me nervous. They cut us off before, but now we're getting ready to fight. This could get very bad."

She noticed Ebber's clarity above all else. It was unusual. He didn't have any problem saying that, as if he knew he could speak freely. She guessed the Friends weren't minding the store right now, so, where were they?

"Do you think it could be the necromancers?"

"I wish. I think our Friends have started to figure some things out. Now they're watching, waiting."

Brita's heart fluttered. She tried to imagine what the Friends would do if they discovered that Ebber, and now Brita, could avoid their control. It wouldn't be good for her, she was sure.

Ebber continued his chaotic thoughts, whispering a string of disconnected words. "Collaborating, dicing, ruminating."

He reached out and took her hand, holding it across the gap between their horses. Brita paused. There was no connection between them. Only what she'd felt before. She'd become accustomed to how the Friends helped them communicate; now it felt empty. "Why do I think something is getting ready to happen? I can't sense the others." She waved her hand at the column of footmen and riders behind them, then toward the column in front of them. "I can't sense them anymore. It's kind of like being normal again, but I know they are still watching me."

"We won't ever be normal again. We'll be lucky to simply exist, let alone be normal."

She squeezed his hand. "Speak for yourself. This isn't over yet."

Their ride continued with only the sounds of horses on the mud road. They moved closer to the tower. She wished she had the Friends nearby. Black clouds were filled with dancing bats, screaming their anger at her.

Deep in her heart, she knew why Ebber was being so quiet. Some kind of doom was coming their way. When a shepherd's herd started getting sick, the shepherd had to protect it. They separated the sick from the healthy flock, and then culled them. The sick were permanently removed from the flock.

Brita felt it coming. They were going to be culled sooner or later. This journey could be the end of the path in more than one way. Would it end at the final door?

They rode on in silence. The closer they came to the tower, the greater her fear grew.

Brita couldn't tolerate the silence. "Might be the White Hand. They could be making us feel fear, maybe a bit of uncertainty. We need to be focused and keep our aim on target."

"Sure. If it helps you, keep telling that to yourself."

The tower didn't look like it cared what they needed to do. They had entered a line of trees, but they could see the outline of it past the trunks. Gray, tall, judging. She could feel it, a single stop before her end. The dark cloud overhead made it look like certain doom. She could use a little bravery now.

The column emerged from the strip of woods. A village lay on the side of a gentle slope. The tower perched in the middle of it. Its gray stone contrasted with the green summer fields surrounding it. Two dozen houses, three workshops, an old inn, and a sprinkling of huts made up the village. A group of forty villagers were visible in the distance. They stood still, watching the column of horses approach.

Ebber spit. "Something isn't looking right. I thought they would spook."

She followed his pointing finger toward the village. A peasant lay unmoving in the road. The other people gave it no mind. They didn't panic, they didn't mingle, they didn't even send a message. They simply waited.

"Creepy."

Gardin rode to the front of the column. He signaled the riders and they turned from the road. The column quickly became a broad row two ranks deep and a hundred riders wide. They made last-minute adjustments to their armor and weapons as the footmen ran up behind them. It looked like this was going to be a massacre. The village didn't have a chance. She could see no real defense, no pits, no armed defenders. So why was she so terrified?

She reached out and grabbed Ebber's sleeve. He nudged his horse, bringing it closer to hers. "Don't worry, this is going to be quick and easy. We've got the numbers."

The villagers had barely reacted, and only to turn and face

them. They stared across the grass field, motionless, with no fear and little regard. She remembered Miller and the tales he had told her long ago, when they were younger and perhaps happier. Long ago the White Hand had come to the cities and to the towns. They used their magic to get what they needed from the people, including their gold, and more precious yet, their children. They were masters of the mind; masters of the dead. Miller wasn't a fool, she didn't expect him to wait in there.

"I don't like it."

"I don't like it, either, but we really need to go with the others."

Brita watched the first wave of their men attack. They descended on the villagers, charging with fury. The villagers didn't flee. They fought. She watched as swords and axes cut into the defenders with little result.

She could hear Gardin calling out to the group. "Ready Weapons!" It was almost time. She had better come up with an idea quick.

"I don't think this is going to be so easy."

Gardin called out to the group again. This time his voice carried clearly over the fields. "Ready shields!"

She pulled on Ebber's sleeve, then grabbed his wrist. "Stay in the back with me. Don't be first."

"But—"

Gardin's voice rang clear. "Kill them all! Go!"

Screams erupted from their company as they launched toward the village. Horses pounded over the soft ground, throwing grass and dirt in all directions. The footmen called out their war cries and sprinted forward, following the row of horsemen down the gentle hill toward the village. She held on to her bridle with both hands, neglecting to draw her knife. The horse tried to keep up with the charging wave, but she held it back.

The footmen quickly began passing her. Ebber struggled with his mount, too. The crowd of armed men, foresters, bandits, and taken commoners descended on the village. The people did not run. They only stood in place. She began to make out details. A silver-haired woman held a heavy club. A young boy stood unarmed, and fearless. A fat old man in a formal suit slowly reached down and picked up a wood ax.

The man's skull had been split open. A handful of rotted brains fell out of the crack and landed on the ground. She tried to call out, but the fear had her in its grip.

Gardin led the charging line toward the risen dead. Brita watched him yell out in anticipated victory.

Then the ground collapsed beneath the horsemen. Dead skeletal hands reached from beneath the ground to grasp horse legs and riders. The risen crawled from the ground, swarming over wounded horsemen and mounts alike. Brita's horse decided that charging into the fray wasn't its best idea ever. It slowed down and She let the horse choose its own path. Ebber wrestled with controlling his mount, and approached her, cutting through the charging footmen.

Screams came from the melee. Men fought with skeletons, rotted corpses awoke and gave battle to their archers. Arrows had no effect as the defenders shambled toward the invaders. Ebber gripped his sword blade tightly, watching the carnage. Brita looked on, filled with fear and terror. The dead were strong, but they would not be enough. The taken had the numbers.

"To me!"

She saw Terp running by the side of the fight. More than twenty footmen followed closely behind.

"Spears! Halberds!"

A line of footmen descended into the fight, stabbing and hacking with lethal efficiency. They kept close, not letting any of the dead get by their tight line. The enemy did not run, nor did they waver. Soon more footmen entered the fray from the other side. Brita watched the dead being herded by two walls of heavy footmen, directly into the dismounted horsemen. The battle began to shift. Working in tight cooperation, the living began systematically butchering those doomed defenders. Cheers went up from her men, as their steel-tipped war arrows began to rip apart the remaining dead.

"We've got this!" Ebber called to her, filled with battle lust. "By the goddess, we've got this!"

The door of the tower opened. A dozen warriors emerged from behind it, each wearing mail of iron, and carried swords. "Terp! The tower! Look to your rear!"

It was too late for the dead. Terp called orders and turned half of his men around. Screaming, he led them into the new threat. Brita watched Terp slice a cursed warrior's arm off completely, cutting through rusted chain mail and brittle bones alike. Gardin staggered out of the melee covered in mud and gore. He commanded the men, dismantling the final half dozen of the original dead warriors with heavy blows. She could see the men. They knew the day was theirs.

"Into the tower!" Terp screamed at his men. He charged past the last few dead soldiers and sprinted in. A dozen men followed him closely behind.

"Not yet!" Gardin screamed out to slow Terp's advance, to keep the men closer together. The men were in a frenzy, they wanted more blood and the door to victory was open before them.

Almost three dozen of the men began to form up according to Gardin's commands. "Keep together! Stay alert! The tower might be a trap, so stay tight!"

Brita started, snatching her gaze away from the fight and toward the tree line. Dogs howled from the trees, hidden within its dark undergrowth. There were no footmen behind her. The only thing that lay between the dozens of hulking, growling black dogs emerging from the trees was open grass. Gardin had begun leading the men toward the tower.

"Ebber, I think I know how we are going to escape from the Friends."

His reply was calm, sad, and resigned. "Yeah, me, too."

The dogs began to dash forward.

43

BETRAYAL

Chamise slowly turned her head until she could see Master December. He held the handle of his long knife. It was impaled deep in Miller's chest. December gently laid him down on the floor. She wanted to scream, but her lungs hurt, and she was terrified.

December had betrayed her. Anger and brute rage took over her mind. She swore to kill that man, today. In the back of her mind, she would hear the code of the Eisenvard. It was calling on her to sacrifice everything for this task, this greater good. There was no more honorable deed than to strike down a necromancer. Today, she was going to do her duty by the code, no matter how much she despised it.

After a moment, December bowed down and whispered into Miller's ear, but he didn't respond. Chamise felt anger and rage overcome her, along with sadness. She had liked Miller. It made her sad to think of life without him. He could have been a lover, or better yet, a true friend. She had begun this journey hoping to discover a few of Miller's secrets, and she had found so much more. She began to tremble as she felt the tear fall softly across her cheeks.

December stood, looked down at Miller for another moment before shaking his head. Then he walked out of the room and down the stairs.

"You'll pay." She gasped out the whisper as she took stock of her injured body. December had picked the perfect time to betray them. She was disabled, and Miller was probably dead. The tales said that the White Hand could overcome death. But could Miller? He was still an apprentice. She didn't think he'd be coming back so easily. Even if he could, he shouldn't.

Memories of her father came unbidden to her. He spoke to her in the training yard, holding his great sword mid-blade and gesturing with the massive weapon to articulate his words. "Never forget why we are here. The necromancers are out there. We have to stop them no matter the cost. Our bodies are sacrifice so long as we hold our souls. We must fight the good fight. We are Eisenvard. There is no other path for us."

She remembered when he gave her the blade. "Keep it safe, little one. Keep the lessons that I've taught you."

She remembered when he reached out to her, holding her shoulder in a kind embrace. "Sometimes you need to decide to do what is right, no matter the cost to yourself. I hope it never happens to you, but you are my blood. You should always be prepared to make this decision."

Chamise drew the knife slowly from her belt scabbard. The battle hadn't changed in all these years. The Eisenvard had left her one more gift. Gray metal shone dully against the sunlight. Runes of power lay etched up and down its thick blade.

She struggled to her feet, nearly losing her balance as she righted herself. She raised the knife and began the ritual she had learned all those long years ago. She chanted the old words, and channeled spirit power into the blade. The runes burst awake, vibrating with magical forces. She rested for just a moment, long enough for the runes to quiet, then she began casting her Free Mage art. Forces of hiding and obscuration wove about her, attempting to distract anyone who searched for her.

Her father had told her that there would be a decision. Chamise made it. She knew what she had to do.

War cries filled the room as Terp led the raiders into the tower. He sprinted forward, trying to enter before someone could close the door and block their passage. Only ten feet of open floor lay between Terp and piles of mismatched wooden crates that lay strewn across the far side of the room. The only light came from the open door, and a single dying torch bracketed to the wall. They'd left the lower tower unprotected! He felt joy at the call of his Friends. This was the victory they had so long waited for.

The rest of his raiders began to jam into the room. Gardin called out. "Come on! Let's take this tower before the dogs get here!"

The cries of men and beasts filtered in from the open door. The Friends announced their joyous agreement by filling his heart with joy and energy. "Now! Victory!"

The men in the room shouted their agreement and surged forward. Terp led by knocking over boxes, spilling their contents to the floor. He climbed over the scattered contents, trying to get to the tower stairs.

A scream of pain erupted behind him but he ignored it. He could see the door to the stairs ahead. He expected it to be barred from within, but it wouldn't be thick. He knew they had victory in their grasp.

Then he fell.

At first, Terp tried to scramble back up, but he couldn't gain purchase with his left leg. It had begun to hurt. He reached down to clear the broken boxes and scattered contents from the leg and felt the warm sticky blood that covered the box.

Then he saw the foot. His severed foot. It lay on its side. Something had cut him so cleanly and quickly that he'd never felt it. His pants were severed in a straight line mid-calf, cutting through clothing and leg with the same exact slice.

The torch sputtered and died. The door he had charged through earlier slammed closed, shattering a box someone had used to prop it open. A moment later, soft green light began to pulse from different places within the pile. Terp grabbed his belt and began to bind his bleeding leg. Then he recognized the sources of light. Dozens of human skulls lay scattered among the boxes. Their empty eye sockets glowed with a sickly illumination. He could see the rest of the men, most lying on the floor, screaming in agony. Only two were left standing, but they were frozen, unsure where to move next.

He called out in a panic. "Necromancy! Look for the caster!"

They scanned the room, searching where this cutting had come from. They couldn't find it.

As one, the skulls began to rise, slowly climbing into the air. Tendrils of green light flared out, connecting skull eyes with the eyes of the men. The light burned into Terp's eyes, causing agony. It felt like something was trying to rip open his mind from within. He screamed.

The door opened at the far side of the room. A tall man stepped from the stairway beyond. Terp could barely see him through the pain. "There he is!"

The man wrapped his black traveling cloak around himself and with a raised hand began to direct the skulls in their tasks. All the men began to scream at once as the life force was sucked from their bodies, then channeled back toward the caster.

The pain went away. He could feel the Friends shielding him from it. He had only one function to fulfill, and he knew what it was. Find the White Hand Master, he must kill the White Hand Master!

The wounded men began to crawl forward. Most had only

minutes left to live. Blood covered the floor as they moved toward their doom. They ignored the pain, ignored their failing bodies. They answered the call of the Friends with every gasp of their dying breath.

"Yes! Come to me!" The dark man laughed as he harvested their souls. The men began to falter, stopping their mad crawling rush toward this man. They began dying on the floor, one at a time.

Terp knew he wasn't going to make it. Terp crawled forward another pace. The man was six feet from him but might as well be six miles.

The green light flowed faster, pulling energy from Terp, and sending it through the skull toward this new threat. He could feel the Friends scream at him. Even if it was his last act in life, he must kill this thing!

He looked up to see the White Hand Master. His smile filled his face with terrible anger.

Then the knife emerged from the Master's neck. His surprised look struck Terp as funny. A woman stepped from behind him, then pushed the White Hand Master to the ground. She recovered the knife, then stabbed him three more times in the back. She screamed out words that Terp didn't understand, yet somehow, he knew them for what they were, words of power.

She held the Master down until the death throws stopped. Then she stood with the knife in her hand, and walked toward Terp.

"Thank you for helping—"

Chamise reached down and grabbed him by the neck. They looked at each other just a moment until she muttered a single word of accusation.

"Taken." She hissed.

She cut Terp's throat.

DOGS AND DECISIONS

The dogs were among them. Brita tore her gaze away from Terp as he charged into the tower. She had more pressing matters to attend to, a pack of ravenous mastiffs were currently foremost on her mind.

Standing on all four paws, they could reach her chest. If one of the dog's stood on it's hind legs, it would tower over her. Their short black fur was splattered with fresh blood. One of them stared directly at her. The dog's eyes were focused, sharp, like no other dog she had ever seen. It was like they could see into her, see what her next move would be.

She wished the Friends hadn't deserted her so quickly. She could use their help right now. She felt weak, exposed, vulnerable.

Ebber stared at her with a strange look, was he in conversation with the Friends? Was he plotting something against her? She felt her heart quicken as she gazed at into his eyes. She was concerned. What was he up to? Was Ebber going to betray her?

Ebber drew his knife as well. "You were always going to kill me, weren't you?"

"No, not until I figured out what you were up to."

She wondered if the Friends were trying to get them to fight each other. It would be an easy way to clean up this mess. She couldn't understand why she was so angry with Ebber but she was furious. Somehow she suspected the Friends of engineering this encounter. In truth, she had always liked Ebber, even if he was a bit off. Now she felt only hatred toward him, and couldn't explain why.

The dogs continued their attack into the midst of their remaining company. Brita could not look away. She had to kill Ebber before he murdered her.

Men screamed out behind her. She only had eyes for Ebber. He might try to stab her in the back, as soon as she looked away. They circled each other, preparing for a decisive strike, one that could end this betrayal.

She saw carnage everywhere around them. The circle they walked in was clear, but men and women lay scattered across the ground beyond. Huge dogs, none shorter than her waist, filled the village. They tore and rended wounded men. It was horrible, yet she still felt no fear. She knew what her task was, what her destiny was. Ebber had to die.

Then Ebber did an unexpected thing. He skipped back a few paces and threw down his knife. Its point struck into the ground, burying the blade deep.

"What are we doing? Brita, wake up! Look around!"

She realized what was happening. The Friends had her in their grip. Icy fear shot through her, then she calmed down. She needed to be afraid. The Friends were going to kill her. Fear was her only ally. The culling has begun.

Their company of men was dead or dying. Bodies littered the ground around them. She saw Gardin struggling with three of the giant dogs. He slashed his knife wildly as they tore his legs, then a great black dog seized his neck and began to shake him back and forth. His head turned at impossible angles, and he was still when the beast dropped him.

Ebber took another step back to view the carnage. She tried to break through the Friends' control, to find that vein of fear and embrace it. Tears came from her eyes. She tried to flee, but she remained frozen in place. The Friends were not going to let her leave. They didn't like being tricked.

She began to glance about quickly, trying to find a way, any way, to escape this madness. Half of the men that arrived in the village lay dead on the ground. Dogs continued to tear at their flesh. There must be a hundred dogs, and only twenty men near her.

Then she gazed at the closed tower door.

"I don't think they are coming back."

"No, I don't think so, either." Ebber looked sad, lost in some sort of inner turmoil. He gazed down at his feet as if preparing to make a decision. She continued to feel the need to stab him. She wondered if he was going through the same thing. The Friends were cleaning up their mess.

The urge to slay Ebber rose up again, but now she had a grip on her fear. She knew what had to happen. The Friends whispered it to her. One of the two of them was going to die right now. It was up to her to decide, unless she waited too long. Then Ebber would make the decision.

She stopped trying to resist, and let the Friends in. They seized control of her emotions, overcoming the fear and dread.

Ebber smiled at her, trying to look comforting. "Don't worry. We can get through this. Let's just leave. We can be far away from here by tomorrow."

She smiled back. A small tear fell down her face as she walked up to him, snuggling in his arms.

"We can make it."

"But we can't. We're Taken. Where would we go?"

Her hand found her small belt knife. She let the Friends have their way. Ebber tried to pull back but she grabbed his shirt. She cried out "I'm sorry! I'm sorry!" as her knife stabbed into his chest over and over.

THE MASTER'S RING

The ring began to change.

Miller stopped. He stared at it. Its blackened edges had begun to shine. A layer of silver emerged from below the black, transforming it. Miller stared at it in curious fascination. The thing that had been constructed from fear, anger, and despair had transformed into another object. This new ring was clean. It was free of those harsh emotions, and now showed a simple reflection of his soul. He knew it just by looking at it.

The ring was a reflection of the self. It was the identity of its maker, no, of its mold, and he was that mold. Now the ring was clean! Had he become clean?

The creatures were swarming on him. One had locked its jaws onto his left forearm. Another crawled on his neck, trying madly to choke him with its tentacle. The silver ring continued to float just out of reach. He tried again to move toward it, but the pile of biting, stabbing creatures drove him to the ground. He felt the ground shifting, threading to suck him in.

It was everything or nothing! Miller screamed as he surged forward to grasp the ring. The ring transformed again, returning to its earlier black, terror-imbued state. *No! It is made of my emotions! The ring is changing because of me!*

The creatures buried him. He felt cuts and bites. Something stabbed into his gut. His chest screamed in agony. The creatures were biting into him and crushing him under their weight.

Suddenly the weight became less. He felt a hand grab his arm and pull him up. He saw the bodies of these creatures lying impaled and dying all around him. Faust stood in the midst of the swarm of creatures, swinging a dark iron blade with one hand, and pulling Miller up with the other.

"I thought I told you not to cast spells!" Faust yelled at him, attempting to make himself heard over the growls and screams of the beasts.

Miller staggered as he gained his feet. He was covered with his own blood. Faust might have just saved him or sacrificed himself. "I didn't!"

"Well, you did something!"

The swarm of beasts redoubled its efforts. Twenty of them rushed forward. One immediately died at the end of Faust's blade.

They only had one weapon.

He grabbed at the arrowhead. It remained fixed to a small portion of shaft. The shaft had begun to splinter. He didn't think this was going to work for long but it was better than nothing.

Faust skewered another of the beasts as two more leaped onto him. Miller ignored the danger and grabbed one with his hand, pulling it toward him. He drove the arrowhead into it with the other hand. The beast exploded in a spray of gore and stink. Screams erupted from the beasts as he pulled another from Faust's back and struck with the arrowhead. Miller saw the reflection of a blue pattern on its body just before it exploded in a cloud of cursed meat and sinew.

The beasts cried out and began to flee. In less than three heartbeats, the room was empty of them. Miller collapsed down to his knees.

"I don't think I can walk. My legs are torn up."

His pants were coated with blood. His craftsman tunic was missing, discarded in three pieces on the floor. Blood flowed from a half-dozen wounds in his chest, stomach, and shoulders. Blood poured from beneath his left armpit in a constant dribble.

Faust looked down at him. "The bad news is that you will probably be dead in ten minutes. The good news is that if you get up and start moving, I can get you out of here in eight."

Miller struggled to his feet. He tried not to fall down as his head spun.

Faust grabbed him and held him steady. "More good news, you don't have a body here, this is just your soul's way of projecting. You don't have any bones to break. Just keep your mind focused and you can make it."

"Focused." Miller didn't know what else to do. He entered the meditative state. This time it came quickly. He fear and concerns washed away and left him in pain, weak, but able to move.

"Let's go."

The pair of them stumbled forward, out of the space. They entered another of the dark, plant-encrusted halls. The pain began to grow, and Miller had to concentrate to stay moving. They passed a lake whose surface reflected golden light. Any other time, Miller would have liked to stop and see that. He didn't look back, he just kept moving.

Faust urged him forward. They turned at some point, and after a few moments, Miller found himself staring at a broad and dark wooden frame. It looked like a huge decorative window box or a door frame. This frame held no door. It held a surface of blackness within.

"That is the way out. You should arrive back in your body. You probably won't see any wounds, but they are still there spiritually. Go see one of the Masters. They can help you heal from this."

"I just want to ask you a question."

Faust began urging him toward the portal.

"Did Aileen just try to kill me like she did K?" The words were out before Miller could stop them. He only had minutes to live. He could feel his blood dribbling down his arm onto the floor. "I've got to know. Is she finished with me?"

Faust paused. He relaxed his grip. It was odd. Faust has been a soldier, a torturer, and an inquisitor. But he had always been the most even-tempered of Mistress Aileen's company. Even when he had left the House of Questions, and roamed aimless through life, he had always kept things in perspective. He wouldn't keep her secrets. He didn't even care.

"All right. Let's spend your last few minutes of life talking about this. Here is what I know: Aileen had a conversation with Easter. Easter suspected you might draw out some sort of enemy. I'm not sure who or what. He asked her to send you forward. She got in an argument with him but agreed to send you alone."

"Easter? What does Easter care about me? He barely knows I exist."

"Easter doesn't care about you. He cares a lot about the Takers, the Diggers, and White Hand itself."

"What do I have to do with all of that?"

"You're in the Order, aren't you? You have everything to do with all of that."

"But Mistress Aileen—"

"Mistress Aileen is a Master within the White Hand. She has dedicated every breath of her life to that, plus some. Come on, Miller, you're an apprentice. You are as expendable as a person could possibly be. Look, December is awaiting trial at Conclave for killing a dozen of you. He isn't in trouble for killing apprentices, he's in trouble for killing someone else's apprentices. Face it, you are a cog in a larger machine, you should probably be used to it by now."

Miller knew it was true. His time with Aileen had changed him. Now he saw her as someone human, and approachable. But she was still a White Hand Master, no matter what their companionship might bring.

It made him sad. He had seen her as more than just a Master. He had seen her as a friend, a close friend. In that instant, he remembered Mistress Sword's final words before she gave his service away. "In time, you will realize that the hurts I did to you are nothing compared to what life holds. I had hoped you'd grow some sort of armor around your heart. Your soft feelings will drive you to madness here. If I were you, I would kill myself now and save everyone else the trouble."

Miller grasped Faust's shoulder like warriors did. Without a word between them, Miller walked through the portal.

"But why did you have to kill Madam K?"

Those were on his lips as he awoke. He lay on the floor where December had placed him. His chest ached with a deep pain, but the wound seemed to have closed up. A small, thumb-sized bloodstain occupied his shirt where the wound had been.

But his legs were coated in blood. *Did I keep the wounds?*

He looked around. Chamise was gone.

He stood and walked toward the stairs. He could hear dogs howling outside. Faust made it, he'd brought help.

Miller walked into the stairwell and looked down. December's body lay sprawled at the bottom of the stairs, just outside the door. Blood had poured from his neck, now it had thickened. His throat had been cut. He had been taken from behind.

There was only one logical explanation: Chamise had killed December. *How did she recover after the healing draft? She must have more Eisenvard training that she told me. That wasn't good. December was going to be irate with her when he came back.*

He moved down the stairs. He looked down at December's body, and then at his hand. The black Master's ring stood out from his pale fingers. Miller did a rough calculation of the entropy forces involved. She had about a week until December recovered. Miller decided he'd better warn her.

December would not be happy when he returned. He had seen Mistress Aileen return from the dead before, and it wasn't a pretty, or a painless process. He walked across the room to the door and gazed out. The attack had ended. Three large mastiffs were busy tearing a corpse to pieces, dismembering it beyond all recognition.

Master Easter used dogs for many things. These dire beasts looked like something he would create. But that didn't explain how Faust got him here so fast.

He began walking toward the exit. He noticed his chest didn't hurt, but he didn't remember being healed.

The odor of blood and meat filled the chamber. Miller drew his sword. Not long ago it had contained a maze and a riddle. Now it contained only body parts and the dead. Blood had started to thicken on the floor. Arms, legs, and heads randomly decorated the floor. Each looked as if it had been expertly removed, leaving only a single perfect cut on each hunk of meat.

His spine shivered, thinking of how close he must have come to that same fate.

December really did have a good defense. Miller was very glad that he had solved his riddle earlier in the tower.

Chamise wasn't in the cairn of body parts. He felt for channels, and found the normal flows of this world. The defensive traps had finished their task and now lay dormant, finished. He walked quickly through and emerged outside.

The sword felt heavy in Miller's hand. He moved across the road and began searching the bodies for Chamise. He stumbled twice, and then noticed that he had lost track of where he was, and how long he had been out there.

Spirit damage. He figured he'd better find her quick before it got worse.

Chamise could not be found. But someone else found him.

BATTLE

"I've been looking for you."

The voice was familiar, yet so unexpected.

Turning, Miller stared at Brita. She had changed in the few days since he'd last seen her. Her cute, smiling face wasn't the same. There was a new edge of cruelty there. Five men armed with short swords and bows stood behind her.

Fresh blood stained her right hand. He tried to pass their meeting off, as if it were a normal day.

"Me? Are you well? What are you doing here?"

"Like I said, looking for you. I met some new Friends. They want to have a talk with you. You can talk to them, can't you? For me?" She smiled at him in her coy way. Her look said, "I've got a secret, and I want to share it with you, alone."

Her eyes didn't say that. Her eyes told a different story, where he was the bug that she would crush. She was playing with him. Why?

The men started advancing.

Miller felt for his spirit channels. They were there, but weak. He needed an hour or two to restore them. It wasn't going to happen. He saw only one good choice. He started to stall.

"Why did you follow me out here? I could have stopped on the way back."

"You always promise, but you never deliver." She kept that same teasing voice, but it continued to feel wrong.

He knew what that meant. She was fully in the power of the Takers.

"Brita, when did they take you?"

Instead of denying it, she simply began to laugh. "Take me? I'm giving myself away! You could have had me! But I guess you lost your opportunity. Now I am part of something so much bigger, and better."

He channeled a small bit of energy toward his protections. Preparing for their attack, he pulled his cloak tightly around his neck, closing the front and placing his enchantments between himself and this new Brita.

"So, let's talk then. What do you need? Can I help you?"

"Oh, it isn't that kind of talk. We are going to have a different kind of conversation. A deeper kind." She gestured toward him, pointing the way.

The men rushed forward. One pulled out a thin knife, and Miller could feel the channeling emanating from it.

Then the dogs attacked. A group of twelve mastiffs emerged from behind a hut and leaped into the fray. Each of the beasts stood shoulder high. They were silent as they charged from behind the building. The taken raiders were ready for an attack but were incapable of standing against the mass of dogs. The dogs were too big, too ferocious, too merciless. Four taken raiders turned to flee as the first man went down beneath the fangs of beast. Its midnight colored fur was splashed with his blood. The dogs didn't bark, or howl. They were silent as the night.

Within seconds the men were in disarray, trying to flee. The dogs were too fast. Eight more dogs came into the open, dashing from behind a different building. Two of the taken raiders stood back-to-back, drawing blades to fend of the mastiffs. The other two continued their effort to flee.

They had no chance.

The newly arrived dogs gave chase, rapidly catching up to the two men. The lead dog snapped at a fleeing raider, catching his pants in its teeth. The dog shook its head brutally and the man lost his footing and slammed into the earth. Three more dogs closed in, tearing, rending, ripping his flesh. The other man glanced back in panic. His Taker-given calm had deserted him. He ran another ten paces before two of the dogs leaped on him. One sprinted forward to seize the man's arm. The other leaped high, snapping his jaws around the man's neck. The dog began to shake him violently. His neck snapped to an unnatural angle and he stopped moving. The dog continued his shaking.

After what Miller had just gone through, he felt momentarily sorry for the raiders. Then he saw Brita. She was trying to join her men. The dogs held her, preventing her from rejoining them. They seized her clothing in their teeth then pulled her back like she was a mere toy. Somehow, she had dropped her dagger. Two enormous dogs had seized her arms in their jaws. Her struggles only created more torn, bleeding skin.

Screams began as more dogs moved in toward the men. They faced the blades of the Taken. One dog would move forward and draw a blow, while the others closed and seized legs and arms, pulling the men down to the ground. Within moments the attackers lay dead on the ground. Brita screamed, somehow trying to fight the beasts with her bare fists.

Miller kept far away from them. It would be best not to be taken today. Their blood was poison and he knew it.

Brita had been taken. How could he get her back?

He needed a sample, something to experiment with. But he didn't want to give the Takers any opportunities.

"Master Easter!" Miller called out loudly, hoping the leader of their cabal was in range to hear him.

Easter calmly walked from behind the same house the dogs had rushed out from. He looked immaculate in his black robes. Easter normally traveled dressed as a merchant or commoner. Now he stood before Miller in his Master's robe. A leader of a White Hand cabal in his full power.

His appearance had an effect on Brita. She began to scream and to curse at Easter. Miller calmly walked up to Easter. He was shorter than Miller's near six feet in height. His close-cut black hair stood in contrast to Miller's shoulder length brown.

He felt like he had to do something. Could he save her? He decided he had to try. It was his fault she was like this. But he was dealing with Master Easter. He had better go about this the right way.

Bowing to Easter in the formal way, Miller spoke. "Master Easter. I am but a humble apprentice with a small request. Please let this young woman live. I have known her well, and she could be of use to the Order."

Brita screamed out her defiance, struggling wildly against the dogs that held her.

Easter returned his formal greeting with a smirk. "Of use? She has been taken. Her days of being useful are done."

He bowed to Easter again. He tried to be calm, sincere, and analytical. Easter didn't like making decisions based on emotion. "No, her days of being useful are just beginning. We have needed a sample of the new takers, and now we have a live one. She can help us out, if only by allowing us to experiment. We cured it before, can't we do it again?"

Miller stared back at Brita. She cowered beneath his gaze. The Takers were in there, moving her emotions, speaking to her choices. Miller had seen just how bad this could get within the cracks.

Easter paused, then showed him a smile. After a few moments of thought, he nodded. "Brita, you are going to do something wonderful. You will help save a lot of people."

She began to scream even louder. She let out her rage and

pain. Miller stared at her as the dogs pulled her away. He felt sorry for her. He could not let her go. Nor would he kill her. He needed her to fight these new Takers. He needed to discover how to save her. Right now, there was only one person in the world who could teach him that, her.

Easter walked forward and put his hand on Miller's shoulder. It was the same warrior's gesture he'd just shared with Faust. "I was always going to keep her. You didn't need to worry."

"I had hoped so. If we can just keep her in Home's Hearth, then I can reach her. If you brought her back to the encampment, she would be gone before I could examine her."

"Home's Hearth? Are you staying then?"

"If I can find my Free Mage guardian. She killed December, so I think that Home's Hearth is the best place for her, at least until those she can make some sort of amends."

"Yes, he does take things like that poorly."

"So does Aileen."

"Yes, she does." Easter took a dozen steps in the direction of the tower. The large dogs formed a protective mass around him as he moved away. He stopped and turned back. "I will get you to Home's Hearth. Why don't you contact your Mistress? I spoke with her a short time ago. She is eager to hear from you."

47

CLOSURE

"Mistress, Mistress. I await your call."

It took only moments for Aileen to contact him. Miller felt the old contact come quickly, sending him back to his link to Aileen.

Is this the final time?

"Miller, oh, that's good. You're back. That's good, I mean."

She was clearly flustered. The imagery was different now. Her study they normally projected into had transformed. Miller had grown accustomed to its neat organization, its perfect symmetry. Now the study was there, but books lay askew, furniture was missing, and even some of the portraits had changed.

Miller could see that something was bothering her. These scenes came from her mental state. She looked terrible.

"Where are you now? You've returned from the cracks?"

He bowed slowly. "I have just arrived in Home's Hearth. I will be going to the Temple tomorrow. I hope to register for an audience."

"She will see you tomorrow. Wear your good wardrobe."

Aileen continued to surprise him. She could normally predict exactly what Phyllicitus would do. How did they grow so close? And why did she leave?

"You heard about December, and the tower?" Miller could not help but rub the sore place on his chest.

Aileen looked at him and quieted for a moment. "Yes. I heard you'd journeyed into the cracks within the world."

"I found something there."

Even with just the mental connection, Miller could hear her quick intake of breath.

She went right for the meat of the matter. "Did you find your ring?"

He thought for a moment. He hadn't found his ring, but he might have found something much better. He just needed time to experiment, and a way back into the cracks.

"I found Faust."

She seemed let down.

"You sent him to me. You had him ready for me. You knew that I would need him."

"Yes, I spoke with him, asked him to scout ahead. Just in case. It's a good thing he was there."

Aileen got up from her lounge chair. She worked her hands nervously, fidgeting with her black ring as she paced. "I thought you might need help. There were rumors about raiders. "

"Of course, it is your prerogative not to share this kind of information with your apprentices. But Faust wasn't waiting for me here." He gestured to the wide world. "He was waiting for me there. I guess the plan was always like this? To have December stab me?"

Her voice cracked as she responded. "I had a feeling. I get them now and again. That's how I got selected into the Temple. But I thought it was time. Your ring. Well, you've been there now. It's a hard place to get through without a guide."

"My ring? That is hardly the point." He paused then continued. "Mistress Aileen. All I ask is that you be honest with me. I only have one question."

Aileen stopped fidgeting and turned toward him. Her eyes were shot with worry and fatigue. It was obvious that she hadn't slept in days. Was she worried that he wouldn't return? Or that he would?

"Was I supposed to die out there, like Madam K?"

She stared back, mouth dropping open, confusion taking hold. "No, oh no, by the goddess no."

"I had some time to think and remember. I remember that you told me that K had to die for her own sake. When will it be time for me to die for my own sake?"

Aileen walked forward and took his hands in hers. She stared up into his brown eyes. Her blue eyes were full of sorrow. "I didn't want to do that. She killed Sword. K even hunted down her apprentices and killed them as well. She was still Eisenvard in her heart, even though she had left the Order when it was disbanded. The cabal would not tolerate it. The Order would have done something." Aileen shuddered. "I loved her. It would have been a true eternity of pain. I could not let her suffer like that."

Madam K had been his confidant. She was the one person that Miller knew would never betray him. She knew his secrets and hurts. She knew what Sword had done to him.

There was only one thing that he could say to Aileen. "I still miss her."

Aileen's arms wrapped around him and hugged him tightly. She rose to her tiptoes and kissed him on the cheek. "So do I."

AFTERWARD

The brown mare walked toward the gates of Home's Hearth. The granite entryway stood open as well as its two oaken doors. Four city militia stood there waiting to check new arrivals. Two of them were in conversation with an old man pulling a cart laden with lettuce and melons.

The mare was covered in mud. It bore wounds from the journey. Evidence of the hard ride decorated both of them. Dozens of scratches covered the horse and rider.

One of the guards, an older man with a wide mustache and a light-red uniform, walked forward. "Hey! Rider! Are you hurt?"

The other three guards stopped, turning to look.

Chamise slowly raised her head. Her hollow eyes spoke of a long ride without comfortable inns or companions. A smile emerged from cracked lips. "Home's Hearth?"

"Aye, you've made it. I don't know what you're running

from, but you're safe now." The guard reached up to help her down.

She took his hand, then slowly dismounted from the saddle, settling her feet on the firm ground. She turned from him and looked at the mare. Miller was right, this was an amazing horse.

The horse stared back at her. "Thanks for coming back for me. I think those White Hands would have killed me, if I had stayed." She moved closer to the horse and scratched it on the neck.

It moved closer, enjoying the touch.

The guard cleared his throat. "If you are done chatting with your horse, we have a healer available. Can we escort you to the temple? At least you can get your clothes washed."

She smiled back. Looking at the gateway, memories came back to her. Knights drawn up on their mounts, archers drilling in the yard, three hundred men shouting the Eisenvard credo.

"I appreciate the offer, but I know the city. I just need an inn. My trip to the temple isn't scheduled for a few more days."

"Trip, eh? You got an appointment?"

"Something like that."

AUTHOR'S NOTE

Thank you for reading my first novel, A Necromancer's Apprentice. If you want to know about the next book, Enemies Within, please check out my web site at

http://whitehand.brianphillipswriter.com

for the latest news. I've left a simple map as an added gift on that blog site (on the menu bar, click 'The Map'). Some of us just love maps!

If you enjoyed the book, please leave a review on whatever platform you received the book from. Reviews from readers cause small independent writers to either survive, or fade away. You, dear reader, are as much of the writing ecosystem as am I and I thank you for joining me on this journey.

Brian Phillips
brian@brianphillipswriter.com

.

ABOUT THE AUTHOR

Brian Phillips lives in Northern Virginia, writes books, plays games, and lives life to its fullest. He has been in turn a sailor, a student, a Doctor of Philosophy, an engineer, and an author.

Made in the USA
Middletown, DE
13 April 2019